80S GHOSTS

V.S. LAWRENCE

Book Cover by We Got You Covered Book Design

Edited by Alexa Thomas at The Fiction Fix

For Mom

The best cheerleader and friend anyone could ask for.

ONE

CLOSING HER EYES, CHRISSY took a deep breath and reminded herself that it was only a house. There were no monsters lurking in the shadows, nothing lying in wait. If things worked out, there may be a restless spirit but, in her experience, those were harmless. Besides, she had her team with her.

Through the darkness of the room, she looked over to where Rodney stood, only able to spot him from the glow of the thermal imaging camera screen. She knew if anything happened, Rodney would have her back, and if that wasn't enough, she took comfort in knowing Bill stood only a few paces behind her, a large camera balanced over one shoulder.

Still, in these moments of waiting in empty houses filled with nothing but the typical creaks and groans, Chrissy always felt on edge. The anticipation in the silence grew into a smothering weight that pressed heavily on her chest.

"Is there anyone here with us tonight?"

The sound of Rodney's voice cut through the quiet of the kitchen, making Chrissy jump. She shot him a dirty look through the dark, even knowing he wouldn't be able to see it.

"Could you please come forward and tell us your name?" Chrissy asked.

Silence.

"The owners of this house tell us you've been messing around with these cupboards." Rodney reached out and grabbed the handle of a cupboard door, giving it a little rattle. "Do you think you could show us what you can do?"

Everyone held their breaths, waiting for the slightest movement, the hint of a whisper. Once more, they were met with nothing.

Rodney took a step away from the cupboards and shrugged. "It doesn't seem like they want to play. Maybe we should head up to the master bedroom."

"Good idea." Chrissy nodded. "Could be that whoever is here is upstairs. Let's go." She turned after Rodney, allowing him to take the lead, Bill bringing up the tail.

As Chrissy looked down at the floor, watching her steps, she thought back to her walk-through of the old mansion earlier that day. The floors were cherry and during the day the sun spilled in through the windows, showing off the rich red of the wood. Once night settled in, the floor had transformed into an inky black, bottomless pit. No matter how many times she did these investigations, it always surprised her how much a place changed once the sun went down.

The group reached the staircase and started up single file as stairs groaned and creaked beneath their heavy boots. As soon as they reached the top of the staircase, an explosion of sound froze them in their tracks.

"What the hell was that?" Rodney half-whispered.

"It sounded like it came from downstairs," Chrissy said.

"Yeah, like, from the kitchen, right?"

Chrissy nodded. "I think so."

"Let's go. Hurry."

Rodney took the stairs two at a time and rushed back in the direction of the kitchen, Chrissy hot on his heels, Bill jogging awkwardly under the weight of his camera behind them. Rodney reached the kitchen several moments before the others, and he let out a startled yell just before they rounded the corner.

"Guys! The cupboards!"

Chrissy looked up to where Rodney was staring, bug-eyed, while Bill panned the camera around the kitchen.

One of the cabinet doors stood wide open.

"Is that-" Chrissy started.

"Yeah! It was the one I was just messing with," Rodney said, his excitement making his voice rise an octave.

"Did you leave it open when we left?"

"No way. We can check the cameras, but I know I shut it." He raked a hand through his long blond hair. "That's so wild, man."

"If that was you," Chrissy addressed the empty kitchen, keeping her voice calm and steady, "do you think you might be able to do that again? Or perhaps make some kind of noise so we know you're here?"

All three went quiet, ears straining to catch something. Just as Chrissy was about to open her mouth to ask another question, another bang came from behind them, somewhere deep in the house. Chrissy whipped around to face Bill.

"Was that you?"

Bill shook his head. "It came from behind us. I think from the staircase."

Rodney pushed past the two of them and rushed towards the stairs. He paused at the base, one foot on the next step, and looked up. For about a minute, the team remained silent, hoping to catch another sound. Eventually, Rodney turned around to face Bill.

"Whoever — or *what*ever — is here in this house, I think they're messing with us." He spoke directly into the camera and then turned his gaze back to the top of the stairs.

Chrissy rolled her eyes before turning towards Bill herself, waiting for him to pan over to her, as she assumed her trademark no-nonsense expression and addressed the camera.

"Rodney, why don't you go to the top of the stairs, and I'll stay down here in the kitchen? That way, if whoever is here makes another sound, we won't be chasing after it like a chicken with its head cut off."

"Sounds good. Take the EMF detector with you," Rodney said, passing her the small black box. "I'll take the thermal and see if anything decides to come back up the stairs."

The two split up, with Bill following Chrissy with the big camera. Rodney was well equipped to record any anomalies with the thermal, as well as any of his own reactions with his mini cam.

Arriving back in the kitchen, Chrissy gestured for Bill to pan to the open cabinet door, then back to focus on her as she placed the EMF detector on the bottom shelf of the open cabinet.

"If you're still in here, I would love it if you could look at the device I just placed inside the cupboard. It's called an EMF detector, and it will help us to know if you are here with us. You can also use it to communicate if you'd like. The closer you get to the device, the more it will light up."

Bill panned over to get a close shot of the EMF detector, waiting to catch the little row of lights go off in response to the line of questions he knew Chrissy would launch into.

"Did you live in this house?"

No response.

"Do you know the people who live in this house?"

No response.

"Do you feel like you're trapped here?"

No response.

"Hey Chrissy?" Rodney yelled from the top of the staircase. "You getting anything down there?"

"Not yet. You?"

"Nada. I think this ghost is messing with us."

Chrissy cringed and yelled back, unable to keep the irritation from her voice. "Othersiders, Rodney, or at least spirits. You know better than to call them ghosts."

"Okay. I think this *Othersider* is messing with us. Better?"

Bringing her attention back to the EMF detector, which still sat lifeless on the bottom shelf of the open cabinet, she started back in on her questions.

"Are you messing with me and Rodney?"

She squinted at the black box. Was the dark playing tricks on her, or did the device just flicker? She turned and gave Bill a questioning look. He raised an eyebrow and nodded, acknowledging that he had seen it too and encouraging her to continue.

"Did you just light the EMF up?"

No response.

"I guess not. Or maybe you really are messing with us."

Another flicker of green, just the tiniest flash, but this time Chrissy was positive she had seen it. Her pulse quickened as she turned, giving the camera her best angle as she continued with her questions.

"Do you not like having us here in the house?"

This time, the first two lights flashed green.

"I understand," Chrissy said, her voice as gentle and soothing as she could make it. "It can be hard having strangers invade your space, but we mean no harm. We just want to get to know you, find out why you're here."

No response.

"Do you think it's fun teasing the people who live here?"

Three lights now, two greens and a yellow.

"I see. Well, you know, they don't really think it's funny."

No response.

"They actually think it's pretty scary."

Four lights this time, all the way up to the orange one.

Chrissy looked into the camera and shook her head in amazement. "I'm currently speaking to whoever is inhabiting this space on the other side. This spirit doesn't appear too happy to have us here, and they seem to really enjoy messing around with the current inhabitants and visitors. This is such an incredible connection. I don't think I've ever had an encounter like this before."

She knew Rodney would be annoyed if she continued without him, but Chrissy turned back to the cabinet and pressed on. She didn't want to share the spotlight for this one, not yet.

"Are you angry or upset about something?"

The lights flashed up to yellow.

"Are you angry about the way you passed on?"

No response.

"Do you know you've passed on?"

No response.

"Are you aware you're dead?"

No response.

Bill stood with Chrissy in the kitchen for a few more minutes, but the lights on the EMF detector had gone dark again.

"Alright. Thank you for talking to us," Chrissy said to the empty room before addressing the camera again. "That's probably good for down here. Let's go see how Rodney is doing upstairs."

As she stepped out of the kitchen, the EMF detector's lights began to flash rapidly, all the way up to the red light, as it emitted a constant, high-pitched beep. Chrissy whipped around, and in the same moment, every single cupboard door began to open and close, hinges squealing and doors banging. Chrissy's hands flew up to cover her ears as the noise filled the room, and she called out to Rodney.

Footsteps pounded on the staircase, and moments later Rodney appeared in the doorway, eyes huge as he took in the commotion in the kitchen. Then, just seconds after his arrival, all movement stopped. The lights on the EMF died away, and the three of them were plunged back into silent darkness.

TWO

"CUT!" RODNEY SAID AS he reached out to flip on the kitchen lights. The sudden onslaught of light drew a groan from both Chrissy and Bill. "That was fantastic. I think we got everything we needed, so let's call it a night."

Bill hefted the large camera off his shoulder and nodded, leaving the kitchen. A minute later, the sound of the front door slamming shut echoed through the house.

"You could have told me about the trick with the cupboards, Rod. Almost gave me a heart attack." Chrissy shot him a dirty look while opening the cupboard to retrieve the EMF detector.

"This way, we were able to capture genuine surprise," Rodney replied with a smirk.

"For a minute there, I thought I was going to pass out on camera." Despite her gripes, she had to admit the trick was impressive. In the moment, with her adrenaline surging, she was certain they had finally made contact with a spirit from the other side. But as soon as the lights came on, she could tell by the dopey grin plastered on Rodney's face that it had been one of his special effects.

"How did you get the cupboard doors to open and close at the same time?"

Rodney shrugged, tossing his long blond hair over his shoulder as he bent to unplug a cable from the sound equipment. "It was pretty simple. This place is already super unlevel — old houses, you know? — and the doors naturally want to swing shut." He straightened to prove his point, pulling open one of the doors and letting it swing closed with a thud. "All I had to do was create a little device that would push them open so they could slam on their own. See?"

He reached inside the cupboard and pulled out a small box with a thin metal rod attached to it.

"I press a button to remote activate them, and then..." The little metal rod shot forward, retracting into the device before shooting forward once more. Rodney looked up from the box and shot Chrissy a lopsided grin. "Simple."

"You didn't do any damage to the cupboards, did you?"

Rodney waved a hand dismissively. "Nah, it shouldn't have left any marks. But even if it did, it's not like the owners are gonna be pissed about it. They'll just get it taken care of during renovations."

"Still, we don't want to upset them." Chrissy peered inside the cupboards, scanning for any stray marks on the doors that looked fresh. "They did us a huge solid by letting us film here."

"Yeah, yeah. I know. Listen, if anyone complains about any damage, I swear I'll come back and fix it myself. Cross my heart." He slashed his finger over his chest, giving Chrissy such an earnest expression, she couldn't help but smile.

"Fine. But let's grab our stuff and head out now."

"Deal. My stomach is starting to make some strange whale noises."

Chrissy rolled her eyes and began moving through the house, going from room to room, collecting their gear. During set up, they had placed a handful of mini cameras and audio recorders in different areas of the house, and cables snaked through the lower levels like twisting vines down to where the larger recording items were. Leaving the heavier stuff for Bill to deal with, Chrissy packed away the last of the recorders and left the house, not bothering to turn the lights on as she went.

Once everything had been collected and loaded up, the group reconvened in front of the van they used for their investigations — a monstrous old beige Chevy G20 made sometime in the mid-80s, which they had affectionately dubbed the Ghostmobile.

Although she had lectured Rodney earlier inside the house, Chrissy didn't have any issue with calling the things that go bump in the night ghosts. The whole "othersider" thing was purely for the camera. With so many ghost-hunting shows out there, they needed something to help them stand out from the crowd. Streaming their show online was a start, but they needed more to show they weren't just echoes of what was already being made. As a result, they became the show that treated the spirits with kindness and sensitivity. That came easily to Chrissy, who had a firm belief in spirits and truly did want to help them pass on, or at least find some peace.

"Well, guys, I think that went well," Chrissy addressed the others. "We got a lot of great footage-"

"Can we please recap over food?" Rodney interrupted.

"Alright. Come on, then." Chrissy turned and hopped into the passenger seat while Bill took the wheel and Rodney eased into the back behind him. "What did you find that's open?"

Rodney glanced up from his phone. "Looks like there's a little 24/7 Mexican joint a few minutes away."

"Sounds like Bill's going to regret it in the morning."

Bill snorted and keyed the van to life. As they pulled away from the old house, Chrissy gave it a parting glance, and it struck her how perfect the location had been. The dilapidated Victorian was a stark silhouette etched against the night sky. The delicate wooden scallops of the house's facade were crumbling away, and the time-worn turret loomed, cutting the face of the moon. It was easy to tell that, at one point, it had been a beautiful home, but whoever had owned it before had let it fall into ruin. When Chrissy had first seen the place, her heart hurt to see the ornate details of a bygone era so worn down and left to decay for so long, but she had to admit, it made for a perfect location for a ghost hunt. It screamed haunted house. Too bad it hadn't been.

Facing forward once again, Chrissy let out a long, low sigh. They had enough footage to make a new episode, and it would probably do alright in terms of views. Rodney's trick with the cupboard doors would at least create a lot of chatter in the comments section. But the evidence Chrissy was so desperate to capture — the *real* evidence — simply wasn't there.

Arriving at the Mexican joint, the team spilled out of the van, appearing very much like a group of sleepless zombies. The restaurant was tiny inside, and the orange tile floors were dotted with standing puddles of what Chrissy hoped was water. She was too exhausted to argue that they should get back in the van and look for a different place to eat, so she followed Rodney, giving the questionable wet patches a wide berth. Besides, there were a few other groups of equally sleep deprived patrons devouring their meals without an ounce of concern etched on their faces, so it couldn't be that bad.

After ordering and retrieving their food, they plopped down in a booth and dug in. Chrissy bit into her bacon breakfast burrito and moaned as her mouth filled with salty, greasy goodness. The place may look like something out of a health inspector's nightmare, but it was the type of artery-clogging food that was needed after a long night's work.

Wiping the grease from her lips, she turned her attention to the two men at the table. "As I was saying, I think we got some great stuff tonight. The house was perfect, and that trick with the cupboards was inspired."

Rodney saluted with his burrito.

"Did you know what he had planned, Bill?"

With a guilty grimace, Bill nodded. "Yeah."

"I had to tell him so he could capture your reaction," Rodney said through a mouth of eggs and hot sauce. "How was it, dude? Was she freaked?"

Bill's smile grew a fraction. "Her eyes were bugging out."

Rodney let out a cackle and banged his fist on the table. "Epic. I bet you thought there really was a ghost for just a second, didn't you?"

"Ha, no way," Chrissy scoffed.

"Come on, Chrissy, admit it. You thought there was actually a ghost in that house."

"I can tell the difference between a real spirit and a hoax." She peeled the wrapper off her straw and held it up to one eye. After peering down the length of the tube, she stabbed the straw into the lid of her Diet Coke and took a swig to wash down the cheesy bacon and potatoes.

"Why do you do that?"

She glanced up, surprised to see Bill's gaze fixated on her.

"Do what?"

"Look in your straw."

"You don't know?" Rodney asked, his face breaking into a grin. "She's afraid of finding a spider in there."

Bill's usually placid face lit up with a look of pure surprise. "Is that true?"

Chrissy felt her cheeks burn, and she shot the dirtiest look she could muster at Rodney, who still wore that insufferable grin.

"Yeah, it's true." She crossed her arms. "So what?"

"Can you believe that?" Rodney asked. "She can face down a house full of ghosts but is terrified of finding a spider in her straw."

"First of all, Rodney, I'm not afraid of ghosts because they can't hurt me, whereas there are several deadly varieties of spiders. And second," she turned her attention to Bill, "when I was little, I really *did* find a spider in my straw. I took a drink and felt something in my mouth that was decidedly not lemonade. Ever since, I make it a point to check my straw. It was the most traumatic thing I have ever experienced."

Bill considered this, then nodded. "Makes sense."

"Thank you, Bill. If only some other people were as understanding and sympathetic as you."

Rodney bumped Chrissy with his shoulder and reached up to ruffle her hair. "Aww, I'm only teasing ya, kid. I probably wouldn't feel so great if I sucked up a spider either."

Chrissy batted his hand away but gave him a playful bump back. "You are forgiven, but don't call me kid. I'm not that much younger than you are."

"Well, you're too old to be my kid, but you could definitely be Bill's."

From the corner of her eye, Chrissy saw Bill wince at the comment, but he covered it with a good-natured smile.

"It's called experience, Rodney," Chrissy said. "We couldn't make this show work without Bill."

Bill's cheeks flushed, and his attention zeroed in on his burrito like it was the most fascinating thing in the room.

"True," Rodney said, taking a massive bite and continuing to talk through a mouthful of food. "I still don't know how we were lucky enough to get you on our team."

Chrissy nodded. It was true; Bill had serious talent as a videographer and editor. She had met both him and Rodney at a networking event a year ago, right after she had graduated from college. She had been drifting at the time, working double shifts as a waitress to pay the rent on the adorable little two-bedroom home she had moved into. The job market was a mess, and although her school had promised she'd find employment mere weeks after graduating, she was still struggling to land a job in her field. Each month that passed, she widened her reach, which was how she found herself attending a digital creators conference.

Seated at a table with people deep in the techy trenches, Chrissy was questioning if she had made a mistake in attending. She was only into technology at a basic level. Who did she think would hire her in a field where she had zero experience? It was just as she was debating whether she should leave early that Rodney had pulled out the chair beside her and introduced himself.

"Honestly, I'm not sure what I'm doing here. My degree is in journalism, not anything tech related," Chrissy said.

"Well, you know, there's a lot of interesting stuff happening on the web right now. I mean, look at YouTube. That place is really picking up steam. Sure, most of what's on there is cat videos and silly skits now, but who knows what it might turn into. Maybe you could have your own talk show," Rodney shrugged with a grin.

At first, Chrissy had laughed the idea off, but the more they talked about it, the more it began to feel like there might be something to it. It was when Rodney jokingly tossed out the idea that they make an online version of one of those popular ghost hunting shows that something ignited inside her.

"Yes! We should totally do it!"

"It was a joke," Rodney laughed. "Besides, there's a million of those fake-ass shows around."

"Sure, but they're all on TV. We would be the first to take it to the internet. Plus, we could do something the other shows don't. We could, I don't know, come at it from a different angle maybe."

Rodney began nodding. "Yeah. Okay. Like, maybe we go in there, guns blazing, calling out ghosts and demons. Really put on a big show. Maybe we could even have exorcisms!"

Chrissy shook her head. "That's already a thing. It's called Ghost Battles."

"Oh." Rodney slumped in his chair.

"Anyway, it's not super smart to approach the spirits so aggressively. They were living people, and they deserve to be treated with respect."

A large man seated beside Rodney who had been observing their conversation spoke up then. "You could come at it from the other side."

Surprised, Chrissy and Rodney turned their attention to the large man. He shifted his gaze away and mumbled, "Sorry to interrupt."

"No, don't be! I think you might be on to something..."

"Bill," the man said, offering a meaty palm.

"Chrissy." Chrissy shook the man's hand. "I like it. We could go for the softer approach. We can try to befriend the ghosts we come across. In fact, we won't even call them ghosts. We'll come up with some other word for them."

Rodney straightened in his chair. "That might work. We'll be cool about it, though, no super fluffy shit. But what can we call them?"

They sat in silence, mulling it over for a few moments before Chrissy's face lit up. "Just what he said," she said, pointing at Bill. "Other side. *Othersiders*."

From that chance meeting, the three decided to team up and make a go of it. There were several kinks to work out and schedules to work around, not to mention the fact that Rodney firmly did not believe in ghosts. But the world was changing, and people were making legitimate money with videos of themselves playing video games online. The potential was there, Chrissy was certain of it. It was simply a matter of time.

60 DAY NOTICE TO INCREASE RENT

Re: YOU HAVE 14 DAYS TO RESPOND TO THIS LETTER

Dear Ms. Rodriguez

In line with current market rents, I am hereby giving you 60 days' notice that the rent will increase to $950 on 10/31/2009.

Please make provision for this increase.

If there is no response to this notice within the given time-frame, it shall act as acceptance of the new rental amount.

Yours faithfully,
Landlord / Agent*
Alma Ford

Dated 07/31/2009

THREE

THE SUN WAS ALREADY slanting through the windows of Chrissy's apartment at a steep angle by the time she woke up the next morning. A quick look at the clock and she found it was already midafternoon. Mornings — or afternoons — following investigations were always rough. Shuffling into the kitchen, she went through the motions of brewing a pot of coffee, still shaking the cobwebs of sleep from her head.

With steaming mug in hand, she settled down on the sofa, pushing the neat stack of bills and notices aside. Those would have to be dealt with later, she knew, but work would come first. Flipping open her laptop, she began to sift through the *Othersider* e-mails. On occasion, in the sea of spam, she would find a request or two from fans to come and investigate. These places were typically too far away for them to travel to, with the cost of gas and motel rooms being what they were. As much as Chrissy would have loved to tell the fans they would come, the trip would devastate their meager budget, and there was no guarantee they would make enough off the episode to recover costs.

Chrissy spent much of her time hunting down locations she thought had potential as a haunted location and would reach out to see if the owners were open to the idea of letting her team film. More often than not, the owners would give her a resounding no or would ignore her inquiries all together. Some loved the idea and offered the use of their homes for free. One or two — like the owner of the old Victorian from the night before — asked for a couple hundred dollars for the privilege. With their minuscule funds just keeping their heads above water, she had to let the owners know it wasn't in the budget, but the Victorian had been absolutely perfect, and Chrissy had believed there was a possibility they would capture some legitimate footage during the investigation. And so, with funds running on fumes, Chrissy dipped into her personal checking account to pay the owners of the Victorian. A decision which, after finding not even a whisper of anything paranormal, she was beginning to regret.

There was also the issue that the supply of spooky looking houses within a hundred-mile radius was officially tapped out. If the team was going to continue with investigations, they would either need to shell out money to pay the homeowners, or they were going to have to start hitting the road. Either way, it meant spending more money than they had.

As she deleted the final email in her inbox, Chrissy sighed. No investigation requests. No sponsorships coming in. Shooting a glance at the pile of bills now teetering on the edge of the sofa, a solid lump of dread formed in her belly. Sooner or later, she would have to deal with them. Things were tight since she quit waitressing to focus on *Othersiders* full time, but so far, she had been able to scrape by. Sure, her sodium levels were sky-high due to all the packaged noodles she lived off of, but she was making it work. Now, with the cost of everything going up and rent being raised, it felt as though she was staring into the face of an oncoming train. Something had to give.

She took a quick glance around the place she had been calling home for the last couple of years. Though the house was on the small side, she worked hard to make the space as comfortable as possible. That started with purchasing organizers for every area of the apartment. A place for everything, and everything in its place was her motto. There were special dividers for her silverware, a rack for her coffee pods, and her makeup drawer was cordoned off into neat sections for foundation, eyeshadow, lipsticks, and lip gloss. There was never a stitch of clothing left on the floor of her room, nor a towel hung sloppily on the rack. Even her so-called junk drawer was tidy and compartmentalized. Everything was orderly and neat, and that feeling of control over her space was comforting. When life began to get too chaotic, there was peace in knowing exactly where every item was. Still, she knew that if things didn't turn around soon, she would be saying goodbye to her home.

With a small shake of her head, she packed all thoughts of her looming financial crisis neatly into a box in the back of her head and returned her focus to the work in front of her.

Next item of business was sifting through comments left on the previous videos they had posted. She sorted through the usual remarks about how parts of the investigation looked fake (they were, but she didn't think they looked it), how Rodney was being a bit of an asshole (he was), and how Chrissy was personally invited to investigate a ghost residing in some guy's pants (no, thank you). Dealing with the unsolicited comments from men was a pain, but one she had soon learned to ignore. They ranged from graphic details of what they'd like to do to her, to telling her she was a fat bitch who should kill herself, and everything in between.

Once she finished deleting all the nonsense spam and replying to some of the followers' comments, she stood and stretched the muscles that had started to cramp from sitting in one position for so long. She made another trip to the kitchen and poured herself a second cup of coffee. Adding the creamer, she allowed herself a rare moment of calm satisfaction as she watched, mesmerized by the forming swirls. A soft chime came from her laptop, bringing her back to the present.

Carrying her cup to the sofa, she eased back down into the small groove created from sitting in the same spot every day, ready to delete what was sure to be just another piece of junk mail. Her finger hovered over the trash can symbol before she started to read the subject line, but once she realized it was marked as an investigation request submitted through their website, she shifted the cursor over and opened the email.

She skimmed the words with suspicion, but as she took it in, a small blossom of hope bloomed in her chest. The email was from a man the next state over. He claimed to be a fan of *Othersiders* and had invited Chrissy and her team to come investigate a unique case.

I worked at Merlin High School during the 80s, up until part of the building tragically burned down, taking the lives of 67 students and teachers. The school was shuttered after that, and for the last twenty-odd years, nobody has known what exactly to do with the building.

I live just down the road and have become a sort of caretaker of the old place. I check in on it and make sure there are no squatters or trespassers and, over the years, I have had several experiences that can only be explained as paranormal.

I would be thrilled if you would be willing to come on out and investigate the school. There's no other group I would entrust this task to, as I know your team would treat the deceased students who are still residing at the school with love and compassion. They've gone through so much, and I know if anyone has the ability to help them move on, it's you.

Chrissy read through the email once more, a plan already beginning to take root as she considered the sheer size of the thing. This case could be monumental. Instead of focusing on house calls, they could start working on public buildings, and that, in turn, would force people to take them more seriously. This had the potential to be their big breakthrough.

Thoughts and ideas piled up, one on top of another. Opening a new tab on her laptop, she pulled up MapQuest and typed in the name of the high school. The town of Merlin was an eight-hour drive from her house. She figured they would need one day to drive there and one day back, plus a day to investigate, and one for interviews. More, if she was able to convince the caretaker to let them film for multiple nights. The whole thing would require at least four days. Difficult, but not impossible.

Next, she did a quick search for anything related to the school, hoping to learn more about the fire the caretaker had mentioned in his email. Something that large, with so many casualties, was sure to have been the major story across most of the state. As she expected, several old articles from different news archives popped up, and Chrissy plunged in, absorbing all its tragic backstory.

According to the accounts, the fire occurred during the homecoming dance in the fall of 1987. The dance had just gotten under way, and as it was still so early in the evening, the gymnasium wasn't at full capacity. Around 6:30, someone smelled smoke.

Each article became a bit vague from that point on. There was no mention of where the fire had originated, and it was only touched on in passing that for some unknown reason, the doors of the gymnasium had refused to open. Reports claimed that as students attempted to flee for the exit, they began to pile up against the doors, leading to several being crushed under the weight of their classmates.

A handful of students who had congregated near the back of the gymnasium were eventually able to escape through the rear doors that lead out behind the back of the building. Some of those same students returned through the front of the school and attempted to pry the doors open from the other side, but by the time they reached them, the fire had spread, becoming a raging inferno, and all those still trapped inside had perished.

Chrissy sat back, horrified by what those students had experienced – the blind panic as they tried to escape, only to be pressed against locked doors, pressure increasing as more and more of them tried to push and claw their way out. Their last moments must have been pure terror. It was easy to see why the building had been boarded up and abandoned after the incident.

From everything Chrissy knew about ghosts, it always seemed to be those who died unexpectedly who tended to stick around. There was a certain type of logic to it, she supposed, and with so many people meeting their end far too early at Merlin

High, she believed that the chances of finding at least one spirit still lingering in the school were very good.

Snatching a notebook from the table, she started to sketch out the details. An investigation this monumental, this steeped in tragedy, had more potential than anything they had come across before. Having a story viewers would be able to verify themselves would be huge. They could go online and find the articles covering the Merlin High fire themselves and see that *Othersiders* wasn't making things up. With this much potential, Chrissy was certain that this time they would find solid evidence proving there was something more after this life.

Satisfied with the rough outline in front of her, Chrissy picked up her phone.

FOUR

THE CONVERSATION WITH BILL had gone as expected.

"We've got an opportunity to go to Illinois to investigate an old high school. Isn't that fantastic?"

There was a brief pause on Bill's end. "In Illinois?"

"Yeah. We'll most likely have to take a few days to go out and do it all. I'm thinking we go really big on this one. We can find former students and do interviews, make it an hour-long episode, maybe even break it into a two-parter. The place has a pretty crazy history, so we might get some real footage this time."

Bill made a small, noncommittal noise.

"Do you think you could make that work? I know it's a lot of time to take off."

"I don't know, Chrissy, I've got a deadline coming up for a freelance project I'm supposed to be working on."

"Please, Bill? This is a massive opportunity for us. When is your project due?"

"Well, not until the end of the month," he admitted.

"Perfect! I promise we won't be gone longer than four days. Five tops, and Rodney and I will go over all the footage ourselves."

Chrissy held her breath, waiting for his reply. After a long silence, Bill agreed. "Fine. I suppose I can make it work."

She hurried to end the call, not wanting to give him a moment to change his mind, then punched in Rodney's number. Bouncing on the balls of her feet, she mentally urged him to pick up.

"Rodney! I have big, big news."

"Oh yeah?"

"We've been asked to come and investigate an old high school. We've actually been *asked*."

"No way. That's so rad! Where is it? When do we head out? I have some ideas for some new tricks, but it might take a little time to work out the kinks."

Chrissy grinned, his enthusiasm amplifying her own. "It's in Illinois, a little town called Merlin. During the 80s, the local high school burned down. Really tragic case. The guy who sent the email seems to think the place is haunted, so I'm hoping we have a chance to capture something real this time. I've been working out some of the logistics, and I was thinking we might go in a couple of weeks, as long as we can get everything sorted out. We could air it in the fall, around the same time that the fire happened. There are so many possibilities here."

She paused, waiting for Rodney to pitch in some of his own ideas and thoughts, but was met with uncharacteristic silence. When he spoke, he sounded almost annoyed.

"This doesn't sound like such a good idea, Chrissy."

"What do you mean, not a good idea?" she asked after a moment of stunned silence.

"I dunno. It sounds a little bit...ghoulish. I mean, all those kids died..." He trailed off.

"Yeah, and? That's what the show is all about, Rodney. At least, it's what the show is supposed to be about. It's what we set out to do, to investigate real hauntings. You know, of people who have died."

"It's what *you* set out to do, Chrissy. You know I don't believe in this stuff. Anyway, we don't have the budget for this kind of thing."

"I've worked all that out. We'll use what have in the budget, and I'll cover the hotel and gas on my credit card. If you and Bill just pitch in and pay for your own food, it's doable."

"You can't put it on your credit cards, Chrissy. It's too much."

Chrissy was about to object, but Rodney continued before she had a chance to say anything.

"I'm sure you think this is the right way to go, but what if the families of the kids who died come after us? What if they don't want us poking around, dredging up old emotions? It could cause a lot of pain."

"I always treat the dead with respect," she said, offended that he would think she would approach the situation with anything other than delicacy. "I wouldn't do anything to disrespect the families or the spirits, if we're lucky enough to come across one."

"Lucky?" Rodney let out a humorless laugh. "People are dead."

Chrissy sat back, stunned by Rodney's reaction. "Well, this is new. You've never had an issue with going to investigate before."

"This is totally different. The houses we've investigated didn't have much history. Maybe a couple of really old people died in them, but mostly, it was just stuff I made up for the show. What happened at that high school was horrible, and it was real."

"It was, which means there's more chance we'll find something real this time. We can use the investigation to honor those who died in the fire. Even if you don't believe, there may be spirits trapped there, and we'd be in a position to help them move on. This could be huge for us. We've worked our asses off to build *Othersiders*. It's been our dream to make something of this show, and I think that this is the break we've been hoping for. Please, just promise you'll think about it."

There was a long moment where all she heard was his steady breathing on the other end. "Fine. I'll think about it."

"Thank you. And if you could let me know as soon as possible, that would be great. I need to get back to this guy and tell him if we'll be taking the case."

"I'll let you know."

He hung up before Chrissy could say any more.

She flopped back into the sofa and stared at her phone. Rodney's reaction was unexpected. He was always the first one out the door, ready to charge into whatever place they were investigating, but she realized he might have a point. Although they had investigated houses where people had died on the property, they had all been single deaths, and most of them occurred over 50 years ago. None of them had been brutal or gruesome ends, just your run-of-the-mill deaths from old age or illness. Merlin High was...well, it was monumental.

A little shiver ran up Chrissy's spine at the thought. Rodney and Bill may not have seen it the way she did, but they would come around. With an investigation as significant as this, she didn't see how either of them would be able to resist for long.

Two days passed with no word from Rodney. When his name finally flashed up on Chrissy's phone, she just about jumped out of her skin to answer.

"Hey Rodney," she said, reining in her voice to sound as casual as possible. "How's it going?"

"Let's do it."

A wave of relief flooded her chest. It was as though a tight cord running through her had been snipped, releasing her shoulders which had been pinned to her ears for the past two days. Determined not to give Rodney any excuse to change his mind, she kept every ounce of enthusiasm from bubbling over into her reply.

"Sounds good. I'll send an email to the school's caretaker."

What she didn't tell him was that she had already sent the man a reply an hour after receiving his invitation, telling him that they would come. If Rodney continued to dig in his heels, she would go to Merlin and investigate herself. She would sleep in the Ghostmobile, if she had to, if it meant capturing the proof she needed.

"Alright. Well, that's all I really called for. But Chrissy..."

"Yeah?"

"Let's do this the right way, okay? I don't want to piss anyone off."

"Absolutely. Nothing but respect. Leave all your tricks at home if it makes you feel better."

After ending the call, she sat back and allowed herself to breathe a huge sigh before dragging her laptop over and sending off a group message to Rodney and Bill. The last two days were spent sketching out a rough itinerary for the trip, and she sent it off, asking the two of them to let her know if any adjustments were necessary.

It was settled. They would leave in two weeks' time. When Chrissy had messaged the caretaker — whose name she learned was Sam Cleeves — to work out the details, he told her they could come as soon as was convenient. He also seemed thrilled when she brought up the possibility of stretching the investigation out to a second night, going as far to say they were welcome to spend a whole week in the school if they liked. Although Chrissy did, she knew there was no way she could convince Rodney and Bill to extend their stay that long. It was a miracle they even agreed to four days.

With things beginning to fall into place, a weight fell from her shoulders. The stack of bills was still perched on the edge of the coffee table, the big red "final notice" stamped across the top envelope taunting her, but now she had a plan. Or, at least, the beginnings of one. Gnawing on her lip, she moved the aggressive final notice envelope to the bottom of the pile. She had a plan. All she needed now was for Merlin High to provide the rest.

FIVE

THE NEXT TWO WEEKS dragged on with a tortuous slowness. Summer was nearing its end, but the muggy heat still hung on, reluctant to release its grip. Even with dawn just beginning to break, the temperature was climbing, causing Chrissy's scalp to prickle as she stood outside her apartment, overstuffed duffel bag at her feet. The day had finally arrived for the team to set off, and as soon as the Ghostmobile lumbered around the corner, her heart jumped into her throat.

The beast of a van pulled up, tires squeaking against the curb as it rolled to a stop. Rodney slid down from the passenger seat and grabbed Chrissy's bag, tossing it into the back with a grunt.

"Jeez, do you think you packed enough?"

Sticking out her tongue, she scrambled into the back of the van, stuffing herself in between the rest of the bags and bins full of equipment. Nothing was going to put a damper on her excitement, not even being crammed in the back next to Rodney's smelly backpack.

Rodney hopped back into the passenger seat and twisted around to face her. "You ready to hit the road?"

"You know it!" Chrissy grinned cheesily and flashed two thumbs up. "Morning, Bill."

Bill met her gaze in the rear-view mirror and smiled. Popping the van into drive, they lurched back onto the road, and were soon slipping into the steady stream of commuters on the interstate.

The back of the van was a chaotic mess, with long black cables looped in great coils and plastic bins filled to the brim with all the gadgets the team used for investigations. With the three of their bags thrown into the mix, it made for a cramped ride, but Chrissy didn't mind one bit. Excitement and nervous energy bubbled up, keeping her thoughts only on the case at hand.

"It's going to be a long ride, guys," she piped up from the back.

Rodney reclined his seat as far as it could go without smashing into Chrissy's knees and threw an arm over his eyes. "I'm going to try and get some sleep. The only time I'm used to seeing the sun come up is when I'm heading to bed."

"How are you doing, Bill? If you're tired, I'm happy to drive the first few hours."

"I'm alright. Nothing coffee won't fix." He reached over and pulled a thermos up from the cup holder between the seats.

"Why didn't I think of that?"

"I'm surprised you didn't," Rodney mumbled. "You've pretty much planned out every other aspect of this trip, right down to the minute."

Chrissy leaned forward and gave his shoulder a playful swat. "I just want to make sure everything goes smoothly. This is going to be-"

"Huge," Rodney and Bill said at the same time.

For the first half of the drive, Chrissy's attention was glued to her laptop. She had downloaded each of the articles she found that covered the case of Merlin High, and she used the time on the road to read them over once more. In each article, the sequence of events was described the same way — homecoming dance, smoke, main set of doors stuck, then death. The one thing every single news outlet failed to mention was what had been the cause of the fire. Electrical wiring? Space heater? A careless toss of a cigarette? Not one word was said about that.

There was also very little mention as to why the doors had been impossible to open. Chrissy found it strange that they had even been shut in the first place. It was early in the night, and students were still arriving at the school. Thinking back to her own high school's events, the doors were usually left wide open for the entire evening.

The one or two articles that did bring up this point suggested the toggles on the doors that kept them locked had not been flipped, meaning once the doors shut, they reverted to being securely locked. It was the most likely reason, Chrissy supposed.

Her eyes drifted from the glowing screen of her laptop to the van's window. Low-slung buildings dotted the landscape, each one displaying a flashy sign declaring that they carried all of the goods you might need, from lawn care to storage, Jacuzzis to commercial baking. A giant phone number painted in red against a concrete wall urged passersby to call and ask for Steve. It didn't say what for, but Chrissy guessed from the massive piles of gravel surrounding the building that you were supposed to call Steve and ask him about gravel.

Buildings blurred together in an endless stream of commerce, and Chrissy found her thoughts wandering once again to the fire at Merlin High. The idea that it had been the work of an arsonist was brought up on some of the internet forums she stumbled across where people discussed their theories about the case. However, none of the newspaper articles had posited that as a working theory. The whole thing nagged at her. With a fire that deadly, the arson angle must have been looked into at some point, but it was never addressed in the articles. Still, she made a mental note to do some more digging once they reached their hotel. If she was lucky, she might be able to snag an interview with the lead investigator and put an end to the arson theory.

Rodney made a quiet grunting noise in his sleep, the movement of the van swaying his head back and forth and drawing Chrissy's attention. Why had he been so hesitant to take this case on? It made no sense. The weeks leading up to their departure, he hadn't shown any of his usual excitement about the investigation. Instead, he was withdrawn and subdued, responding to her questions with one-word answers. The whole thing left her with an uneasy feeling she was desperate to shake off.

Part of what had drawn her to Rodney during their first meeting had been his passion for life and everything in it. At the convention dinner, he met each idea that was thrown at him with equal excitement. Even the ones she made up only to make him laugh, he found some aspect of the idea that he was "super stoked" about. His enthusiasm was infectious, and it was impossible not to like the guy.

The dramatic shift in his personality was worrisome, but Chrissy tried to convince herself that once they made it to the school for the initial run-through, he would perk up. Even though he didn't believe in ghosts or the afterlife, he was most committed to the entire production. He never expected to find anything in the hours of recordings they collected, but still, he listened to and watched every minute of footage looking for something they could use for the show.

Yes, she was sure once they got going, he would be just as into the investigation as always. She found herself smiling at the back of his head as he snored away. A small cough from the driver's seat pulled her attention away. Two intensely blue eyes stared back at her in the rear-view mirror, giving her a little start.

"Doing okay back there?" Bill asked, his voice barely rising above the sound of the traffic.

"Yeah, doing great. Need a break from driving?"

He shook his head and returned his eyes to the road.

Bill. Now there was a conundrum. Where Rodney was full of excitement and jokes, Bill was the quiet one. The enigma. No one had never gotten a straight answer from him on where he sat on the believer spectrum. Rodney and Chrissy debated over it at length, but Bill never once said outright if he believed in ghosts. When Chrissy presented an audio clip that might be evidence, Rodney was more likely than not to dismiss the sound as a cough or normal house settling sounds. Bill, on the other hand, would give a little tilt of his head and only say something along the lines of "Interesting."

They were a bit of an odd trio — Rodney with his long blond hair and surfer dude persona; Bill, towering over all of them, giving off some serious Edmund Kemper vibes (though Chrissy would never say anything, as it would undoubtedly crush him); and Chrissy, the youngest, and shortest, of the group, and clearly the one in charge. Despite their differences, they fit together seamlessly and worked like a well-oiled machine from the get-go, and there was no reason to believe this investigation would be any different.

A long stretch of road later, a big green sign flashed by, announcing that they were now entering Merlin. Chrissy peered out through the window, hoping to catch a glimpse of the town's personality and coming up empty. It was like every other mid-sized town in America — fast-food chains, a handful of budget hotel chains, gas station chains, and acres of used car lots.

Disappointed, she leaned back and tried to tell herself that this was simply the newer, built-up part of Merlin. Somewhere there had to be an old street, with a name like Center or Main, and it would have all the charm she had given the place in her mind. At the very least, she could probably count on the high school to have an air of mystery and tragedy clinging to it.

They pulled into one of the more budget friendly motels in town, and the Ghostmobile shuddered to a stop, the scent of hot metal wafting up from the overtaxed engine. The three of them spilled out onto the blacktop, groaning in relief as they stretched road-weary limbs.

"I can't believe the old girl made it," Chrissy said, pulling open the rear doors of the van and dragging her duffel bag out.

"Never had a doubt," Rodney said, giving the broad side of the van a thump.

"Once we check in and put our stuff in our rooms, we should swing by the old school. There's still enough light, and we can get some great golden hour shots of the exterior. I could even call up Sam and ask him to come over-"

"Aw, come on, Chrissy. It's been a long drive, and I'm exhausted. We should just settle in and rest for the night."

Chrissy turned to Bill. "What about you, Bill? Want to come with me?"

Bill rubbed the back of his neck awkwardly. "It has been a long day..."

Frowning, Chrissy shifted her bag from one hand to the other, the weight of the nylon handles digging into her palms. "Fine. Let's go get checked in."

Once they had retrieved their keys and marched up to the second floor, they headed down the hallway until they found rooms 212 and 213. Bill and Rodney would be bunking together, using the second bed and extra space in Chrissy's room to store their more valuable equipment.

Chrissy shoved her key card into the door marked 212 and entered. The room was standard hotel fare — exceptional only in how unexceptional it was. Two queen-sized beds took up the majority of the floorspace, draped in inoffensive sage green and terra cotta comforters. Watercolor paintings of ducks taking flight adorned the wall above each bed.

Tossing her bag on the table in the corner of the room, she immediately unzipped it, moving her clothes into the dresser drawers she was certain hadn't been used for their intended purpose in years.

As soon as everything was placed in neatly folded stacks, she shut the drawer and flopped down onto the bed nearest the window. Rodney and Bill were probably right. It would be wise to rest up tonight so they could head out early the next morning, but excitement raced through her, making her itchy with the need to move, to get out there and have a look at the school for herself. She tried to lie down for a few moments, coaxing her mind to relax, but the roughness of the comforter did nothing to help the restlessness clawing at her insides.

She couldn't take it anymore. She needed to go. There were still a couple of hours of sunlight left, and even if Rodney or

Bill didn't want to come along, she could still grab some decent footage of the school with one of the mini cams. In fact, she thought, it might be better if she went on her own. It would help her to get the lay of the land and an initial read on the place.

Her mind now made up, she crossed the room and slipped into her chunky combat boots, impatient fingers fumbling with the laces. Stepping through her door, she headed towards room 213 to tell Rodney and Bill she was heading out for a while, but a thought popped into her head that gave her pause. What if they had changed their minds about coming? The idea of going out to see the school on her own had solidified in her mind, and she was actually looking forward to the time alone. Instead of knocking, she turned away and headed straight for the parking lot.

Chrissy drove through the streets of Merlin with a familiarity acquired through hours of poring over Google Maps. It was almost like visiting an old friend. She knew every twist in the road as she headed east, where she knew the school sat surrounded by quaint little suburban homes, as though it had been dropped right down in the middle of a neighborhood.

The roads narrowed, and the houses seemed to age backwards the nearer she drew to the high school. Newly constructed communities sat near the center of Merlin, each house identical to the next, before giving way to older constructions. The next street over, the yards were slightly overgrown, a stray dandelion or two poking its head up through the emerald blades, the paint on the homes a little worse for wear. The houses themselves seemed to be in good shape, only suffering from the beginning stages of neglect.

Further down the road, the deterioration became far more pronounced. The immaculate lawns two streets back were gone, replaced with scorched yellow grass, balding in some areas, overgrown and weed-choked in others. These houses were more weathered and worn, patches where paint had flaked away with the passage of time lying bare the wood beneath. A few homes had had their windows shattered, the gaping holes now covered with bits of pieced-together plywood.

Chrissy was so wrapped up in witnessing the gradual decay of the neighborhoods that she almost missed the sharp bend in the road. She pulled the wheel to the left, narrowly avoiding a dented mailbox perched on top of a stack of cinder blocks. Heart still in her throat from the near miss, she glanced up to see the school just ahead, rising behind a rusted chain link fence. In some ways, it was just like any other high school building — a couple of stories tall, earth-tone brick. Institutional, but inviting. The only difference was here, where the left wing ended, the second floor had collapsed into a large area that Chrissy assumed had been the gymnasium.

By contrast, the entrance to the school, as well as the right wing, had been untouched by the fire. No doubt water and smoke damage covered the walls inside, but the exterior remained pristine. She could almost picture the dismissal bell ringing, kids bursting through those wide front doors, yelling and chattering as they made their way home.

Chrissy pulled the van to the side of the street and hopped out. The sun slid lower towards the horizon, bathing the building in a warm, toasted kind of light. The school was beautiful, in its own way. Doric columns framed the double doors at the entrance, and tall, skinny windows ran down the length of both wings of the building. Most of the windowpanes were empty, the glass likely having been broken by punk kids with a penchant for throwing rocks. But unlike the windows of the homes down the street, nobody had bothered to board these up.

Reaching the chain link fence, she raised the viewfinder of the mini cam she had brought along and panned across the front of the building, moving from the right wing to the left. The golden bricks grew darker, consumed by soot and scorch marks the farther she panned. She focused the camera on the rubble at the end of the left wing for a few moments, capturing the devastation from long ago. Once she was certain she had gotten a decent shot, she returned the camera to her purse and hung her fingers through the diamond-shaped holes of the fence.

After reading so much about the history of the school, she had hoped that she would feel something the moment she saw the place, but she wasn't prepared for the heaviness that clung to the building. Waves of sorrow radiated from every shattered window. The longer she stared at it, the more it felt as though she had swallowed a black hole that continued to churn and grow in her gut.

"Gorgeous, isn't it?"

Chrissy jumped, choking back a yelp. Turning, she came face to face with a short, balding man with a thick white brush of a mustache, smiling up at the building.

"Sorry about that," the man apologized. "Didn't mean to startle you. Sam Cleeves. Caretaker."

With a shaky laugh, she reached out to shake the man's offered hand. "It's nice to meet you. Chrissy Rodriguez from *Othersiders*. I'm the one who responded to your email about investigating."

"Knew it was you. Recognized you from your show." Sam grinned then turned his attention back to the school. "That evening sun really makes her glow, wouldn't you say?"

"It's a beautiful building."

"I spotted your van and had to come check it out. There's been some trouble with vandalism, as you can see," he said, pointing a gnarled finger at the smashed-in windows.

"That's too bad," she said. "I just wanted to take a quick look before the team comes by tomorrow with all our equipment."

"I tell you, I was just thrilled when you agreed to come. It's such a lovely old school. They really took great care when they built it, but the town doesn't know quite what to do with the place. Some folks want to tear it down, say it's a danger, an eyesore." He paused. "A reminder of a terrible thing."

Chrissy could feel that reminder herself, the unpleasant sense of despair that gnawed away when you looked at the place. She couldn't blame people for wanting the place gone.

"Other folks want to try to salvage the exterior, gut the inside and rebuild it. They did something similar out in Utah some years back, but that would cost a small fortune, which the city doesn't have."

"What do you think should happen to it?"

"Well now, I think it should be left as is. Not as a reminder of tragedy, but as a memorial to all those kids we lost back then. A home for their spirits to rest in."

Chrissy studied the old man's face, searching for any hint of a joke. Finding only sincerity, she stared at the building again, shadows now deepening and filling the classrooms behind the windows with inky darkness. She wondered if Sam felt anything when he looked at the building. Did he not feel the waves of heaviness crashing over him, the riptide of grief pulling him under?

"I should probably get going," she said, dragging her gaze away from the school. "But it was good to meet you, Sam. I'm really looking forward to getting the guys out here tomorrow and diving into the history of the place with you."

"Oh, pleasure was all mine, my dear."

As Chrissy retreated to the van, she felt the presence of the building still looming behind her. Never before had she encountered a location so...alive. It was an exciting prospect. If she was able to sense it — whatever it was — from the street in broad daylight, she could only imagine what might happen when the sun set and the cameras were rolling.

SIX

AFTER RETURNING TO THE hotel and dropping off some burgers she had picked up for Bill and Rodney, Chrissy retreated to her own room. Neither of the guys seemed too interested in hearing about her little field trip, and truthfully, she didn't have much to tell them, except for the strange heaviness that hung over the school like a storm cloud.

She grabbed the mini cam and flopped down on the bed, skipping the video that she had shot of the school back to the beginning. She watched the slow pan across the face of the building on a loop, pausing now and then to admire some of the building's little details.

A sudden motion in the corner of one of the windows caught her attention. She skipped back a few frames and paused, squinting at the screen. Where all the other empty windows allowed light to filter into the abandoned classrooms, the corner of this particular window was completely blacked out. She tried to make out the shape of what could possibly be blocking the light, but the further she zoomed in, the more pixelated and distorted the image became, making it impossible to determine what it might be.

Looping back, she pressed play once more, this time keeping an eye on that one window, hoping that as the angle shifted she would be able to get a better idea of what had been blocking the light. As she slowed down, the window crept into view. There, in the corner, was the dark shape, which was still nothing more than a blob on the screen. The window slid across the camera's display and was almost out of shot when the shape disappeared. Pausing the clip, she skipped it back and played that part again frame by frame. One moment, the shadow was there, and in the next, it had simply vanished, allowing the sunlight to fill the entire window. Whatever the shape was, it had moved.

"Looks like we'll be dealing with raccoons or feral cats," she mumbled to herself, squinting once more at the shadow.

A loud, jangling chime shattered the silence. Startled, Chrissy dropped the camera into her lap, as though it had suddenly transformed into a ticking bomb. Realizing it had only been her cell phone ringing, she tried to laugh at how jittery watching that clip over and over had made her, but seeing the name of her landlord flashing on the caller ID brought her nerves back home to roost.

"Hello?"

"Ms. Rodriguez. This is Alma Ford."

"Oh, yes. Hello Alma. How are you doing?"

"I'm calling because I haven't had a response to the letter I dropped off regarding the new rent situation."

"Right. Well, I haven't had much time to look it over. Things have been a little crazy with work. I'm actually out of town-"

"It's been weeks, Ms. Rodriguez," Alma interrupted. "I need an answer as soon as possible. In the event that you won't be staying, I'll have to put an advertisement in the paper and arrange showings so I can find a new renter."

Chrissy squeezed her eyes shut, pressing the heels of her palms into her eye sockets until she saw stars. She had been putting off contacting Alma, not wanting to drag out the mental file stored away with all her financial worries. Once the box was opened, there would be a spiraling. There always was. She could feel it starting to happen already — images of her every possession crammed into boxes that filled up her parents' condo, of her mother giving her that loving "I-told-you-so" look but never saying it outright, the overwhelming knowledge that she had failed, would never find work in her field, would never be able to leave her parent's house, would never-

"Ms. Rodriguez? I need you to let me know one way or the other."

"Well, like I was saying, I'm out of town right now. Once I'm back, I'll let you know. Is that alright?"

The prim woman on the other end huffed. "I suppose, but just as soon as you return. We really do need to proceed with things if you won't be staying."

A knock at the hotel door drew Chrissy's attention from the conversation and she hurried across the room to answer. Rodney stood in the doorway, and she waved him in, gesturing for him to have a seat while she wrapped up the call.

"...and walk-throughs for potential renters," Alma was saying. "I do give you the courtesy of a 24-hour notice before bringing anyone through to look at the place, so you can tidy things up."

There was a way she had emphasized tidying things up that set Chrissy's teeth on edge.

"As I said before, I'll let you know my decision when I'm back in town."

"Be sure you do, Ms. Rodriguez. As soon as you're back."

Chrissy muttered her thanks and ended the call. Staring at the black screen of her phone, she sat on the edge of the bed. With

a deep, shuddering breath, she tilted her head back and stared at the ceiling, willing the prickling of her eyes to stop.

A small cough from the other side of the room brought her attention back, and she looked over her shoulder to where Rodney had made himself comfortable on the other bed. With a quick wipe of her hand, she brushed the tears that had spilled down her cheeks away and turned to face him.

"Hey, Rodney. What's up?"

"Everything good?"

"Sure," Chrissy said, pasting on a weak smile. "Just peachy. Did you need something?"

"I was just going to ask how things went at the school — yeah, I noticed you left — but it can wait." He stood and made his way towards the door, pausing as he reached for the doorknob. "Is there anything I can do?"

She stared down at the phone in her hand once more and shook her head. "Not unless you want to pay my rent," she said with a bitter laugh.

Rodney's face creased with concern. "You can't make it this month? I'm happy to lend you whatever you need."

Chrissy waved a hand dismissively. "No, no. I just got notice a couple of weeks ago that rent was being raised an extra two hundred a month."

"Ouch. You know, if you ever need a place to crash, my futon is always available."

Chrissy let out a small sigh. "Thanks. Hopefully, this investigation will work out as well as I think it will and bring in more sponsors, more ad revenue, more investigations, the whole shebang. If it goes well enough, we could even keep Bill on full time. Wouldn't have to schedule our investigations around his other projects."

"That would be pretty dope," Rodney agreed. "Think he would?"

Chrissy shrugged. "We can hope."

"You ever seen his other work?"

"A little bit, stuff from before he joined the team. I haven't seen anything that he's done since. Have you?"

"Nah. Hell, I have no idea what he does on the days he's not investigating with us. Dude's a little weird."

"He just likes to keep his business private. Not everyone is as open about the details of their life as you."

Rodney grinned and raised a shoulder. "You going to be alright, though?" he asked.

"Yeah. Thanks. You go on and get some sleep."

Rodney gave her one last glance before leaving her alone with the conflicting thoughts darting around her head. It seemed impossible to have so many emotions coursing through her yet still somehow feel like an empty husk. Everything rested on the success of this one investigation, which, if she was honest with herself, terrified her.

Instead of dwelling on the fact that she very well may be homeless if things here didn't work out, she turned her focus back to the high school, stuffing all of those worries back in their neat little box and cramming them into the far corners of her mind. Alma would have to wait. Chrissy couldn't afford any distractions.

Turning off the lights, she slipped out of her clothes and under the covers, reaching for the mini cam and pressing play.

SEVEN

CHRISSY FOUND HERSELF IN the halls of her old high school. At least, it felt like her old high school. The halls were the same, but they stretched out for miles in both directions. She was overcome by a sudden sense of urgency and knew that, for some reason, she needed to find her locker. She approached the row nearest her, searching for number 344, but the numbers this far up the hall were in the thousands.

Locker 2,433.

She made her way down the hall.

Locker 2,434.

Locker 2,435.

Wrong way, she thought hazily before she turned, starting back the direction she had come. The hall stretched out infinitely this way as well, and she stopped looking at the numbers. It would be quite some time before she reached 344.

Opposite the rows of lockers, the wall was covered in students' artwork, massive pieces of colorful construction paper streaked with thick black lines of finger painting. Piece after piece showed the same scene, black swipes against different colored backgrounds. She wouldn't call it art herself, but there was something jarring about it. Something felt off, though she couldn't quite say what, just some vague notion that it was...wrong. Ignoring the feeling, she glanced back towards the lockers to see how far she had come.

Locker 2,433.

She continued walking.

At some point, the paintings had lost their colorful backgrounds and were now thick finger strokes of black paint smeared against plain white paper. Further down the hall, the pages doubled in size, and the streaks appeared to be less haphazardly slashed across the paper. The lines were more evenly spaced and lined up, heavy black strokes running from the top down and off the edges.

Locker 2,433.

Her steps quickened as the urgency to reach her locker grew. Whatever she needed, she knew she had to retrieve it before class started, and at the pace she was moving, she would never make it on time.

More paintings flashed past as she jogged. The black lines, she soon realized, looked as though someone had dipped all five fingers into a bucket of tar, dragging them down the paper, almost like huge, black claw marks. But no, she thought, that wasn't right. Not claw marks. But what?

Locker 2,433.

Sprinting now, the artwork flew by. She tried to drag her eyes away from them, but they kept drawing her back. The paint had started to drip from the ends of the papers and onto the walls, and it hit her: they weren't claw marks. They looked like bloody black handprints. Fear squeezed her throat at the thought, but she forced her legs to propel her further, the idea of being late to class more terrifying of those bloody-looking prints.

Locker 2,433.

She stopped, breathing heavily from the exertion. She would never make it to her locker and back to her classroom in time. Whatever she was trying to get to would have to wait. Resigned, she turned around and headed towards her class and away from the unsettling paintings. But after only a few steps, she noticed something that struck her as odd, something she was surprised she hadn't noticed sooner.

There were no doors.

No classrooms.

Only a long hallway stretched out impossibly far. At the end of the hall, she could just make out the pinprick that was the exit, but it didn't matter. Deep down, she knew she wouldn't be able to make it. Besides, she still needed to get back to her classroom before the bell rung.

Chrissy started to run once more. She had only gone a few steps when a low, squelching sound came from beneath her sneakers. She glanced down and saw that the black pigment from the art on the walls had run off the pages and was spreading out across the floor. She tried to keep running, but her feet slipped and slid on the paint-slickened floors.

Soon the paint had risen over her shoes and past her ankles, inching its way up her legs. A seed of concern rooted itself in her mind as the thick acrylic continued to fill the halls, but still, she was more concerned about finding her classroom door. She absolutely could not be late.

Once the paint crawled up her thighs and over her hips, however, the reality of her situation set in. Half-walking, half-swimming, she tried to move further down the hallway. All thoughts of getting to class now abandoned, she kept her eyes on the double doors at the far end of the hall, her means of escape. Her breath hitched in her chest as she took shallow, panicky breaths, the black paint rising and splashing up over her chin and lips.

And just like that, she was submerged in the inky, viscous paint. It ran into her nostrils and coated her lips, tongue, teeth. Black sludge flowed down her gullet, invading and filling her stomach. Coughing, sputtering, she fought her way forward, desperate to reach the doors that never seemed to draw any nearer. Unable to hold her breath any longer, her body betrayed her. Her chest spasmed and hitched as she gulped for air, only to feel the paint flowing directly into her lungs.

Chrissy's eyes flew open as she gasped for breath. Bringing her hands to her face, she tried to clear the paint from her airways, her chest heaving as she gulped down great lungfuls of air. The darkness of the dream began to fade as her gaze darted around the room, trying to make sense of her surroundings.

The comforter lay on the floor in a crumpled heap, tossed aside as Chrissy had thrashed in her sleep, and she found the sheet twisted and tangled around her body. The room was sweltering, and her skin was covered with a thin sheen of sweat. She struggled to free herself from the sheets before stumbling into the small bathroom. A plastic cup, wrapped in more plastic, sat beside the sink. She peeled off the wrapping and filled the cup to the top, gulping the water down in one go. Still able to taste the bitter paint coating the back of her tongue, she filled the cup once more, swishing the last mouthful of water around and spitting it out in the sink.

Once she had cleared out most of the taste, she returned to bed, looking at the flashing red lights of the hotel's alarm clock.

It was too early to be up, but the thought of going back to sleep didn't appeal to her either. She shuddered to think she might find herself back in that never-ending hallway.

Perched on the edge of the bed, Chrissy realized it had been years since she'd had a bad dream. She rubbed the remnants of sleep from her eyes, allowing the images to slip away. But the feeling of being completely consumed and drowning in paint wouldn't leave. Dropping her hands from her eyes, she glanced at the clock once more and decided she might as well get up and shower.

Warmth flowed across her skin, and she closed her eyes against the spray, letting the water work its magic. As the tension in her back eased, she created a new little box in her mind to file her nightmare away into. It was something she learned to do a long time ago. In an attempt to find some order in her life, she began tucking anything unpleasant away into neat little boxes, pushing them far back in the dusty corners of her mind. Most of the time, it worked, or so she told herself. At the very least, it relieved some of the immediate pressure, allowing her to forget about the problem and continue as though she had no cares in the world. And so, she tucked this new box containing the nightmare right next to the much larger one that contained her financial situation. That box was harder to ignore. She would have to deal with it eventually. There would be no way around it. But for now, she did her best to keep it at bay.

Chrissy stepped from the shower and wrapped a thread-bare towel around herself. The oppressive heat from earlier had seeped out, abandoning the room and leaving only a chill behind. Grabbing the TV remote, she turned on the local news, needing the background noise. The announcer droned on about the forecast — still hot — as she went to the dresser where her clothes sat in tidy stacks. Suiting up in a pair of faded jeans and a tee, she raked her dark hair into a ponytail. It was just about time the hotel would start serving its continental breakfast, so she gathered her laptop and made her way downstairs.

The savory smell of bacon pulled her in the direction of the small dining room. The place was empty this early in the day, save for the attendant who was setting out the last tray of pastries, and she set her laptop down on a table nearest the television set in the corner. She piled her plate with fruit, scrambled eggs, and a bagel, balancing a Styrofoam cup full to the brim with coffee on top. A cup that would require at least four more refills, she thought, frowning at its tiny size.

Guests began to trickle in, and an hour later, the room was filled with the clatter of silverware and noisy conversation. Chrissy looked up from her work at the same time Bill appeared behind a group that had congregated at the entrance. She waved him over, pushing her empty plate aside.

"Morning, Bill. How'd you sleep?"

He gave a halfhearted shrug. "Rodney snores."

She grinned and scanned the room, looking for Rodney's unmistakable long blond hair. "Did he come down with you?"

"Said he'd be here in a minute."

"Too hungry to wait for him, huh?" she teased. "Well, don't let me stop you. As soon as he comes down, I want to go over the itinerary for the day."

With a nod, Bill slipped between the clusters of folks standing around and made his way to the buffet. When he returned a few minutes later, he was balancing his plate along with two cups of coffee, one of which he slid over to Chrissy.

"Figured you could use another."

"Definitely," she said, taking a grateful sip. "Do I really look that bad?"

Bill flushed a deep shade of pink, and he stumbled over his words, trying to backpedal.

Chrissy held up a hand, unable to keep herself from giggling. "I'm sorry. I'm just teasing."

Rodney suddenly appeared over Bill's shoulder, carrying two plates, each stacked with a sampling of every dish from the buffet. He dropped the plates on the table with a heavy *plop* and eased himself into the chair beside Chrissy.

"Morning, Chrissy!" he said, his voice far too chipper for so early an hour. "How did you sleep? Did you know that Bill snores?"

"That's not what I heard," she replied.

Bill shook his head.

"Must have been nice without someone honking away all night."

Chrissy made a non-committal noise, and Rodney looked up from his plate.

"Didn't sleep so good, huh?"

"Not really. Bad dreams."

"You had a nightmare?"

"I guess. I can't remember most of it," she said. "But it woke me up way too early. I'm going to need at least fifty more of these tiny cups of coffee."

Wordlessly, Bill took her cup and pushed away from the table, giving it a good rattle with his knees as he stood. Once he left, Rodney leaned forward.

"Was it about that call you got last night?" he asked, keeping his voice low. "You know...the apartment sitch?"

"No, nothing like that."

"You sure? Do you want to talk about it? Need a day to deal with whatever it is?"

She shook her head vigorously. "No. It was nothing. The best thing for me to do right now is to focus on the investigation. It's the key to solving the 'apartment sitch,' as you called it."

Rodney's gaze lingered on her face for a moment. He opened his mouth to say something more, but she held up a hand to stop him.

"Listen, Rodney, I need you to act like you didn't overhear what happened. Treat me like you normally do. No kid gloves, alright? It's not like I'm going to end up on the street or anything like that."

Rodney leaned back, putting his hands up in a gesture of surrender. "Whatever you say. I didn't hear a thing. But...just let me know if there's anything I can do."

"Thank you."

Bill reappeared then, easily holding three cups of coffee in his hefty palms. As soon as he set them down, Chrissy turned her laptop so the screen faced the others.

"Let's go over everything that needs to get done today. We'll meet Sam at the school right after lunch. He'll walk us through, show us where we can film and what areas will be off limits due to safety concerns. We'll set up all the equipment, film Sam's interview and another walk through, and get some shots of the school as the sun is setting. Once it's dark, we'll launch into the investigation." She turned to Bill. "How's the editing of the last investigation coming along?"

"On schedule."

"It'll be ready for tomorrow's upload?"

Bill nodded.

"Perfect. Then I suggest we use these few hours before lunch to get some work done. Bill, keep doing what you're doing. Rodney, I was thinking we could shoot a little teaser this morning. Give me thirty to get ready, then come over, and we'll shoot something. Sound good?"

Rodney flashed a thumbs up, and Chrissy scooped up her laptop, leaving the others to finish their breakfasts.

When she entered her room, evidence of her fitful night greeted her in the form of her sheet and comforter, both still laying in a discarded heap on the floor. Thoughts of the never-ending hallway tried pressing in, and she turned her focus to the application of her eyeliner to try to distract herself.

The crumpled sheet reflected behind her in the mirror, the sight of it pulling another fragment of her dream forward, a memory of a thick blackness sweeping over her. Stalking across the room, she snatched the bedding from the floor and flung it onto the bed just as a knock came at the door.

"Come on in," she said, opening the door and ushering Rodney into the room. "Where's the big camera?"

"So, Bill bounced right after breakfast. I didn't have a chance to grab it from the van before he left."

"He left?"

Rodney shrugged, nonplussed. "Said he had stuff to do."

"What kind of stuff? Where did he go?"

"Didn't ask, but we'll be fine with this little guy," he said, waving the palm-sized video camera. "I'm not great with the big one anyway. Too many buttons."

Chrissy gnawed at her bottom lip. The camera — a Canon XH-A1 — had been a huge expense for the team, one that had maxed out their credit card. She wasn't too thrilled about the idea of it bouncing around in the back of the van while Bill was off doing who knows what. Hell, she wasn't thrilled that it had been left in the van in the first place. She would have to talk to the guys about making sure that didn't happen again, but right now wasn't the time.

"You wanna just do it in here?"

"What?" Chrissy's attention snapped back to Rodney.

"Do you want to do it up against the wall?"

"Do I...what?" Chrissy opened her mouth, her cheeks burning, before she realized he was talking about shooting the teaser. "Oh! Right, um, yeah. That's fine."

Rodney raised an eyebrow and attempted to hide a smirk by turning his attention to the display screen of the small camcorder.

"Alright, let's get this done," Chrissy said, trying not to make eye contact.

Rodney raised the camera and nodded. "Ready."

"Hey guys, Chrissy here!" She beamed into the camera. "We have a huge announcement to make. We are on location! Now, I'm not going to tell you where we are — not just yet — but what I can tell you is this investigation is going to be intense. Be sure to stick around for more announcements and clues about where we're investigating. And as always, we hope to see you on the other side!"

Rodney lowered the camera. "Want to do it again?"

Fixing her face into a bright grin, she turned to the camera once more, running through the whole thing a few more times until she felt it was as close to perfect as it was going to get.

"Good enough." She let the fake smile fall from her face. "Bill can pick the best one and edit it onto the front of tomorrows upload."

Rodney nodded absently as he glanced around the room, taking in the surroundings. Chrissy watched him out of the corner of her eye as he walked down the narrow space that separated the two beds.

"Hey. We've got the same ducks," he said, gesturing to the paintings above the headboards. She saw his gaze land on the twisted sheets, the disheveled mess looking out of place in the otherwise tidy room. His gaze flicked toward Chrissy but made no comment.

"So, Bill didn't say anything about where he was going?"

Cocking one shoulder in a half-shrug, he shook his head. "Nope. Just said he had to take care of something and jetted."

"Maybe he got sick of being cooped up with you for so long," Chrissy teased. "He's such an introvert, he probably needed some time alone before spending another night with you and your snoring."

Rodney clutched his chest, feigning hurt. "Harsh, dude. Anyway, I've never had any complaints about my snores before."

Chrissy rolled her eyes but couldn't help but laugh.

"Right. I'll go get this uploaded onto the laptop for Bill to mess with later."

She followed him to the door. "Let me know when he gets back, alright?"

"Sure thing, boss."

EIGHT

WHEN IT GOT TO be noon and Bill hadn't returned with the van, Chrissy tried calling his cell. After the third attempt went unanswered, she flung her phone down onto the bed with a frustrated growl.

"Still no answer?"

She bit her tongue, recognizing none of this was Rodney's fault, but she was tempted to snap at him regardless. Instead, she just shook her head.

"Dang. Well, we can call a cab or something."

"Sure we can call a cab, but the point is that he has the camera. How are we supposed to get any footage without it?"

"We'll get what we can until he shows up. It's not a big deal, Chris."

"It's a huge deal!" She whipped her head around, the last hold she had on her anger slipping. "You might not care about this whole thing, but you know how important this investigation is to me. We can't have crappy looking footage. It has to be perfect, okay? Nobody's ever going to take us seriously if we mess this up, and then I'll be royally screwed. I can't go back to my family. I can't."

The room grew heavy with a tense silence as Chrissy fought to keep the tears that threatened from falling. Rodney shifted his weight from foot to foot, his eyes glued to the floor. She wanted him to say something, anything, that might help her focus on her anger. Anger was better than tears, but he kept his mouth shut. She sniffed and straightened, snapping her phone off the bed.

"Fine. I'll call a cab. You...just be ready to go as soon as it gets here."

"Sure thing," Rodney said, hurrying out of the room.

Her hands shook as she gripped the phone. Rodney didn't understand how much was riding on this. Leaving home was one of the hardest things Chrissy had ever done. Her family was close — perhaps a bit too close — and her parents had quite literally begged her not to go. Once it was clear she was determined to leave and start her own life, her parents let her know in no uncertain terms how stupid they thought she was being.

"You think you can make it out there on your own?" her mother asked. "You really think you can make money from those silly internet videos?"

"People do it all the time, Mama."

"And how many of those people fail? If you do this, you will end up on the street."

"It's going to take some time to build a following, but I have it all planned out. I'm going to stay at the restaurant, waiting tables until the videos take off. I'll have a steady income."

Her mother threw her hands up. "This isn't what we want for you, Christina. Please, listen to your father and me. You don't have to go. You always have a home here, with us."

She looked to her father, who remained silent through the entire thing, hoping to find a sliver of support. Finding nothing but disappointment, she turned back to her mother.

"I love you, Mama, but I want my own life. I know I can make this work."

"I can't force you to stay, but know this: when you come crawling back after you realize how foolish you've been, we will welcome you home with open arms."

Her father finally contributed to the conversation with a grunt. Her mother turned and shot him a warning glare, but the man wouldn't be quieted now that he decided the time was right for him to put in his two cents.

"You can welcome her home with open arms, but don't expect the same from me."

"Michael," her mother warned.

"No. She's our only child. She should be here, helping her parents, not swanning off to make stupid little videos for some internet weirdos." He turned to Chrissy. "Real life is going to come and hit you hard, girl. Your mother won't allow me to forbid you from coming back when everything falls apart, but you sure as hell won't get a single ounce of sympathy from me."

Those were the last words her father had spoken to her before she left. He refused to acknowledge her presence the last few weeks she was still living at home, going so far as to leave the room whenever she entered. She had tried desperately to mend the relationship before she left, to put a bandage over the wound, but her father was intent on letting it fester and rot.

Chrissy's grip on the phone tightened, knuckles bone white. Crawling back home on her knees was impossible. She refused to allow her father the satisfaction. Even if it meant going out and hunting Bill down herself, she would get the investigation back on track and make sure it was a success.

The cab driver had been surprised by his riders' destination when he arrived to pick them up just after noon.

"What you folks heading out that way for?"

"We have a ghost hunting type show," Rodney said, settling his backpack on his lap in the passenger seat. "Got called in to investigate."

"No kidding?"

"No kidding."

Chrissy stuck her head between the front seats. "Do you know anything about the school?"

"Not much, but I only moved here a few years back. I always wondered about that old place. Creepy as hell."

"Think we'll find some ghosts?" Rodney asked.

The driver chuckled. "Wouldn't surprise me if you did."

They arrived at the school, and after paying the fare and watching the cab disappear, Rodney let out a low whistle.

"I know," Chrissy said. "I felt the same way when I saw last night. It's beautiful, but kind of dark."

A sound came from deep in Rodney's throat as he stared at the building. Chrissy scanned the area and spotted a car parked beside the fence that surrounded the lot. A man in faded green coveralls leaned against the beat-up sedan, his own gaze resting thoughtfully on the school. Chrissy tugged at Rodney's elbow and tilted her head in the direction of the man.

"That's the caretaker, Sam Cleeves. He's the guy who called us out to investigate. I met him last night when I was here. Let's go say hi."

Rodney reluctantly turned from the building and allowed himself to be pulled away. The sound of their footsteps drew Sam's attention as they neared, and Chrissy gave a friendly wave.

"Hey, Sam. Nice to see you again."

"Well hello there, Miss Rodriguez. How is this fine day finding you?"

"Pretty good, thanks. How about you?"

"Oh, not bad. Not bad at all." He shifted his gaze to Rodney. "And this must be the other half of the team."

"This is Rodney Smith, my co-investigator."

Sam extended a hand. "Pleased to meet you, son."

Rodney shook the old man's offered hand with a terse nod.

"I think she's looking forward to your visit." Sam grinned, showing off a perfect set of dentures.

Chrissy's brow creased in confusion. "Sorry...who is? The building?"

"Yep. Came to me in a dream last night." He thumped a finger twice against his temple.

Forcing a little laugh, she cast a glance down the road. "You haven't seen a big guy in a beat-up van around, have you? Our camera guy went out earlier. I thought he might have come by to scope the place out."

"Can't say have."

"Well, I'm sure he'll show up," Chrissy said with feigned confidence. "In the meantime, why don't you give us a little background on the school. Once our other teammate shows up, we can do a walk-through of the building with you. You can take us to some of the locations where you've had experiences, and we can shoot some footage."

"Be happy to. Do I need to have my makeup done?"

"Nope. You look great just as you are."

Sam grinned and fixed his eyes over her shoulder. "I think your camera fella's here."

Chrissy turned at the same moment the Ghostmobile pulled up, lurching to a stop against the curb. Her eyes narrowed as Bill stepped down from the driver's seat and lifted a hand to shield the sun.

"Finally," she muttered.

"I'll go unload," Rodney said, making her flinch. He had been so quiet since their arrival, she had almost forgotten he was standing beside her.

"Alright." She turned to Sam. "I'm going to go get Bill up to speed, and then we'll get started."

Gravel crunched beneath Chrissy's boots as she stalked to where Bill stood beside the van. He raised a hand in supplication as she closed in.

"Where the hell have you been?" she asked, keeping her voice low, not wanting Sam to overhear and think something was wrong.

"I'm sorry. I just needed a little fresh air."

"For two hours? And you had to take the van?"

"I lost track of time."

"And why didn't you answer any of our calls?"

"My phone died."

Chrissy gritted her teeth and closed her eyes, taking a steadying breath before she completely lost it on him.

"I'm sorry, Chrissy. It won't happen again."

"Fine. Go help Rodney unload. We need to get to work."

Bill hurried around to the back of the van to help Rodney, who was struggling with one of the hefty plastic bins full of equipment.

Everything was carted over to the school's entrance, where it was then stacked in organized piles. Once the van was empty, Bill hoisted the camera to his shoulder and joined the others for the first walk-through. Rodney palmed one of the mini cams and Chrissy shot him a questioning glance.

"It's a big place," Rodney said with a shrug. "Figured it wouldn't hurt to have two shots of the walk-through."

Sam stood in front of the double doors and raised his arms in a grand, sweeping gesture.

"Welcome to Merlin High School. I'm pleased as punch that you folks have decided to come and investigate. I'm sure you're aware of the history, but in case you aren't, the school was built in 1924. Used to be, when Merlin was more cornfields than folks, this was the only school that served the area for miles. Of course, once things started getting built up, new schools were built to accommodate the growing population. None of them were ever half as pretty as this place, though.

"It continued to serve as the town's high school until 1987, when the fire occurred. It was a terrible time for Merlin, one that those of us who still call the area home never fully recovered from. I've been the building's caretaker for the last 15 years or so, and I have a real love for the old gal," he said, patting the doors with clear affection.

"It's a gorgeous building," Chrissy said. "Can you tell us why you called us in to investigate?"

"Well, as I said, I've been caretaker here for a while now. In that time, I've done my best to keep the place safe, keeping vandals from doing more damage. I usually walk through the building about once a week, make sure there are no squatters and such. I've had my share of...let's say, unusual occurrences here over the years. But the reason I called you in is the bigwigs in city hall have been having serious discussions about the future of the building. Many folks want to knock it to the ground and build something new. A strip mall, apartment buildings...something to reinvigorate the neighborhood." He snorted.

"And how can we help?" Chrissy asked.

"I'm hoping you folks will be able to show the town what I know to be true: this school houses the spirits of many of those students and teachers who passed here. If they go ahead and destroy the building, where will they go?"

A tremor grew in Sam's voice, and by the end, he had pulled a yellowed handkerchief from his pocket and honked into it. Chrissy placed a hand on his shoulder. He nodded his thanks and took a deep breath.

"With that said, shall we?"

Gripping a handle in each of his gnarled hands, he threw open the double doors, allowing the team their first glimpse inside Merlin High.

NINE

SLASHES OF SUNLIGHT FROM the open doors cut through the darkness, adding to the illumination from the broken windows lining the halls of Merlin High. It resembled any other high school, if you didn't take into account the peeling walls, fallen ceiling tiles, and detritus that littered the hallway. The wings stretched out to either side of the main entry while a wide set of stairs climbed upwards to the second floor.

Almost immediately, the creeping sensation of dread settled over her. It was similar to the heaviness she experienced outside the building but dialed up several notches. It made her skin prickle and she found herself wanting to look over her shoulder, certain something was standing right behind her. She risked a glance once, but the only thing behind her was Bill with his camera.

Chrissy took the scene in, trying to imagine the school in its heyday, filled with students weaving expertly between groups as they made their way between classrooms, the halls echoing with chatter and laughter. Now, the only sounds echoing through the halls were the sounds of their own footsteps crunching over layers of dirt and water dripping somewhere to her left.

"Now, the right wing of the school is perfectly safe," Sam said, breaking the silence. "It looks a sight, but the only real thing to worry about is the possibility of one of these ceiling squares falling on top of you. But that shouldn't happen, unless we get an earthquake."

"What about animals?" Chrissy asked. "I thought I saw a cat or something when I was here yesterday."

"Yep, plenty of critters have made the school home. Cats, raccoons, possums. Might even spot a bat or two in here at night if you're lucky. I do my best to secure the place but, well, I just don't have the budget to board up every window. Besides, they'd still somehow manage to find a way in."

He started down the right wing, giving them their own little walking tour of the school. They passed by a row of drab olive-green lockers and past a classroom. Chrissy hesitated before approaching the door, cupping her hands to try to peer in through soot-stained glass.

"Will we be able to go into the classrooms during our investigation?" she asked Sam, who continued down the hall.

"Everything on this side of the school is yours to roam. If there's a door and it lets you open it, then you're free to explore. The left wing has the most severe damage. There are some places you won't be able to go, even if you wanted to."

"Down here is the old home ec room." Sam nodded his head at one of the doors at the end of the hall.

Chrissy poked her head through the door and was hit with a wave of nostalgia as soon as she saw the room lined with cabinets. Drawers were left open, cooking utensils scattered over the floor. At some point someone had salvaged most of the appliances, but one lone oven remained, its door missing. Chrissy thought it looked like a creature frozen in a silent scream. She shuddered and looked away.

"Of course, these days nobody teaches home economics. Too expensive, they say," Sam said.

"Home ec was my favorite when I was at school," Chrissy said wistfully. She turned to Rodney and Bill, who followed along behind in silence. "Either of you guys take home ec?"

Bill shook his head.

"Wasn't an option at my school," Rodney said, sounding almost bitter.

Sam's gaze shifted to Rodney. He peered at him for a moment, then nodded sadly. Turning, he headed back up the hall towards the entry where they had come in.

"Sam, could you tell us about what kind of activity you've experienced in this part of the building?"

"Besides the possums, you mean?"

"Have you had any encounters in any of the rooms down here? Anywhere we should focus our investigation in this wing?"

"I've heard footsteps on occasion, but that's about all for down here. Now, the second floor's another story, pun not intended." He gestured for them to follow as he began to climb the staircase, kicking aside bits of fallen ceiling and debris to clear the way. "Pardon the mess. Haven't been up this way in a bit."

The second floor was identical to the first, with the hallways stretching out on either side of the staircase, but due to the gaping hole down at the end of the left wing, the lighting was far better. A bright streak of open blue sky made the location of the gymnasium obvious. The intensity of the fire led to the ceiling falling in, burying the area below and leaving the end of the hallway exposed to the elements. Even now, a gentle breeze blew through the hall, slightly tainted by the smell of soot. It surprised her that, after so many years, the scent of smoke still clung to the place.

The sound of footsteps caught her attention, pulling her attention away from the hole. Sam moved further down the right wing until he came to a door with a plaque that read "Ladies." The letters bubbled up into an almost alien font, the plastic sign a warped testament to the heat of the long-ago fire. It was a miracle it survived at all.

"You asked about where you should focus your investigation," Sam said. "Well, this room here has given me its share of stories."

"What types of activity?" Chrissy asked. "Have you been pushed? Scratched? Did it feel malevolent?"

A warning flashed across Rodney's face.

"No, no. Nothing like that. The young lady who spends her time here is actually rather lovely. I caught a glimpse of her once." Sam's mouth quirked up into a sad smile. "But mostly, I hear her singing."

"Singing? What kind of singing?"

"It's very soft, to the point where I can't quite tell what song it is, but I've never been much into modern music."

"Anything else we should know about in here?" Chrissy asked.

Sam scratched his head, the thin wisps of white hair shifting to expose a bald patch. "There's no water in the building, as I'm sure you've guessed. However, on occasion, I'll hear the taps in this room turning on."

Chrissy looked to Rodney with excitement, but his gaze was fixed on the dark corners of the bathroom, a faraway expression on his face, the camera in his hands forgotten and recording nothing but the tiles.

Sam moved on out of the bathroom, and Chrissy nudged Rodney with her elbow, signaling him to follow.

He took them along the hallways, pointing out the remaining classrooms down the right wing of the second floor before shifting his attention to the left wing, the scene of the tragedy.

"Now, up here is where you folks need to be careful."

"It does look pretty sketchy down there," Chrissy said, glancing toward the open hole.

"It is, but that's not what I'm talking about." Sam shuffled forward and pulled a coil of twine from out of one of the pockets of his coveralls. Attaching one end to one of the doorknobs of a classroom about halfway down the hall, he strung it across to the opposite wall, tying it to one of the lockers. Back and forth he went, roping off the hallway and securing the twine.

"It's easy to tell where the floor gives way during the daylight, but it's just about impossible to see in the dark. That twine should at least keep you folks far enough away that you won't accidentally wander out where the floor's weak."

"Good point. Thank you for that, Sam."

Chrissy glanced over her shoulder, hoping either Bill or Rodney would voice their thanks as well, but neither said a single word. Frustrated and tired of having to be the one to carry the entire conversation, she turned back with an apologetic smile. Typically, Rodney asked all sorts of questions in an effort to debunk any claims. At that moment, she wished he would say something, anything, so they could dig deeper and fully flesh out the story. Still, he remained tight lipped.

Sam's stride had slowed to a hobbling shuffle, and Chrissy realized his energy was waning.

"Why don't we take a quick look at the gymnasium, and then you can have a seat so we can do some talking head stuff."

"Well, gym I can do, but I don't know anything about a talking head," Sam chuckled, making his way down the stairs.

"That's what we call the up-close interview footage. Nice and simple," Chrissy reassured him.

At the bottom of the stairs, Sam led the group down the left-wing corridor. Evidence of the fire became more and more obvious the further they went. A set of metal lockers near the end of the hallways were so warped and twisted, they seemed better suited to a modern art museum. Sunlight struggled to filter through the soot-covered windows, casting everything in a strange muddy light that only amplified the uneasiness continuing to build in Chrissy's gut. The sense that someone was behind her, pressed against the back of her neck, sent a chill through her. Once again, she fought the urge to look back, knowing she would only find Rodney and Bill.

Reaching into another one of his pockets, Sam pulled out a penlight and flicked it around, the weak beam making almost no impact on the darkness. The light landed on a set of double doors at the end of the hall, rubble and debris from the ceiling piled in front.

"Do they still open?" Rodney asked, his voice barely a whisper.

"Melted shut."

Chrissy shuddered, all too aware it hadn't only been the doors that melted that day.

"Is there any other way to access the gym?"

Chrissy snapped her head around, surprised that it was Bill who asked the question. The camera was still hoisted up on his shoulder, but his head was tilted away from the viewfinder as he stared at the doors.

"Out around the back." Sam turned and led the way back into the sunlit portion of the hallway. "The building is just the brick shell over there. You can peer in and see into the gymnasium, or what's left of it. Might be able to go in a ways, but there's so much roof in there, you won't get too far. You're welcome to try, but be careful."

They stepped through the school's entryway and back out into the fresh air, and a weight slipped from Chrissy's shoulders like a heavy coat. The darkness from inside the school hadn't gone, but the sun's rays seemed to dilute it, making it far easier to tolerate.

"It's a bit later than I expected," Chrissy said, noting the length of the shadows. "Bill, you and I can start on the interview, and Rodney, do you mind starting set up?"

Without a word, Rodney went to the stack of equipment and began to rummage through the contents. Inside the building, he had been so withdrawn, even more than he had been on the drive out, and Chrissy wondered if it was possible he felt the same heaviness she did. Brushing that aside, she addressed Sam.

"Let's focus on the events of 1987 and the experiences you've had with the spirits here."

For the next hour, Chrissy peppered Sam with the standard questions, throwing in some unique to Merlin High and the activity surrounding it. By the time the interview wrapped up, the sky was a deep purple, and Rodney had almost finished setting up cameras throughout the school.

As Bill swapped the camera for a length of extension cord, Chrissy walked with Sam to his car.

"Thank you so much, Sam. You've been such a big help."

"Happy to do it."

"The guys will finish setting up the equipment, and then we'll get started. We usually stay at the location until about 4:00 in the morning. We'll do our best to keep quiet as we leave the neighborhood."

"Oh, no need to worry. Most of this neighborhood is empty. Nobody around to wake."

"I was going to ask you about that. It seems like a lot of the homes around here are abandoned."

Sam scanned the homes closest to the school, his eyes narrowing to slits. "Being so near the memory of a horrendous thing is difficult to live with. The energy." He fixed his gaze on Chrissy. "I love this old school. It was a beautiful place. Still is, but there's something dark about it, too. When an event that evil occurs, the energy stays. You feel it, I can tell. That energy has been leeching out of the building, moving into the neighborhood, spreading like an infection."

Chrissy's brow furrowed. "You said an evil event occurred. Are you talking about the fire? I was under the impression it was an accident."

Sam's eyes clouded over. "It wasn't an accident."

"The reports all said-"

"I know what the reports said. I also know that those doors were unlocked. I know it because I unlocked them myself."

Chrissy stared at him, stunned by this revelation and wishing she had thought to ask him more about the circumstances surrounding the fire when the camera was rolling.

"You were there that day?"

"I was."

A million more questions piled up, eager to be asked, but were silenced by Rodney calling to Chrissy. Throwing a quick wave over her shoulder in acknowledgment, she leaned toward Sam eagerly.

"Mr. Cleeves, would you be willing to answer a few more questions? I'd love to cover more about what you remember from the day of the fire."

"That would be fine," he said, easing himself into the driver's seat of his little sedan. "Might have to wait a few days, though. I've got a fairly packed schedule this week, but like I said, I'm happy to assist in whatever way I can."

After thanking him profusely, Chrissy jogged across the gravel and hardpan back to the school to help finish setting up. She had just reached them when she heard Sam's window rolling down and calling something out.

"What was that?" Chrissy shouted back.

"I said, you folks be careful in there."

TEN

BY THE TIME CHRISSY made her way back to the building, Rodney and Bill had gotten most of their equipment set up. Chrissy had them shift a couple of the stationary cameras to improve their angles, but she was impressed by how much they had been able to cover with only a handful of cameras.

"Great job, guys," she said once she had finished surveying their work.

"We've got audio in the upstairs bathroom, as well as Camera C," Rodney said. "If there's any singing going on in there, it'll get picked up."

Chrissy dug into one of the equipment boxes and pulled out the sandwiches she stopped to pick up on the way to the school, passing them out to the others. Settling down on the steps in front of the building, they chowed down on slightly soggy sandwiches and warm sodas. It hit her how quiet the neighborhood was. It was the tail-end of summer, and the streets should be full of children trying to eke out the last bit of freedom before school started up. Instead, the only sound came from the chorus of night bugs in the tall, dry weeds.

"Feels like I'm back in high school," Chrissy said.

Rodney snorted. "Thank God we're not."

"Not a fun time for you?"

“Was it a fun time for anyone?”

Chrissy shrugged. “It wasn’t that bad for me. Not great — I wasn’t Miss Popularity — but it was alright.”

“Of course it was. You’re cute. Things were different for a long-haired freak like me,” Rodney said in a tone that hinted he was only half-joking.

“What about you, Bill?” she asked.

Bill shook his head. “School’s rough when you’re the quiet new kid.”

“Well,” she said, trying to lighten the mood a bit, “I would have been friends with both of you if we went to the same school.”

“You would not,” Rodney snorted. “None of us would be in the same building, let alone class.”

She stood, brushing crumbs from her shirt. The sun had disappeared, and a smattering of stars flickered against an umbral sky. A light night wind blew away the last of the heat of the day, sweet and invigorating.

“Time to get a move on.”

Grabbing one of the audio recorders and a flashlight from the nearest box, Chrissy stepped through the double doors and into the pitch-black halls of Merlin High.

They paused inside the entryway, allowing their eyes to grow accustomed to the dark. In the stillness, she flexed the fingers of her free hand, searching for a shift in the atmosphere now that the light had gone. The darkness amplified the oppressive feeling that filled the school. Her hand trembled, and she chastised herself for being so nervous. Rodney came up behind her, his mere presence helping to calm the bundle of nerves going off like fireworks in her belly.

“Where to first?”

"Let's focus on the right wing." She turned to Bill, who stood beside her, camera perched on his shoulder. Raking her hands through her hair to smooth down any flyaways, she steadied her voice and spoke into the camera in a low tone.

"Hey, all. This is our first night investigating Merlin High School. Tonight, we'll be focusing on the right wing, where there have been reports of disembodied voices, sounds of taps running, and full-bodied apparitions. We're going to start on the first floor, paying extra attention to the audio in this area, as the caretaker has reported hearing footsteps here. After we've spent a few hours investigating down here, we'll head upstairs, where the ladies' room is a hot spot for activity. We're hoping we can make a connection with the spirits who may still be lingering here, get to know them and their stories, and help them move to the other side if they're interested."

She took a couple of steps deeper into the inky gloom of the hallway. Debris crunched beneath the soles of their sneakers as she led the procession past the first row of lockers towards the first classroom door, the one with the soot-darkened window. Placing her hand on the doorknob, she turned and pulled, meeting with some resistance before the door relented, its rusted hinges squealing in protest.

Peering through the darkness inside, Chrissy tried to make sense of the shapes lurking in the shadows. Rodney was soon beside her with the thermal camera, giving the room a slow scan, his face lit by the glow emitted from the screen.

"Any heat signatures popping up?" she asked, sneaking a quick glance at the camera's display.

"Nothing."

Now that her eyes had adjusted to the dim light, Chrissy glanced around the room again. Someone had piled all the students' desks on top of each other in the center of the room. Chair legs jutted out in every direction, and the entire structure looked as though it could topple at any moment. At the front of the room stood the teacher's desk, a thick layer of dirt and debris covering the piles of paper and books left behind. Gingerly, she reached out and picked up one of the textbooks, brushing her hand across the cover to clear some of the grime away, but the soot and age appeared to be baked in. The pages, brittle and wavy with damage, crackled as she carefully worked them apart, looking for a hint of what had been taught in this room. The contents of the book were faded, but if she squinted, she could make out faint numbers on one of the pages.

"It looks like this might have been a math room," she said, setting the book back down in its original spot on top of the desk.

Rodney stepped into the shot and gave a dramatic shudder. "Math is scarier than any ghost I've ever encountered."

He sounded more like his usual self, which was good — great, even — but hadn't she just gone over this with him during their last investigation? Realizing he couldn't see her face, she nudged him with her elbow. "How many times do I have to tell you to stop using that word on camera? It just makes more work for Bill."

"Sorry," Rodney replied, not sounding it at all.

With a shake of her head, Chrissy turned her attention back to the classroom, pulling the flashlight from her back pocket.

"I want to get a better look at this room." The beam of light cut through the shadows, sweeping over the desk and up to the blackboard on the wall behind it. If anything had been written on it at the time of the fire, it was long gone now. Moving the light over the walls, it surprised her how much damage the fire had caused this far down the hall. The dingy gray of smoke damage covered the walls, broken up by splotches of lighter gray where paint had peeled away, revealing the drywall beneath.

With a better feel for the room, Chrissy clicked off the flashlight, plunging them back into darkness. Letting her eyes adjust once more, she stepped up to the teacher's desk and motioned for Bill to move the camera back to her.

"Hello," she addressed the empty room. "My name is Chrissy. These are my friends, Rodney and Bill. Mr. Cleeves has asked us to come so we can hopefully talk to the people who might still be residing here. If there's someone here who would like to come forward, we have some gadgets here that will allow us to hear you, possibly even see you. We would love it if you would come talk to us."

After ensuring the little red light on the audio recorder was on, she placed it on the desk and extended a hand to Rodney, who deposited an EMF detector in her palm. She set that right beside the recorder.

"If there's anyone here, could you please come over to this device with the red light and speak into it? Or you can touch the device next to it to make it light up, and that will let us know you're here with us."

Chrissy took a step back and turned to Rodney, waiting for him to start his line of questioning. That was how it always went: Chrissy would make the introductions, and Rodney would start asking the first round of questions. When he didn't begin right away, Chrissy glanced up to see what had drawn his attention and found him staring blankly at the display screen of the thermal camera.

"Are you picking something up?"

He jerked his head up with a guilty expression. "No, nothing."

"Well, do you want to start asking some questions?" Chrissy asked, impatience mounting.

"I'm good."

Chrissy cocked her head. Rodney never gave up the first line of questioning. She shot him another glance, one that asked if he was alright, but he waved her off. Brow furrowed, she shrugged and returned to the EMF device, launching into the standard questions: asking for names, were they happy being at the school, did they have any messages to pass on? The lights on the EMF never once blinked.

"The caretaker said that he's heard footsteps in this hall, right?"

Chrissy glanced over at Rodney and nodded. "Yeah. Said sometimes it sounds like somebody's running."

"Why don't we set up out here for a while, see if we can't catch something ourselves on audio or thermal?"

The group had gone into a handful of other classrooms, but not a single light blipped on their equipment. Chrissy figured setting up in the hallway was as good an idea as any at this point. At least it would break up the monotony of shooting empty classroom after empty classroom.

Placing the EMF on the laminate tiles of the hallway floor, she stepped back until she was leaning up against a set of lockers and repeated the same line of questions she had already used several times that night.

They were a few hours into the investigation now and had nothing but footage of Chrissy talking into empty rooms. She tilted her chin, frowning down at the EMF detector. When she had researched the school's history, the excitement that bubbled up with every article she read had become a kind of high. There had been no doubt in her mind the school would offer up actual proof of the paranormal, a first for her team. But so far, other than the bleak oppression that seeped out from every corner of the building, Merlin High seemed to be as dead as all the other places they had investigated before.

As she chewed on that disappointing fact, something else occurred to her. There were no signs of the afterlife here, but there was also no evidence of life, either. Sam mentioned that all kinds of creatures had claimed the abandoned building as their home, and she had seen a shadow moving in the window herself. Yet, as she looked up and down the hallway, she realized the tell-tale sounds of scurrying feet and scratching in the walls was absent. It was odd. A place this open and exposed, they should have seen some trace of the animals who had taken up residence.

Chrissy was about to comment on the strangeness of it when Bill wheeled around, the camera on his shoulder missing smashing into her face by an inch.

"What the hell was that about?" she gasped, pressing a hand to her chest.

"I..." Bill started, then turned back, shaking his head. "I thought I heard something back there."

Rodney pushed himself away from the wall he had been leaning against and peered down the dark corridor behind Bill. "What, like a raccoon or something?"

Bill remained motionless before offering an uncertain shrug.

"I haven't seen any signs of animal life in here," Chrissy said. "What did it sound like, Bill?"

"I mean, it maybe sounded kind of like a...a breath?"

"Do you think the camera's audio caught it?" she asked, excitement creeping into her voice.

Bill just shrugged again.

Holding her audio recorder forward, Chrissy positioned herself in front of Bill's camera, speaking into the depths of the hallway. "Is someone with us right now?"

A hush settled into the halls as they each strained to catch even the faintest noise. Chrissy's neck prickled with anticipation. After a long stretch of nothing, she released the breath that had been pent up in her chest.

"We would love it if you would come forward and speak with us." Chrissy cringed at how desperate she sounded, and she did her best to pull it back. "We're only going to be here for a couple of days, so if you have something — anything — to say, you need to do it now so we have a chance to help you."

"Do you know they want to tear down the school?"

The sound of Bill's voice made Chrissy jump again. He had never asked questions during an investigation before. He was strictly a behind the scenes kind of guy. Her eyes darted between him and Rodney, marveling at the complete role reversal, but she was grateful at least one of them was stepping up so she wouldn't have to carry the investigation herself.

"They probably should," Rodney said under his breath.

"What?"

"I mean, look...there's no activity here. Yeah, the place is creepy, but mostly, it's just a depressing eyesore. I don't blame them for wanting to bulldoze it."

"We don't know that there's no activity," Chrissy snapped. She'd have to remember to tell Bill to cut this part out of the footage later. "I'm not sure what your deal is, Rodney, but you are really botching this investigation. Do you think you could at least pretend to be interested?"

Through the darkness, she watched his head fall back as he let out a heavy sigh. When he spoke, his tone was light and chipper and dripping with sarcasm. "Sure thing, boss. Let's go catch us a ghost."

She raised both middle fingers in salute, knowing he would get the general idea of even in the dark.

"Alright, let's try this again," she said, turning her attention back to Bill, who was still pointing his camera into the dark behind Rodney. Taking a deep breath, she steadied herself and started back where they left off. "How do you feel about the idea they might tear down-"

Bill took a sudden staggering step backwards. Chrissy spun around and searched the hallway for whatever had startled him but couldn't make anything out in the pitch black.

"Dude, what's wrong?" Rodney hurried over to Bill, placing a steadying hand on his shoulder. "Did you see something?"

Bill shook his head and continued to stare down the length of the corridor.

Audio recorder in hand, Chrissy moved deeper into the hall towards where he had been filming. Nothing appeared out of place, and the only thing she could hear were the shallow breaths coming from Bill.

"Hello? Is somebody down there?"

"It was nothing," Bill said under his breath. From the sound of his voice, she was certain it hadn't been nothing.

A few steps further down the hallway, and she felt it at once: the subtle shift in energy that made the back of her hands all staticky. The heaviness that had been their constant companion turned darker down here, angrier.

"Bill," she said, hurrying back to the group, "I know you don't get involved with the investigations, but would you mind asking some more questions? Whoever it is, they only started to interact after you spoke up."

He shifted his weight one foot to the other and cleared his throat a few times. "I guess so. What do you want me to say?"

"Just ask if they want to talk to us."

Bill cleared his throat again, his voice coming out strangled. "If someone's here, do you want to talk?"

The air was thick, and Chrissy stole a quick glance at Bill, waiting for a reaction. His lips were pinched shut, each exhale whistling through his nose, and she thought if she were to point the flashlight at his face, he would be white as a sheet. When no response came, he turned to her for another prompt.

"Ask them again about the idea of tearing down the school. That got its attention last time."

"Would it upset you if they tore down this building?"

After another stretch of silence, Rodney spoke up. "I think we should move on. If anything was down here, they're done talking now."

Chrissy hesitated before reluctantly agreeing. "Alright. Why don't we go upstairs and try the ladies' room?"

After gathering up the EMF from the floor, the group turned to head up the stairs. Chrissy took one last glance over her shoulder down the hall. She wasn't sure what Bill had or hadn't seen, but she hoped one of their devices had been able to capture it.

Audio Transcript

[00:26] CHRISSY: Alright, we're here on the second floor of Merlin High School in the girl's bathroom. There have been reports of a girl singing in here, as well as the sound of taps turning on and off.

[00:27] RODNEY: Should Bill and I be in here?

[00:27] RODNEY: [Laughter]

[00:27] CHRISSY: If the girl Mr. Cleeves has heard in here is with us, I just want to let you know that there are two males present. We don't mean to intrude. Mr. Cleeves has asked us to come and look into things and see if we can possibly help you.

[00:30] CHRISSY: We've heard that you like to sing in here. Would you mind singing for us?

[00:31] RODNEY: I wouldn't want to sing for random strangers.

[00:31] CHRISSY: Shh.

[00:31] RODNEY: I'm just saying.

[00:32] CHRISSY: Whoever is in here, could you let us know if you can hear us?

[00:33] CHRISSY: If there's anyone in here with us, can you tell us your name?

[00:35] RODNEY: I don't think she wants to talk tonight.

[00:35] CHRISSY: Maybe we should play some music? See if that will bring her out?

[00:35] RODNEY: We can try.

[00:36] Blondie's *Call Me* starts to play.

[00:36] CHRISSY: Oh, I love this song.

[00:37] RODNEY: It's a classic.

[00:37] CHRISSY: Do you remember this song?

[00:38] [Music stops]

[00:38] [Loud bang]

[00:38] CHRISSY: What was that?

[00:39] BILL: Sorry. I leaned against the stall door.

[00:39] CHRISSY: Jesus.

[00:39] RODNEY: [Laughs] Rookie mistake.

[00:40] CHRISSY: Anyway. If you're in here with us, did you like the music?

[00:41] RODNEY: Maybe she doesn't like Blondie.

[00:41] CHRISSY: Who doesn't like Blondie?

[00:41] BILL: Me.

[00:41] RODNEY: [Laughs]

[00:42] CHRISSY: If there's anyone in here, if you could make a noise, bang on the pipes, to let us know you're here, we would really appreciate it.

[00:43] RODNEY: Sam said you like to turn on the taps. If you're too shy to sing, maybe you can try to turn on one of the taps here.

[00:45] CHRISSY: Were you here the day the gym caught fire?

[00:46] CHRISSY: Were you a student here at Merlin High?

[00:47] RODNEY: Were you a teacher?

[00:49] RODNEY: We're not really getting much up here.

[00:49] CHRISSY: We're going to step out for a bit, but I'm going to leave this recorder here...and if you want to say something, you can just step right up and speak into it, and we'll be able to hear you when we listen to it later.

[00:50] RODNEY: Let's hit the art room next.

[00:50] CHRISSY: Sounds good. Bill, follow behind us and get a shot of the art room over our shoulders maybe. There are some abandoned projects that are still up on the walls, so if you want [unintelligible].

[00:57] [Sound of door swinging]

[01:39] [Quiet humming]

[01:39] [Quiet humming stops]

Eleven

THINGS WRAPPED UP AT the school around 3:00 a.m. After an aggravatingly uneventful investigation and a long day of touring and setting up, everyone was ready to head back to the hotel for some much-needed shuteye.

After mumbling their goodnights, Chrissy stumbled into her room, pausing only for a moment to strip out of her grimy clothes before collapsing onto the bed. She was fast asleep minutes after her head hit the pillow.

An hour later, the smell of something burning jolted her awake. Her eyes snapped open to a room thick with choking black plumes of smoke. In a panic, she rolled off the bed and to the floor. She crawled on all fours, the dark billows confusing and disorienting her as she scrambled around searching for the door.

Her eyes narrowed to slits as the smoke burned, causing tears to streak down her cheeks and blur her vision even further. What small gulps of creosote-filled air she was able to force into her lungs were quickly expelled by her panicked exhalations.

This was the end.

She was going to die.

Those thoughts spurred her on. She refused to let her final moments be in a strange hotel room far from her family or friends. Fingers splayed out in front of her, she struggled forward, smashing her knuckles into a wall. With no air in her, she was unable to cry out in pain, but the wall was hope. If she could just follow it, eventually she would come to the door.

Gripping the tiny edge of the baseboard with her fingertips, she inched her way forward, hitting a corner, then continuing on. The smoke grew thicker, an odd metallic scent in it. Something familiar but tainted. It was sulfurous, sweet and sickening, and made her gag. It pressed into her, impossibly growing in weight, pushing against her exposed skin, pushing her down. She crawled faster and ran into the leg of a table.

The table.

On the opposite side of the room from the door.

Whimpering with despair, she turned around, moving as fast as she could on her belly, eyes squeezed shut against the burning smoke. Her knees and elbows stung, the rough carpet peeling her skin raw with every inch forward. Her fingers ached from smashing into the corner again, but at least now, she knew where she was, and she knew she was heading in the right direction.

Lungs on fire and body aching, she risked opening her eyes to search for a beacon, a sliver of light coming through the bottom of the door.

There. Only a few feet to go.

She screwed her eyes shut again, sandpaper eyelids scraping over her dry corneas, and she threw her body forward.

The texture beneath her fingers suddenly changed, eliciting another whimper, but one full with triumph. She had made it to the door.

Shifting all her weight onto her stinging, raw knees, her aching hands clawed for the door handle. Just as she brushed against the edge, something grazed her thigh. She gasped, her chest filling with that foul, charred scent.

"No, no, no..."

Desperate, she gripped the door frame and hauled herself to her feet, lungs burning with soot and a scream that wanted to tear itself free. Another touch, this time across the exposed flesh of her lower back, almost caressing. Desperate to get away, she pressed her body against the door while her frantic hands moved over the expanse of wood, groping around for the doorknob. The smoke pressed back, forcing the air from her. She needed to get away from the smoke, from whatever was in the smoke. She needed to escape.

Her already tender and bleeding fingers struck something hard protruding from the door. The doorknob. Her mind howled with relief. She made it. She wasn't going to die. But the moment her fingers curled around the knob, a set of arms appeared from the billowing smoke. They reached out, encircling her waist, hauling her backwards. The scent of copper and musk washed over her, and her stomach clenched. Using the last of the air in her lungs, she forced her way forward and yanked the door open.

It only moved an inch.

Silent sobs wracked her body as she tried again, yanking the door several times, only to be met with the same resistance again and again. The pressure around her waist increased as whatever was with her tried to pull her back into the room.

As whoever — whatever — continued to pull at her, Chrissy realized what was stopping her. Shooting a hand up, she searched desperately for the security latch. Once she found it, she flipped the bar and tore the door open, collapsing on the floor of the hallway.

Half-naked and gasping for breath, she lay there, tears streaking down her face. She had to stand up, to warn Rodney and Bill, to alert the hotel. Hauling herself to her feet, body trembling, she risked a glance into her room.

Into her now perfectly normal room.

No flickering flames. No smoke billowing out through the door. Peering down the hall, she expected to see guests pouring out of their rooms, yelling fire, but the place was silent. The hotel was peacefully asleep.

Back at her door, she reached into the room and flicked the light switch beside the door, bathing the room in a warm glow. Her room, as it had been hours ago, greeted her. Frozen in place, she stared from her position halfway through the door, unable to comprehend what had just happened.

Had it been another nightmare? It felt so real. Too real. Her eyes were still burning, that disgusting charred scent still lay like a thick carpet on the back of her tongue. Several minutes passed as she stood in nothing but her underwear, staring into the room. It wasn't until she began to shiver that she took a hesitant step inside, allowing the door to shut behind her.

With shaking breath, she did a quick survey of the room, even heading into the bathroom to ensure there really was no fire. Satisfied that the room was clear, she eased herself back into bed, leaving every light in the room on.

Lying on top of the covers, her eyes drifted shut. Two nightmares in as many nights, but the one tonight felt different. Something had been in the room with her, trying to drag her back into the smoke. It wasn't possible, but it had happened. She had felt it.

Shuddering, she pulled her knees up to her chest and tried to banish those thoughts and ignore the faint whiff of smoke that still hung in the air.

A faint buzzing woke Chrissy just before noon. At some point in the night, sleep had returned, shallow and restless. Blinking awake, she rolled over, scooping up her phone and checking to see who had texted.

You up?

She shot back a thumbs up emoji and pulled herself into a sitting position. The phone buzzed again.

Be there in 5.

With a groan, she heaved herself off the bed and shuffled into the bathroom. A worn-down version of her face stared back from the mirror, all eye bags and mussed hair. Raking her fingers through the dark strands did little to improve the situation, but she figured it would have to do. Nothing could fix the eye bags in five minutes, though.

Pulling a pair of shorts and tee from the drawers, she struggled to dress, almost falling over as she tugged the shorts over her thighs, before a light knocking came from the door.

"No way that was five minutes," Chrissy grumbled as she pulled the door open.

Rodney gave a lazy smile and followed her into the room. "Close enough. You're dressed, aren't you?"

Chrissy replied with a grunt and dropped down onto the bed, resting her head in her hands. The lights in here were too bright, and her temples pounded. God, she wanted to go back to sleep.

The mattress dipped under his weight as Rodney sat down next to her. "Don't take this the wrong way, Chrissy, but you look like crap."

She grunted again.

"Didn't sleep?"

"Not much." She shook her head, immediately regretting the motion. "I had another nightmare."

Rodney's forehead creased with concern. "Another one? Is that normal?"

"I'm sure lots of people have nightmares two nights in a row."

Rodney rolled his eyes. "I mean, is that normal for you, smartass?"

"Not really," she admitted.

"I know you said you didn't want to talk about it, but could it be because of the whole landlord thing?"

She opened her mouth to say no, but the thought had crossed her mind. She did her best to compartmentalize, to keep all thoughts of her living situation shoved deep into those dark corners, but she had to admit, there was a possibility the nightmares were a result of her subconscious trying to drag it out into the light and sort through the stress while she slept.

"It's possible," she conceded. "But I still don't want to talk about it."

"Fair enough. My offer still stands. Got plenty of room on the old futon."

She gave him a weak smile and quickly changed the subject. "How long have you been awake?"

"Few minutes. Bill's still dead to the world. Last night really did a number on him."

"I don't think he's ever had any experiences in the field before." She leaned forward, beginning to perk up. "What do you think that was all about?"

"Beats me. Something about the school shook him hard."

"Do you think he saw something?"

"You know me, Chrissy. I don't think these things are anything more than people's overactive minds. The best way to find a ghost is to go into a place believing you're going to see one."

"Bill's never been jumpy like that, though," she said. "He's always been so...neutral about it all. What do you think it is about this case?"

"Dunno. Whatever it is, he'd better sort it out. Having him so on edge is hella annoying."

Chrissy made a noncommittal noise. Nothing about this investigation was what she expected. Despite the overpowering vibes that wound through the school, the night had been excruciatingly uneventful. But Rodney was withdrawn, and Bill was spooked, and she was running on so little sleep and so much stress, she wanted to crawl back under the covers and sleep the rest of the day. The whole thing was off.

Rodney slapped his hands on his thighs, breaking into Chrissy's thoughts. "What's the plan for today?"

"I'm going to head to the library and do some research, put together a list of names and make some calls to see if any of the survivors are willing to be interviewed. I want you and Bill to start going over the footage from last night and see if we picked up anything."

Rodney grimaced. "How did you know I wanted to watch sixteen hours of silence?"

"You can order room service on the company card."

"You mean on your card?"

"Just don't go overboard, alright?"

"Got it." Rodney grinned and stood.

Chrissy bit her lip, hating what she was about to say, but after the complete flop of last night, it might be necessary.

"If you get bored and need a break, you can come up with some ideas to liven things up tonight. Nothing crazy, but...just in case we don't end up catching anything. Do you think one of those cabinet pushers would work on the lockers?"

Rodney paused at the door, his back to the room. The grin he wore dropped like a mask as he turned, and he gave her a troubled look.

"About that..."

"Did you not bring them? That's okay. We can-"

"Maybe we shouldn't do any tricks this time. Bill's good at editing things enough to make them look more dramatic than they are. Lots of jump scare type stuff. And who knows, if we don't have any crazy experiences, it might actually lend to our credibility. Not every house is haunted."

The revelation that Rodney left his gadgets behind on purpose stoked the little ember of annoyance burning away inside her. First, he refused to participate in the investigation, and now, he was purposefully sabotaging the whole thing. The drum in her head picked up its steady beat again, and she squeezed her eyes shut for a moment.

The truth was, it wasn't such a bad idea. Their previous investigations had turned up a lot of "evidence" of hauntings, and an investigation where they found little very well could give them more legitimacy. But it couldn't be this investigation. Not this time. Far too much was riding on it.

"Fine. Since we have no other choice, I guess we'll have to roll with it. Let's just hope the spirits decide to come out and play tonight."

TWELVE

MERLIN PUBLIC LIBRARY WAS a huge, blocky affair, circa 1960, and held all the charm of a prison block. Inside, the long rows of shelves reached almost to the top of the low ceilings, giving the place an immensely claustrophobic feel. Staking out a spot at one of the industrial-looking tables closest to the local history section, Chrissy got to work.

The first item on her checklist was to comb through the library's collection of microfilm. Many of the newspapers covering the fire at Merlin High had been digitized and were available online, but the labor and cost of digitizing meant there was a backlog waiting to be dealt with. The search was tedious, but with some helpful guidance from the librarian, she was able to find two articles she hadn't yet seen.

Each article laid out the same general information she already knew, but one of them contained a few statements from some of the survivors. She jotted the names down in her notebook, hoping that if they were willing to talk to the press before, they might be interested in being interviewed for the show.

The second article regurgitated the same details the others had, and she was about to abandon it when a line jumped off the page at her.

"One witness claimed to have seen a young person with a gas cannister earlier in the evening before the dance kicked off."

None of the other articles she read mentioned this detail, which made her think it was unlikely to have been of significance or was even completely made up. If the blaze had been intentionally set, the other papers would have picked up on it, and there would have been a huge investigation into the matter. Still, she scribbled the information down, along with the name of the journalist who had written the article.

After exhausting the newspaper archives, she turned her attention to the collection of old yearbooks from Merlin High. Grabbing one from the '85-'86 school year, as well as the '88-'89, she carried them back to the table.

Pulling the books towards herself, she decided to start with the year after the fire. A memorial to the staff and teens who perished the year prior took up the first few pages. Name after name, each one adding to a mountain of heartache.

The book was heavy with the weight of grief, and Chrissy could hardly stand it. She closed the cover and pushed it aside.

She slid the yearbook from the year before the fire towards her, opening to a page right in the middle. Rows of permed hair, bangs sprayed to the sky, and new wave styles greeted her. Dozens of smiling faces beamed from the pages, oblivious to the fact that only six months after receiving their yearbooks and filling them with signatures and well wishes for the summer, their whole worlds would shatter.

At the front of the book was a section called Student Life, showing off photos of pep rallies, cheerleaders, kids sitting at desks in classrooms, and a photo that looked to have been taken at a drive-in movie theater. Boys with mullets and patchy mustaches, Ray-bans and denim jackets, leered at the camera, and girls in backwards sweaters and stirrup pants showed off perfect hot-pink pouts.

Chrissy paused at the varsity cheer team's page. A photo of the team making a human pyramid dominated the space, each girl's grinning face forever frozen in time. Beneath was a picture of the captain and co-captain, a blonde and brunette, kneeling on the grass beside a giant megaphone, pompoms resting by their knees.

A few pages further, she came to a spread of pictures from the homecoming football game. On the left was a fuzzy shot of the quarterback getting off a good pass, then another of the team celebrating, fists raised in triumph. The words "Victory!" and "GO Wizards!" splashed across the page in a font so retro Chrissy couldn't help but smile.

On the right were photos of the homecoming dance. Couples filled the page, holding hands or dancing stiffly in their partners' arms. There was a picture of the homecoming queen, and Chrissy recognized the bright face of the cheer captain. She wore that same wide, dazzling grin as another student placed a tiara on top of her voluminous curls, teased to perfection. The amount of hairspray needed to keep it so high and fluffy must have been staggering.

Working her way through the yearbook, the pretty blonde homecoming queen made several more appearances. She was a member of the French club, the student council, and seemingly friends with half of the school.

There was something about this girl, something that made Chrissy feel almost as if she knew her. She pictured her as the type of person who smiled and waved at everyone she knew, introducing herself to those she didn't. She was smart, likely helping out in the language lab or math lab, explaining the concepts to students who didn't quite grasp the material, but she always did it in a way that was encouraging and kind. She probably volunteered at the soup kitchen, not just on Thanksgiving, but at least twice a month, every month. She was the type of girl everyone wanted to be, the type of girl everyone adored. In short, she was the type of girl Chrissy had tried so desperately to be when she was in high school.

The caption beneath one of the photos revealed that the girl even had a perfect name — Alorah Smith — and she had only been a junior. The year of the fire would have been her senior year.

A lump formed in Chrissy's throat. She didn't want to look, but she needed to know. Hesitating, she pulled the memorial book towards her and opened it up to the front page. She held her breath, running one finger down the list of names and offering a silent prayer she wouldn't find Alorah among them, but there it was, sandwiched between Rebecca Robertson and Edward Sorley.

Alorah Smith was dead.

Sorrow hit Chrissy in one powerful, crushing moment, and she collapsed back into the chair. Three full pages of names, each one a life cut short. Before, the story had been almost abstract. Terrible, of course, but she had no ties to the event, nobody to mourn. Now, she had put faces to the tragedy, and the loss felt so pointless.

A text from Rodney stopped her thoughts from spiraling further. The message was brief, but it sent her scrambling to pack her things and race back to the hotel.

We caught something.

As soon as Rodney opened the door, Chrissy barreled into his room, words tumbling from her mouth before stopping to catch her breath.

"What did you find? Is it an EVP? Where was it caught?"

In an attempt to calm her, Rodney held up a hand, but his face betrayed his own excitement and disbelief.

"Chill out. Just sit down, and I'll show you."

Chrissy sat on the edge of the bed but shot right back up to her feet, pacing the length of the room while he got the audio queued up and filled her in.

"I went over the footage from Bill's camera but didn't find anything, not a peep, and there's nothing I could see that would have made him jump like he did."

Impatient, she nodded, then glanced around the room. "Where is Bill?"

"He went to pick up some food." Stepping back from the laptop, he pushed the headphones towards her. "Now, sit down and give this a listen."

She obeyed, perching on the single chair in the room and slipping the headphones on. The audio replayed their session in the bathroom on the second floor. The first thing to crackle through the speakers was the loud bang of the stall door when Bill leaned against it. The team asked a few more questions, played a snippet of Blondie, and then left the room.

She shot him a sidelong, puzzled glance. "I didn't hear anything."

"Not yet. I was just getting you situated. Skip to timestamp 00:57."

Eyes narrowed, she looped it back to listen again. "Is that the bathroom door?"

"That's what it sounded like to me."

"That's super cool. It's not much, but it's a solid start."

Rodney was shaking his head. "Anyone could say that the wind blew it open, or that an animal went in or something."

"There weren't any animals around."

"Not that we saw, but it doesn't mean they weren't there."

Chrissy was about to argue, but he held up a hand and cut her off.

"That's not the point. The thing I texted you about is a bit further. Jump ahead to 01:39."

The way Rodney's eyes drilled into her sent a fluttery shiver through her. Whatever he found must have been big, based on the way he drummed his fingers against the table, eager for her to hurry up. Skipping the audio to the section he highlighted, she concentrated on the sounds. Something was there alright, buried in a burst of static. She was about to replay the segment when it happened, clear as day. It was short, only a handful of notes, but unmistakable: someone was humming. Her hand flew to her mouth, and she looped the section, listening to those few notes on repeat several more times before lifting her gaze.

The look of astonishment on Rodney's face mirrored her own. "Is this... Did that sound like humming to you?"

He gave a baffled shrug. "I've tried to figure out some other explanation for it. It doesn't sound like any animal I've heard of. I cross-referenced the timestamps to make sure it wasn't one of us, and we were all in the art room at that exact time. Plus, we had one of the cameras pointing down that hall, and it didn't pick up anybody going or coming."

Leaning forward, she asked, "Did the camera catch the door swinging open?"

"No such luck, but the audio alone is... To be honest, I have no freaking clue."

A slow smile spread across her face. "Rodney. This is it. This is the first solid piece of evidence we've ever caught!"

"I mean, I've tried to think of anything else it could be, but..."

"Does this mean you're coming around to being a believer?" she teased.

"No way, dude. I admit that this — whatever it is — is super weird. I can't explain what it is, but I'm not going so far as to say it's a ghost."

"Well, maybe by the end of tonight, you'll be singing a different tune."

"Doubtful."

Rodney sat down on the bed and reached up to rake his hair back into a sloppy bun. Chrissy watched, admiring the way his smooth, golden locks looked good no matter how he kept it. Her own hair was dark and wavy, and though there were days when it would cooperate, more often than not, it was a constant battle trying to tame it into something more manageable.

"Hello?"

"Hmm?" Her eyes returned to Rodney's face, a slight flush warming her cheeks. "What?"

"I asked you if you found anything at the library," he said, his lips quirking up into an amused smirk.

Turning her face away, she reached down into her bag, spending longer than was strictly necessary digging around for her notebook. She pulled it free and flipped it open, keeping her gaze down until her face stopped burning. "I made a list of people who might be willing to give us an interview. I'll give them a call this afternoon. I also checked out some of the yearbooks. That was a trip."

"Oh yeah?"

Chrissy risked a glance up, relieved to find the smug smirk had vanished. "Yeah. The yearbook from the year after the fire has a memorial with all the names of the students and teachers who died. It was kind of depressing."

Rodney's gaze dropped to the floor, and when he didn't respond, she continued.

"The year before the fire, everyone looked so happy and excited about everything. There was this one girl who caught my attention, mostly because her photos were all over; captain of the cheer team, homecoming queen, and she was in a bunch of clubs. Basically, she ran the school," she laughed. "She seemed super cool. Even her name was cool. Alorah. I mean, have you ever-"

Rodney stood abruptly, interrupting the babbling stream-of-consciousness Chrissy had fallen into. He stalked across the room to the window, fingers toying with the dingy hem of the curtain.

"You okay?" she asked, staring at his back. When he shook his head, she went to his side. From the corner of her eye, she studied him for a few moments. Veins in his neck bulged, and a tension invaded his body, forcing his shoulders higher and higher with each shallow breath. She placed a tentative hand on his arm.

"What's going on, Rod?"

He shook his head again and continued to stare straight ahead, clutching the grimy sage colored curtain in his fists.

Chrissy gnawed on her lip, feeling very much out of her depth. Until now, she thought Rodney had only two sides: chipper goofball and slightly-serious-but-still-a-goofball. She had never once seen the man upset or even annoyed, not even when the Ghostmobile died on the way home from a particularly frustrating investigation where nothing had gone to plan. The entire time, he had cracked jokes on the side of the road and tried to get the team to find the humor in the situation.

This new facet was unnerving, and she had no idea how to handle it. She stayed beside him, giving his arm the occasional awkward pat while he worked through whatever had disturbed him.

After a few more minutes of silence, he raised his hands and scrubbed his face before turning back to her.

"Sorry about that."

"Don't be sorry. What's going on?"

His body shook beneath her hand as he drew in a shaky breath. Realizing her fingers were still wrapped around his arm, she dropped her hand to her side.

"It's nothing."

She raised an eyebrow. "It sure as hell isn't nothing."

"I said it's nothing." He took a step away from the window. "I'm a little overwhelmed, I guess. Like you said, this place is hella depressing. I'm not getting the best sleep. I wasn't kidding when I said Bill snores like a freight train. Plus, I can't help but feel like we're exploiting this situation, and I think the whole thing is just kind of messed up, and it's wearing me down."

She stared at him uncertainly, struggling to accept his explanation.

"I'm going to go over a few more hours of footage before we need to roll." He moved across the room and eased into the chair in front of the laptop, turning his back to Chrissy, who stood rooted in the same spot next to the window.

As he hunched over the glowing screen, headphones clutched in his hand, she debated whether she should push the issue. His comment about them being exploitative was categorically untrue, and she wanted to fight him on that, but she could see that the combination of bad sleep and the weight of this investigation were wearing him thin. She knew better than anyone that when people were stretched too thin, sometimes small tears formed, allowing unmeant words to seep out.

"Alright," she said, grabbing her bag and stuffing the notebook back inside. "I'll be in my room making some phone calls if you need anything."

He waved a hand at her and slipped the headphones over his ears, refusing to look at her as she left the room.

THIRTEEN

BACK IN HER ROOM, Chrissy tried to push the incident with Rodney aside and focus on her work. Spreading her notebook out on the bed in front of her, she made her way through the contacts she had written down at the library. Most of the numbers were out of service or were screening calls. Those who did answer hung up as soon as she explained who she was and what the project was about. Only one person, a man named Donnie Melton had agreed, and arranged to come down to the school the next day for a chat. After thanking him, she stretched her legs out and leaned back.

Exhaustion from two nights of fitful sleep slammed into her like a freight train. If she didn't get some rest, she would never be able to make it through another night of investigation. Leaving the lights on and curtains open, she crawled under the sheets, relying on the sanitizing properties of the sunlight to keep the nightmares at bay.

Sleep came before long, and Chrissy found herself in the hallways of her old high school once again. Except...it wasn't her high school. She recognized the drab olive lockers and realized she was in the halls of Merlin High, not the burnt out husk that it was now, but how it must have been prior the fire.

The halls were empty. She moved to the nearest classroom and peered through the window. A teacher stood at the front of a room filled with students, droning on and gesturing at the board with a piece of chalk. A young girl in the front row yawned, her eyelids drooping as she lowered her head to rest on her arm laying across the top of her desk.

It was Merlin High as it had been in its heyday. Chrissy knew it was a dream, but it didn't have that fuzzy quality most dreams did. The colors were too bright, and the chalky potpourri of textbooks and body odor filled her nose.

Certain of her surroundings, she made her way up the stairs. The sound of a locker slamming reverberated somewhere below, but on the second floor, the silence was eerie.

Her footsteps echoed off the walls, and suddenly, she was standing in front of the door to the ladies' room. It swung on its hinges, as though someone had just gone in. Taking a step towards the door, she held her breath and listened. Sure enough, a song too faint to make out drifted out from inside.

A sudden movement from the corner of her eye drew her attention away from the door. Lights at the end of the hall flickered once and went dark. The primitive part of her brain begged her to look away, to run, but she had to find the source of the humming. As she turned again towards the ladies' room, her eyes remained glued to the black hole at the end of the left wing.

The sound from the bathroom shifted, and Chrissy realized the girl inside was now singing. She tried to grab hold of the muffled words, to discern what the song was, but the thing hidden in the shadows chose that moment to make its move. Her heart jackknifed up into her throat, cold beads of sweat blossoming across her forehead, and she told herself again and again that it was just a dream. It *had* to be a dream.

The singing in the bathroom grew louder, but she was transfixed by the thing in the hall. Even in the dark recesses, she could tell that, whatever it was, it was huge.

Against the white tiles of the floor, something emerged. A long, segmented leg poked out from the shadows, soon joined by a second. They were about as thick as the wide end of a baseball bat, covered in barb-like hairs all the way down.

The voice continued, but now, the lyrics were impossible to make out. They were distorted, elongated one moment, compressed and warbling the next, changing pitch like an old, warped cassette.

Chrissy grappled with the horrifying reality unfolding before her, unable, or unwilling, to comprehend this monstrosity crawling from the shadows. It wasn't until two thin antennae popped out into the light that she allowed herself to accept the reality of what she was seeing.

Enormous compound eyes locked onto her.

Mandibles gnashed, loud enough that she could hear the click each time they snapped shut.

The distorted, otherworldly song continued, words still too fuzzy and garbled to make any sense.

Now halfway into the light of the hallway, the giant cockroach paused, its bulk filling the corridor. Chrissy froze in place. Her entire nervous system had abandoned her, leaving her unable to do anything but tremble.

All at once, the sweet voice was there, snapping into perfect clarity.

"Once upon a time."

The bathroom door started to swing open, and the roach's head swiveled. It skittered forward, hairy legs scrambling for purchase on the tile as it squeezed itself through the hallways, the metal lockers making an ear-splitting screech as its carapace scraped over them. The sound snapped Chrissy into action, and she slammed her body against the door, keeping it shut. Whoever was in there was in danger, and she was determined to keep them safe from the monster now sprinting towards them on six legs.

She opened her mouth to scream, but instead of her own voice, what came out was the shrill ringing of the class bell. Classroom doors flew open, and students spilled out into the hallway, blocking the view of the giant roach. None of them seemed to notice the bug or act as though anything was wrong at all.

Over her shoulder, the door pushed open, and a sweet voice whispered in her ear.

"Chrissy. Wake up."

Hoping to catch a glimpse of whoever the speaker was, she turned, but the voice remained behind her.

"Chrissy. Wake up."

She spun around a few more times, desperate to see the girl, but her grasp on this dreamworld was slipping.

"Chrissy!"

The haze of dreams fell away, and she rolled out of bed, stumbling to the door.

"Rodney?" she croaked.

"Chrissy! Are you alright?"

Fumbling with the door latch, she managed to open it to find Rodney standing there, the corners of his mouth drawn down.

"What's wrong?" she asked, voice still thick with sleep.

"That's what I should be asking you. You were screaming. Is everything okay?"

Chrissy reached up to rub her eyes. "I was asleep."

"Did you have another nightmare?"

"I think so."

Rodney stepped into the room and put his hands on her shoulders, peering down into her face, forehead creased with concern. "I don't like this."

"It's not all that fun for me either." She choked out a bitter laugh. "I'm exhausted."

Rodney guided her back to the bed, where she sat curled over with her head in her hands.

"Want to tell me what the dreams are about?"

She mulled it over, unsure exactly where to start. The first two dreams still held their clarity — sharp and vivid, as though they had happened moments ago, but this last one was elusive, despite being so intensely clear in the moment. Already, it was slipping away, and trying to remember the details was like trying to grab a hold of smoke.

"I think they're just anxiety dreams."

"Well duh. You're dealing with a lot, with the apartment and how much pressure you're putting on yourself with this investigation."

"I guess."

"Do you remember what made you scream? Cause you were freaking loud. I thought you were getting murdered in here."

She started to shake her head, but an image of the huge bug flashed in her mind, and she gasped. "It was a gigantic cockroach."

Rodney laughed, surprising Chrissy who turned to glare at him.

"It was terrifying, okay?"

"I believe you," he said, struggling to contain his laughter. "But you have to admit that's kind of funny."

"It's not funny! It was horrible. I was at the school..." The memory of the dream crept forward again, giving up a detail here, a snippet there. She spoke slowly as pieces began to fall into place. "I'm pretty sure I dreamed about the school before the fire."

"Makes sense. You've been obsessing over this case for the last couple of weeks. Figures it would seep into your subconscious, too."

Coaxing the images from her memory, she recounted each bit as it came to her. "I think I was looking for the humming girl in the bathroom. I didn't see her, but I heard the song. She started to actually sing the words. In the dream, I was trying to hear them and figure out what she was singing when that...thing stepped out of the shadows and ran at me."

She shuddered again at the image, expecting Rodney to laugh again. Instead, he sank down on the bed beside her and draped an arm over her shoulders, giving her a gentle squeeze.

"Even when you're dreaming, you're trying to investigate."

Chrissy snorted. "Seems like it. It was a pretty song, but I didn't recognize it. It sounded all messed up."

"Well, you must have heard it somewhere. Your subconscious can't just make up a song. It pulls stuff from your real life."

"Maybe." She sighed and leaned into him. "Thanks for coming to check on me."

"No problem, kid." He reached up and ruffled her hair. "I legit thought you were being attacked or something. It's a good thing I didn't have my headphones on."

A pang in Chrissy's stomach made her conscious of the fact she hadn't eaten anything since the soggy sandwiches the night before.

"Has Bill come back with the food?"

Rodney dropped his arm from her shoulders, a strange look crossing his face. "He did. He put some sandwiches in the mini fridge, and then he kind of...left again."

Alarm bells went off in her head. If Bill had taken the van again, they would be stuck at the hotel, scrambling once more to make it to the school to investigate. Another taxi fare was an extra hit their anemic budget couldn't take.

"He just left? Again? Did he take the van?"

"Calm down. He didn't take the van. He set the keys on the table, turned around, and wandered off."

Chrissy sagged with relief, still unsure what to make of Bill's newfound interest in going off on his own.

"Is it just me, or has he been acting kind of weird?" Rodney asked.

"It's not just you. He's definitely not been himself, but, to be honest, neither have you."

Rodney's expression darkened, and he dropped his gaze to the floor. "Yeah. I know."

She waited for an explanation, throwing her hands up when none came.

"You don't have to tell me what's going on, but could you at least try to put a little more effort in? I'm carrying the entire investigation, and there's a hell of a lot riding on this. Maybe if you picked up some of the slack, I might not be so stressed out, and I might be able to get a good night's sleep for once."

Her voice rose an octave, and she knew she was getting close to screaming at him, but she wasn't sure how else to get the point across.

"Yeah, sure. I'll try."

"No!" Chrissy exploded. "Don't say you'll try. You have to *do* it. Listen, this is kind of a huge deal for me. You and Bill have other things going on, but this is my entire livelihood. I have put everything on the line here. Everything. And if this doesn't work out, I don't..." A sob caught in her throat and, despite fighting the burn, tears pooled in the corner of her eyes. "I don't know what I'll do if this doesn't work out."

Silence hung heavy between the two as she continued to fight the tears. As soon as Rodney's arm returned, slipping around her shoulders and pulling her against his body, something inside her broke, and all the emotions she thought were so neatly packed away came spilling out.

"I can't go back to my family. I can't admit that I was wrong. I put everything into *Othersiders*. Why does everything have to be so hard?" she sobbed.

Rodney held her, her face buried in his chest, letting her tears soak through his shirt. She tried to wiggle free once, but he only held on tighter, pulling her close. Several minutes of ugly crying and incoherent and disjointed thoughts later, silence returned to the room, interrupted only by the sound of a handful of shuddering breaths and sniffles.

"I'm sorry, Chrissy."

She slid a hand up between them to swipe at her face. "It's fine."

"No, it's not. I didn't realize you were in such a shitty position. I'm sorry I haven't been putting in much effort."

She pulled back, keeping her face down, not wanting him to see her blotchy red face.

"I need a tissue," she mumbled.

He jumped up and grabbed the box of tissues that sat on the counter in the bathroom, returning and handing them over.

"Thank you."

"No problemo."

"Sorry," she said, wiping away the tears. "I didn't mean to cry in front of you."

He reached forward, brushing a stray tear from her cheek with his thumb. His eyes lingered on her face for a moment before he cleared his throat and glanced away.

"Hey, do you think the ghosts are going to come after Bill again tonight? Maybe you won't be the only one to cry today."

"I hope not." She gave a startled laugh. "I don't know what I'd do if Bill started crying. It would be like seeing my dad cry."

Rodney grinned and dissolved into laughter, with Chrissy soon joining in. The sound of his laugh filled her up, melting away some of the stress she had been holding onto. Without thinking, she leaned forward and threw her arms around him, wrapping him in a tight hug. When she released him, he had a surprised look on his face and turned a shade of pink she hadn't seen before.

"Thank you," she said, trying to ease some of the uncomfortable tension. "You know, for being so cool about me breaking down."

"Oh, yeah. Like I said, no problemo."

His eyes shifted to the door, Chrissy kicked herself internally for embarrassing him and making everything so awkward.

"Sorry."

"What for?"

"Making things weird?"

This time, Rodney was the one to surprise her. He grabbed her hand, firm but gentle. "You didn't do anything wrong, Chris."

His eyes finally met hers, and her stomach flipped over on itself, making it impossible to reply.

Giving her hand a squeeze, he released it and stood, glancing at the clock on the bedside table.

"Getting close to roll out time. I'm going to check to see if Bill's come back yet. You going to be alright if I go for a bit?"

She nodded and waved a hand towards the door. "I'll be fine. You go and get ready."

Shooting her a grin, he made his way to the door.

"And don't forget the sandwiches. I'm freaking starving," she called after him.

Once the door latched shut, Chrissy fell backward onto the bed, feeling lighter than she had in weeks.

Fourteen

IT WASN'T UNTIL THAT evening, as the sun began its descent, casting the town in a golden haze, that Bill returned. Chrissy and Rodney had already wolfed down their sandwiches and started to load equipment into the back of the Ghostmobile when Chrissy spotted him lumbering across the parking lot.

"Bill! Where have you been? We were starting to worry."

Bill gazed at her with a blank expression.

"Bill?"

He shook his head and finally seemed to see Chrissy standing in front of him.

"Oh. Hey."

Rodney came around from the other side of the van and clapped him on the shoulder. "Hey man. Where ya been? You missed out on the good sandwiches. Only have tuna left."

"Just went for a walk."

Chrissy shot Rodney a look. He shrugged and turned his attention back to Bill, who stood staring into the middle distance.

"Alright," Chrissy said slowly. "Well, glad you're okay. Ready to go?"

"Hmm?" Bill's gaze shifted to her, but his eyes remained unfocused. "Oh. Yeah. Let's go."

The rest of the equipment was quickly loaded up, and the group piled into the van for another trek out to Merlin High. They drove in a strange, disconnected silence, the usual banter and excitement that always surrounded an investigation missing.

About a block before they pulled up in front of the school, Bill broke the silence.

"Do you think we should split up tonight?"

Chrissy studied Bill's face in the rear-view mirror for a moment, noting the dark circles under his eyes. Apparently, none of them had been sleeping too well. "Did you have something in mind?"

His massive shoulders bunched up. "Thought I could go alone, since whatever is there seems to like messing with me. You and Rodney could check out the bathroom again."

"I don't see why not," Chrissy answered as the van eased up against the curb in front of the school. "But only for a little while. We still need you to film us during the majority of the investigation."

Bill killed the engine and gave a short nod, jumping out of the drivers' seat before the others had their seatbelts off. Throwing the back doors open, he started carting equipment through the gate and towards the school's entrance at a near jog.

Rodney turned in the passenger seat. "What is his frickin deal?"

"No clue. I don't think I've ever heard him say that many words in a row before."

"Right?"

"But he does have a point. Whatever is in there has been interacting with him, so we might as well give it a try." Through the van's window, she watched Bill set a box down in front of the doors and hustle back towards the van. "It is weird, though. He has never wanted to go off on his own."

"I think he might be dealing with some stuff too. After we got back from investigating last night, we talked about our own high school years. It sounded like he had a really rough time of it."

"High school is bad for lots of people."

"Sure, but the way he was talking, it sounded more like torture for him."

Chrissy wanted to ask what else he had said, but Bill had already returned for another load. Rodney opened the door and hopped out, so she followed suit, getting the last of the equipment carted over to the school.

They decided to begin the night on separate floors, Rodney and Chrissy taking the second floor to try to capture more in the girls' bathroom, and Bill sticking to the first.

"Make sure you stay inside the building," Chrissy called down from the staircase. "We can check out the gymnasium from outside later."

Bill nodded his acknowledgment, swung his camera away from them, and tramped off into the dark corridor of the right wing.

Turning back to Rodney, Chrissy felt like a kid again, stepping into her first haunted house. Though the heaviness had still fallen over her once she stepped through the doors, it had become almost like background noise. It was like an awful stench you became nose-blind to after enough exposure. And anyway, the excitement of their discovery from last night overrode the darkness, and it took everything in her to not reach out and grab Rodney by the hand and drag him along. "Come on, let's head up and see if our singing girl wants to play."

Equipped with a small hand-held camcorder, she lead the way, doing her best to keep the camera level and steady, though she was sure she was vibrating with excitement. The bathroom door appeared, and the sight of it triggered a memory of her dream, making her cast an involuntary glance down to the end of the corridor. The hallway disappeared into darkness, and she whipped her head back around, certain if she were to stare any longer, a pair of grotesquely long antennae would appear out of the darkness. Suppressing a shudder, she panned her small camera over to Rodney.

"It's night two of our investigation of Merlin High, and Rodney and I are back up on the second floor to investigate the ladies' room. Last night, when we went through the footage, we discovered some incredible EVPs caught in this room by the recorders we left behind. We're hoping that whoever was in here last night is willing to come forward and interact with us again tonight."

Looking up from the camera's display, she gave Rodney a nod, hoping their conversation earlier in the day had made some kind of impact. When he actually picked up on her cue and addressed the camera, she sagged with relief.

"The audio caught the sound of this door here opening." He reached out and gave the swinging door of the bathroom a gentle push. "And half an hour after that, it caught the sound of someone humming. It was only a few notes, but it was definitely humming. Wild stuff."

She smiled from behind the camera and followed him through the swinging door into the bathroom.

"Excuse us for interrupting, ladies. I don't know if you remember, but Chrissy and I were here last night. We think we heard one of you humming, and we would be absolutely stoked if you'd be willing to do that again."

Chrissy pressed the back of her free hand to her mouth, overcome with a sense of gratitude. He was interacting with the camera like he had for all their previous investigations, hamming it up and pulling his weight. Whatever it was about this case that bothered him, he appeared to have put it aside for now, and she thought she could just kiss him for stepping up.

"If you're with us tonight," she said, "we'd love to hear some more of the song you were humming."

After asking several more questions, they let the silence of the room settle for a few moments. Chrissy once again thought about how clear her nightmare had been. The oppressive weight occupying the school dulled the edges of her excitement, and she suddenly found the silence unnerving.

"The nightmare I had was set here," she said, trying to fill up the empty room.

"Oh yeah?"

She cleared her throat and tried to steady her voice. "Yeah. I heard the girl singing in here. I was out in the hallway, and this giant..."

A faint sound caught her attention, interrupting her train of thought.

"Uh-huh, that giant cockroach-"

"Shh. I thought I heard something," she whispered, cutting him off.

When the noise didn't repeat itself, Rodney asked, "What did you hear?"

"I don't know. It was a kind of...hissing sound?"

"Fantastic. Snakes are exactly what this hellhole is missing."

"No, it wasn't a snake hiss." She shook her head and listened for the sound to come again. "I'm not sure what it was. Anyway, back to my dream. I was standing outside the ladies' room, and a giant cockroach appeared at the end of the hall. It was massive. It had-"

The noise returned, louder than before.

"Did you hear it that time?" Chrissy asked.

"Yeah. It was sort of like a...*shh*. Is the ghost telling you to shut up?"

Ignoring him, she asked, "Could you please make that sound again?"

"Dude, what's that smell?"

A faint odor seemed to materialize right in front of them. Chrissy sniffed a few times, trying to place the scent. It had a sweet, synthetic quality, with a sharp tinge of alcohol lingering somewhere beneath. There was something so familiar about it that she couldn't put her finger on. "Whatever it is, it smells like some kind of chemical, maybe?" She sniffed again. "It's almost like...hairspray."

"Oh my God." Rodney inhaled deeply. "That's not just hair-spray. That's Aqua Net."

"It's what?"

"Aqua Net. My sister used to have a can of that stuff in her purse." He gave a soft chuckle at the memory. "She carried it around with her everywhere she went. Jeez, that takes me back."

"Are you sure? It's possible a chemical could have spilled in here." Chrissy looked around in the dark, knowing she wouldn't find anything.

"No, dude. It's Aqua Net."

"Well, it's only the two of us in here, and I don't think either one of us uses hairspray-"

"Aqua Net."

"Fine. Neither one of us uses Aqua Net, or any other kind of hairspray, so we shouldn't be smelling that in here. Did you smell anything like it last night?"

"Nope."

Camera pointed forward, Chrissy panned across the bathroom. "There's no soap or cleaning supplies in here, so I guess we can rule that out as the source of the scent."

"Nothing on the planet smells like that stuff, anyway."

"So what's causing it?"

Rodney shrugged, looking around the room at a loss. Suddenly, she saw the whites of his eyes in the light of the camera's display screen.

"What is it?" Her skin prickled, every hair standing at attention. "Do you see something?"

"That noise you heard a minute ago?"

"Did you hear it again?"

"No. I feel stupid even asking this, but did it kind of sound like an aerosol spray can? You know, like hairspray being sprayed?"

Chrissy's hand flew to her mouth. "That's exactly what it sounded like."

Rodney made a noise somewhere between a laugh and a cough, and Chrissy took a small step closer, her shoulder bumping up against his. She leaned in close until a strand of his long hair brushed her cheek.

"Starting to believe yet?" she whispered against his ear, the grin in her voice evident.

He turned his head, his hot breath brushing over her lips as he spoke. "All I'll admit is this is some pretty weird shit."

They stood that way, close together in the dark of the bathroom, for what felt like both an excruciatingly long and achingly short time to Chrissy. She had the sudden, overwhelming urge to stand on her toes and kiss him right then, but she pushed the thought aside as soon as it came. Giving her head a little shake, she wondered where that thought had even come from, and she quickly stepped away. Clearing his throat, Rodney raised the thermal camera and turned his attention to the screen.

"You know," Chrissy said, her words tumbling out in an effort to get past those intrusive thoughts, "I discovered an interesting fact when I was doing my research at the library."

"Oh yeah?"

She looked over, but Rodney's eyes were still glued to the display screen, his tone giving nothing away about what he was thinking.

"Yeah." She raised her voice, forcing herself back into the self-assured tone she always used for the camera. "In every article I've read, the fire was reported as accidental or of unknown origin, except for one. The article I found yesterday said that a student claimed to have seen someone carrying a gas can right before the Homecoming dance started."

When Rodney didn't respond, she glanced over. The thermal camera was still in his hands, the glow of the screen washing his face in a greenish light. He stood stiff-shouldered, eyes burning a hole straight through Chrissy. The coldness of his stare startled her, and she felt all the warmth that had built up between them ice over.

"That's impossible," Rodney said. "The cops would have figured that out."

"That's what I thought, too, but it couldn't hurt to ask some questions about it and see if we get a response."

Reaching into her pocket, she fished out a small audio recorder and set it down on the bathroom sink. She wished she had thought to pull it out sooner, although she doubted the little device would have been able to capture the faint hissing sounds.

"Rodney and I think we may have heard you spraying hair-spray in here," she said, addressing the empty room. "We're pretty sure we smelled it, too. Would it be possible for you to make another sound so we know you're in here with us?"

Silence.

"Were you getting ready in here for the homecoming dance?"

Silence.

"I heard there's a possibility someone started the fire on purpose. Do you know anything about that?"

Rodney went rigid, but a soft noise coming from the furthest stall in the bathroom made all thoughts of him rush out of Chrissy's mind. She spun around, straining to decipher the sound. It was so quiet, so delicate, it teetered on the brink of nonexistence, but it was there.

"Hey, it's getting late. I think we should-"

"Shh. Did you hear that?" Chrissy asked.

"Hear what?"

She pressed a finger to her lips and nodded towards the last stall. Whatever it was, it had stopped.

"Was that you just now? In the end stall? Do you know how the fire started?"

The sound came again, louder this time, prompting Rodney to raise the thermal camera. Chrissy lifted her own camera, trembling with anticipation as she trained it on the stall door.

"Did somebody start the fire in the gymnasium on purpose?"

Gradually, the noise increased in volume, until it became unmistakable. Someone was crying. Chrissy's pulse hammered in her chest. This was it, the key piece of evidence she had been searching for, the thing that would send *Othersiders* into the stratosphere and gain hundreds of thousands of followers. To show the world that there was an afterlife, and she would be the one to prove it. She wanted to grab Rodney and jump for joy, but she couldn't take her attention from the place where a girl was sobbing.

"If you know something about the fire, could you speak into this recording device? We would love to be able to try to help you." Her voice trembled. Keeping her eyes on the spot, she turned her shoulders towards Rodney and asked, "Is anything showing up on the thermal?"

His gaze dropped to the screen briefly, and he shook his head. "Nothing. She sounds so distraught. I think we should stop and leave her alone."

"We need to find out if she knows anything," Chrissy said. She couldn't drop this line of questions, not while the activity was still happening. Whoever was in the bathroom was the key to finding out the truth about the fire, was the key to success.

"Can you please tell us what caused the fire?" she tried again, the sobbing so loud now that she had to raise her voice.

"Stop, Chrissy. It's not right. We shouldn't-"

The bathroom stall door flew open with a bang, cutting Rodney off mid-sentence. The room resonated with the sound of taps being turned and water running, echoing off the tile walls. But the sinks were dry, nothing coming from the spigots but a flake or two of rust. Confirming the bathroom wasn't flooding, Chrissy's gaze darted around the room, pingponging off every surface. Rodney was frozen to the spot, eyes never leaving the open stall door, face a contorted grimace of terror. She pushed past him, running to the far stall, only to find it empty. The sobbing continued, building to a crescendo that filled the room, mingling with the sound of rushing water.

"Please," Chrissy yelled over the noise. Her voice was thick with fear and desperation, and she despised it, but the suffocating despair of the girl was too much. "Please, can you tell us what happened to you?"

The noise stopped. Her ears rang in the sudden vacuum of silence. As she turned to look at Rodney, a blast of icy wind hit her in the face, the chill shooting straight through her and into her bones.

A high-pitched voice tore through the dark fabric of night in an earsplitting scream, delivering a message both Rodney and Chrissy were quick to obey.

"Run!"

Audio Transcript

[11:17] BILL: Alright.

[11:17] [Heavy breathing]

[11:19] [Sound of lockers being opened then shut]

[11:20] BILL: Where is it?

[11:21] [Sound of lockers being opened then shut]

[11:24] BILL: Shit. Where...

[11:26] [Muffled bang]

[11:26] BILL: Hello?

[11:26] [Closer bang]

[11:27] BILL: Chrissy? Rod?

[11:27] UNKNOWN MALE: Hey Bill.

[11:27] BILL: [gasps]

[11:27] BILL: [unintelligible] ... What are you doing here? You're not supposed...You can't be...

[11:28] UNKNOWN MALE: [laughter]

[11:28] BILL: I swear, I never... [unintelligible].

[11:28] [Unknown male screaming]

[11:28] [Heavy breathing]

[11:28] [Footsteps running]

[11:29] BILL: What is that? What the hell is that?

[11:30] [Doors opening and closing]

[11:30] [Heavy breathing]

[11:36] CHRISSY: Bill? Bill?

[11:36] RODNEY: Where the hell did he go? Bill!

[11:37] CHRISSY: Is he still inside?

[11:37] RODNEY: I don't think so. He would have called out.

[11:37] CHRISSY: I thought I heard the front doors a minute ago.

[11:38] RODNEY: Maybe he went around to film the gym?

[11:38] CHRISSY: He wouldn't do that after I told him not to.

[11:38] [Footsteps]

[11:39] CHRISSY: Bill! Rodney, he's over here. What happened? You're not looking too good.

[11:39] [Footsteps]

[11:40] RODNEY: Jeez, Bill. You look like shit.

[11:40] CHRISSY: Did something happen?

[11:41] BILL: I think I need to go back to the hotel.

[11:41] RODNEY: What happened, man?

[11:42] BILL: I'm just feeling...really sick.

[11:42] CHRISSY: Yeah. Alright. Will you be alright waiting in the van while we pack up?

[11:43] BILL: [Unintelligible]

[11:43] RODNEY: Just hold tight, man. We'll get you back soon.

[11:44] CHRISSY: Oh, grab his camera. It's still rolling.

Fifteen

Everything was packed up and loaded in record time. Chrissy jumped into the drivers' seat while Rodney sat in the back with Bill, who was pale and sweating. The sound of his breathing wasn't right. No one spoke.

As soon as they reached the hotel, Rodney helped Bill from the van, tucking himself under the large man's arm like a human crutch, and took him up to their room. Chrissy glanced around the back of the van, too exhausted to do anything about it, leaving most of the equipment inside, taking only what was necessary back to her room.

After the girl in the bathroom had screamed at them to run, all activity came to an abrupt stop. Rodney and Chrissy took that as their cue to leave and rushed downstairs to find Bill. They had gone outside, finding him in a heap next to the Ghostmobile, camera laying on the gravel beside him.

Once inside her room, she collapsed onto the bed, thoughts about the events of the night cascading over her like a waterfall. So much had happened in such a short amount of time, and in the rush of getting out and leaving as fast as they did, she hadn't yet been able to process any of it.

She turned onto her side and caught a whiff of her own ripe scent in the process. Wrinkling her nose, she dragged herself from bed, stripped out of her grimy clothes, and headed to the bathroom.

Steam billowed from behind the shower curtain, and she stepped under the stream, letting the water drum against her back and take some of the tension from her tired muscles. She allowed her mind to wander and soon found her thoughts dwelling on the girl at the school. What had she been trying to tell them? Other than to run, of course. That message had been very clear. A manifestation so loud and dramatic required the spirit to draw vast amounts of energy, which was difficult and exhausting for them. There had to be a reason she wanted them to hear her crying. That it started when Chrissy asked about the origins of the fire made her think there must be something to the idea that it had been arson, but it was strange the police never issued any statements about it, that nobody other than a single student saw anything suspicious.

Shutting the water off, she dried herself and pulled an oversized tee over her head. Hands on her hips, she surveyed the room. Exhaustion seeped all the way down to her bones, and she craved sleep like a man in the desert craves water, but she didn't dare hope it would come easily. She was still jittery from everything that had happened, and even if she was able to fall asleep, she had a feeling the nightmares wouldn't be far behind.

With a sigh, she went to the pile of equipment she had lugged up to her room and began to dig through them, hunting for the audio recorder they used in the bathroom when the activity kicked up. If she couldn't sleep, at least she could go over the audio and try to find any clues they might have missed in the heat of the moment.

She had just found the recorder at the bottom of one of the bags when a soft knock came from the door. Placing the device on top of the bed, she went to answer, checking the peephole before opening.

Rodney stood in the hallway, rubbing the back of his neck and staring at her apprehensively.

"Hey."

"Hey, Rodney. How's Bill?"

"Not great. That's actually why I'm here." He hesitated. "I know it's a huge imposition, and it's totally cool if you say no, but is there any way I could bunk in your room tonight? Bill is puking his guts out. Like, louder than you've ever heard anyone barf. And the smell-"

"Gross," Chrissy cut him off before he went into any more detail.

"Yeah. I don't think I can get any sleep with that going on a few feet away from me. I was hoping — only if you're chill with it — you'd let me use the other bed in here? Again, if not, that's totally cool. No hard feelings whatsoever."

She stared at him for a moment then nodded her head towards the room, inviting him in.

"Come on in."

"Thank you so much. I promise I won't snore."

"I can make no such promise," she said, smiling.

Rodney strode across the room and flopped down on the edge of the bed opposite Chrissy's, jaw cracking with a massive yawn as he stretched his arms above his head. "I'm beat. I know we didn't stay as late as we typically do during these things, but whatever happened back at the school kinda zapped my energy."

Chrissy nodded and glanced at the audio recorder on the bed. She had been looking forward to going over the recording, but it would have to wait, as she doubted Rodney would be thrilled if she kept him up all night listening to it. Besides, she should at least try to get a decent night's sleep. Knowing he would be in the bed beside her, able to wake her if she started to have a nightmare, was rather comforting.

"Is it cool if I take a shower real quick? Unless you need one first. I always feel super grungy after leaving that building."

"Go ahead. I showered as soon as we got back."

"Right on." He jumped up, flashed a lopsided grin as he brushed past her, and stepped into the bathroom.

When she heard the lock click and the sound of the water running, she plucked the recorder from the bed and skipped it back to the beginning of the recording. She might not be able to go over the whole thing before Rodney finished his shower, but she might as well get a start.

Curling up on top of the comforter, she held the speaker to her ear and pressed play. Her own voice came through clearly, replaying her questions about hairspray and homecoming. She listened for anything in the gaps, in the blank spaces stretched out between questions, hoping to discern an answer on the recording they hadn't been able to hear in person. Without headphones, though, the task was much more difficult, and all too soon, the shower shut off. Pressing pause, she hurried to set the recorder on the bedside table before wiggling down underneath the comforter.

Rodney appeared in the bathroom doorway, steam swirling out from behind him, a towel wrapped almost obscenely low on his hips. Chrissy tried to avert her eyes, but they seemed to have a mind of their own, returning to take him in a little at a time. He stepped into the room and shot her an embarrassed glance as he snatched a pair of shorts from the bed.

"Forgot my boxers. Don't worry, they're clean."

She rolled her eyes and looked away, feeling her cheeks ignite, a sensation that was becoming all too frequent around him. “I didn’t need to know that.”

He returned to the bathroom, and Chrissy reached over, flicked the lamp off on her side of the bed, and shifted further down beneath the covers. As she lay in the muted light of the room, she thought about the final days of her previous relationship. It had been several months since it had fallen apart, the driving force behind the split being his inability to accept that she worked with two men. He couldn’t wrap his head around the fact that she wasn’t sleeping with one of them. To him, it was simply a matter of when. After returning one night from an investigation that ran longer than normal, she found him pacing the sidewalk in front of their apartment, raging and unreasonable.

“Which one was it?” he screamed.

“Dean, stop. It’s the middle of the night. You’re going to wake the neighbors.”

“I don’t give a good goddamn! Which one of them were you with? Because I know you were, Chrissy. Don’t you dare lie to me.”

“Seriously, Dean? I can’t go over this again. It’s offensive that you’d even think I’m cheating, but to think I’d cheat on you with one of my coworkers? It’s completely inappropriate. For the last time, nothing is happening.”

“You think I’m stupid enough to buy that?” he spat back. “I’ve seen how you look at the long-haired one. I’m not fucking dumb, Chrissy.”

She had vehemently denied that anything was going on between the two of them, and there hadn’t been, but Dean wouldn’t waver. He was convinced, and in the end, she hadn’t been able to live with his insecurity and kicked him out of their apartment.

Thinking back over the whole ordeal, she did have to admit Dean had been right about one thing: Rodney was, objectively speaking, an attractive man. She wasn't blind to it, but it was only an observation, nothing more. She had never acted on it or said anything about it to anyone, and there was no harm in looking, was there? No, there was not. Even now, she found herself picturing him wearing nothing but a towel, framed by the doorway, and she gnawed at her lip.

At the sound of the door opening, she flipped over, keeping her back to the opposite side of the room, and squeezed her eyes shut. Footsteps, followed by springs compressing in the bed next to her, described his movements, and then the room fell silent. The last of the light in the room died as he clicked off his bedside lamp.

"Night, Chrissy."

"Night, Rodney."

Rolling over, she couldn't resist glancing at the other bed, finding him laying on top of the blankets, wearing only his boxers. Even through the darkness, she could see his body was damn near perfect: lean, but with the strong, muscled physique of a rock climber. His hair had been freed from its messy bun, and for a moment, she wondered what it would be like to reach out and run her fingers through it.

She shoved those thoughts aside. Thinking about Rodney in that way would be the biggest mistake she could make. Her life was in shambles, and getting involved with someone you had to work so closely with almost never ended well. In fact, she thought the only reason she was thinking this way right now was because everything was falling apart so spectacularly.

"Chrissy?"

She flinched at the sound of Rodney's voice, convinced he had somehow been able to read her mind.

"Yeah?"

"Maybe me being here tonight will help keep the nightmares away."

"Maybe."

"Or maybe it'll make them worse. Who knows."

Grabbing a pillow off her bed, she chucked it in his direction. "Go to sleep."

A grin spread over her face and she felt her cheeks flush again. Rolling back over, she faced the wall and tried not to focus on the half-naked man chuckling softly in the bed next to her.

Once again, Chrissy found herself in the hallways of Merlin High as soon as she shut her eyes. The halls were empty, and with a sense of déjà vu, she approached the nearest classroom door and peered in. The same teacher scratched the same lesson on the chalkboard, while the girl in the front row yawned and laid her head on the desk

She was ascending the stairs again, the same echo of her footsteps following her up. Aware that everything was identical to the dream she had the night before, she risked a quick look down the left-wing corridor as soon as she reached the top of the stairs. She knew what was down there, waiting in the deep shadows, and it drove her towards the ladies' room with the hope that she would be able to discover the identity of the girl in the bathroom. This time, she would find the girl and drag her to safety before the thing came for them. This time, she knew what was coming.

The door was swinging, and the familiar, quiet humming drifted out from within. She reached out to push the door open, but it refused to budge. She pushed again, harder this time, but was met with the same resistance.

"Hello? Whoever is in there, can you please open the door? I think you're in danger," she said, keeping her voice low for fear of alerting the giant cockroach at the end of the hall.

Inside, the girl continued to hum as though she hadn't heard Chrissy.

"Please," Chrissy begged. "You need to open the door. We have to get out of here right now."

The humming turned to singing, and any moment the girl would be coming through the door, which also meant that the giant cockroach would pop out of the shadows and begin scrambling down the hallway towards them.

Throwing her weight against the door resulted in nothing but an aching shoulder. The door simply would not budge. She stole a wide-eyed glance down the hall, though every fiber of her being screamed at her not to. Out from the darkness, a long, thin leg emerged in a single, abrupt twitch, the movement so repulsive, she was on the verge of hysterics. Tears filled her eyes, blurring her vision, and she beat her fists on the door.

"We have to go! It's coming!"

The singing paused.

"You have to hurry!" Chrissy screamed, desperate for the girl inside to hear her, to understand the danger.

But the girl picked up the song right where she left off.

"It's going to get us if we don't leave now," Chrissy moaned, letting her hands fall to her sides.

A second long leg appeared, the muted sunlight filtering through the windows and splashing across the tile of the hallway highlighting every disgusting bristle.

With renewed urgency, she pounded her hands against the unyielding door, her palms stinging with the impact. Her screams, now incoherent, continued as she sobbed and clawed at the bathroom door.

The song stopped again for a moment, and the girl spoke through the door. "Sing with me. It helps make this part easier."

She started singing once more, this time much louder, and Chrissy watched in horror as the head of the giant roach came into view. Antennae twitched at the air, sensing...something. Her? Shaking with terror, the beating of her fists slowed and turned to weak, exhausted slaps of her palms on the wood. It was no use. The monster was here. It was coming for her.

With tears streaming down her face, she took a deep breath. She didn't recognize the song, yet the words somehow came to her as her voice, watery and trembling, joined the sweet and clear one of the mystery girl.

The sound of gnashing mandibles pulled her attention away, but the song went on. Again, the lyrics seemed to come from somewhere outside of Chrissy, as she had never heard them before. But there they were, floating off the tip of her tongue with ease, words about music playing and following the sound.

Beneath her aching palms, the door began to move. She scurried backwards, allowing it to open fully, and there, singing the final notes of the song, was the sweet face of a teenage girl, piles of sprayed golden curls fanning out all around her face. She gave Chrissy a sad smile and took her hands in her own.

"I know you," Chrissy managed to say, her throat raw from screaming.

"Close your eyes and keep singing. It really does help."

Chrissy screwed her eyes shut tight and stammered out the next few lines from her burning throat, the sound of giant cockroach feet punctuating each note as it scuttled towards them. Wings beat against lockers and walls. She wanted to cry out in terror, but the sweet sound of the girl's voice kept her going.

The creature pounced. Red-hot pain flared across her skin as the barbs on its legs dug in, making it impossible to yank free without tearing away a chunk of flesh. She let out a piercing scream, jolting herself awake.

Sitting up, she wiped her cheeks, wet with tears. With a trembling breath, she glanced over at Rodney, hoping she hadn't woken him, and was startled to find him half standing-half sitting on the edge of the bed, eyes huge as he stared at her.

"I'm sorry," she said. "I had another nightmare. I'm sorry."

His gaze remained fixed on her, horror-stricken. "You were singing."

"I'm sorry," Chrissy repeated. "I don't understand what's happening to me. It was the girl in the bathroom again."

Every limb began to shake, and her breath came so fast and shallow, she thought she would pass out. Rodney was by her side in no time, gathering her trembling body in his arms and holding her against his chest.

"It was the roach," she sobbed. "And it came...it was there. Its wings...and the bathroom door wouldn't..."

Everything poured out of her in a torrent of dark fragments. She knew she wasn't making any sense, but he continued to hold onto her, listening as she recounted every moment, though they came in jumbled bits and pieces. He just held on tight, not uttering a single word, and when she finally finished, she looked up to find him staring across the room, still wearing that strange expression.

"I'm so sorry I woke you up."

He gave an almost imperceptible shake of his head, and when he spoke, his voice was flat and dull. "Stop apologizing. It's not a big deal. I wasn't asleep yet."

"Oh."

They sat in the dark for a time before he cleared his throat.

"You were singing in your sleep."

"Yeah." Chrissy sniffled and swiped at her nose. "The girl told me to."

He made a small sound in the back of his throat but didn't say anything more.

"She told me it made the next part easier."

"What next part?"

"The part where the...the monster came and got us." She shivered and looked down at her bare arms and legs where the bug's feet scraped and raked over her.

"So you *do* know what song it is."

She shook her head. "No. I'm more convinced now that I've never heard it before. But somehow, I knew it in my dream."

His intense gaze locked onto her. "You were singing all the words, Chrissy."

"I don't know how. Now that I'm awake, I don't think I could tell you what they were. I doubt I could even get the melody right."

Rodney made the same sound in the back of his throat, the one that she now suspected might mean he didn't quite believe her. He kept his arms around her, pulling her against him, and they sat that way until her body began to relax. The trembling had stopped, and now that the haze of the nightmare was falling away, exhaustion crashed over her, eliciting an enormous yawn.

"Think you can go back to sleep?" he asked, releasing her from his embrace.

"I don't want to, but I'm so tired, I don't think I'll be able to keep my eyes open much longer."

He shifted away and made to stand. Without thinking, Chrissy reached out, gripping his wrist. He froze and stared down at her.

"Please don't go. I'm terrified I'm going to have another nightmare."

She swallowed hard, aware that what she was asking was far from professional, but she was frightened beyond caring at this point. After a moment's hesitation, he crawled back into bed, stretching his long legs next to hers.

"If you make a single peep, I'll wake you up. Deal?"

"Deal." Sinking back down beneath the covers, she curled into a tight ball, doing her best to avoid making any physical contact with him. Once she had settled in, Rodney took her hand, lacing his fingers with hers, and gave a gentle squeeze. With his touch came a soothing reassurance, bringing a rush of warmth to her, and she soon dropped into a sleep blessedly free of dreams.

Sixteen

Chrissy woke slowly, consciousness creeping in and whisking away the final mist of sleep. She wanted to stay in the haze, warm and safe. For the first time since arriving in Merlin, she felt rested. Drawing the blanket around her, she turned over and made contact with something solid. Her eyes sprang open, and she found her face inches from Rodney's side. He sat propped up against the headboard, phone in hand, and gave her a quick glance, lighting up as soon as he saw she was awake.

"Morning. I thought you'd never wake up."

With a groan, she rolled away and onto her back.

"What time is it?"

"Just about eleven."

She groaned. "Seriously? Why didn't you wake me up sooner?"

"You needed the sleep," he said, his attention back on his phone.

Chrissy pulled herself into a sitting position, another groan escaping her. The bed shifted, and she threw a look over her shoulder to find Rodney standing with his hands laced together behind his head. The muscles of his back pulled taut as he bent one way, then the other before gathering his hair into a ponytail.

She reached up and raked her fingers through her own locks self-consciously, attempting to smooth her sleep-tousled hair as much as possible.

"Did I do any more singing in my sleep?"

"Nope. Didn't make a sound."

"Thank goodness for that," she mumbled.

Rodney went to the chair where he had tossed his dirty clothes from the night before and gathered them in his arms.

"Now that you're awake, I'm going to head back to my room and check up on Bill."

She nodded, stifling a yawn as the final cobwebs of sleep cleared away. "Let me know how he's doing."

"Will do."

When Rodney reached the door, Chrissy called over her shoulder, "Thanks for staying with me."

Looking back with a grin, he gave her a thumbs up, dropping the shirt from the pile he carried in the process. He bent and snatched it back from the floor, grin still glued to his face as he left the room.

Once he had gone, Chrissy reached over and grabbed her phone from its charger, checking the screen. There were several notifications for emails she would have to deal with later, as well as a weather advisory — severe thunderstorm warning for Merlin — but the one that made her stomach do a little flip was a missed call from an unknown number. They had left a message.

With the phone pressed to her ear, she hopped off the bed and hurried to the dresser, grabbing a clean pair of jeans and scrambling to pull them on one-handed. The message was from one of the people off her list of possible interviewees she had contacted the day before. The caller identified herself as Beverly Walsh, a former student at Merlin High, and she said she would be available any time before one o'clock to speak about "the incident," as she put it. The message ended, and Chrissy tossed the phone onto the bed, proceeding to rush around the room getting ready. She'd be cutting it close.

She gave three rapid knocks on the door of the room next to hers. Rodney opened it, looking at her with surprise.

"Well, hello again. What's up?"

"I got a call from someone who said they're willing to do an interview about Merlin High, but I have to get over there fast. I wanted to check in with you guys first and make sure it was cool if I took the Ghostmobile." She lowered her voice slightly and continued, "How's Bill?"

"He says he stopped throwing up halfway through the night," Rodney glanced over his shoulder into the room. "But he looks like hell."

She followed his gaze. In a chair in a dim corner of the room sat Bill. Even from a distance, she could see that he was pallid and covered in a sheen of sweat that extended from his forehead up to the bald patch on top of his head. His lids were at half-mast, and he swayed gently back and forth, gazing at the floor glassy-eyed.

"He looks awful. Do you think we should take him to the hospital?"

"I don't need a hospital," Bill said from inside the room. His voice sounded thick and queasy.

Chrissy took a step into the room and made her way to the chair in the corner. Even seated, Bill was close to eye level with her. He turned his face up and gave a strained facsimile of a smile.

"Sorry you're having nightmares, Chrissy."

"I'm sorry you're feeling so rotten."

He gave a halfhearted shrug and dropped his head as though it was too much effort to hold the weight of it up.

"I have to head out for a couple of hours for an interview. Can I bring you back anything? Some saltines or ginger ale, maybe?"

With the smallest movement, Bill shook his head. "I'm alright. Just need to rest."

"Okay. You concentrate on getting better." She stepped back towards Rodney, concern creasing her face. "Will you be alright staying here with him?"

"Sure thing. I was planning on reviewing the footage from yesterday anyway."

"And if he gets worse, will you call? Or take him to a doctor?"

"Cross my heart," he said.

"You're the best." She placed a hand on his arm and smiled.

Chrissy left the room and headed out to meet Beverly Walsh, stopping back at her own room to grab the audio recorder from the bedside table.

Keeping one eye on the speedometer and one on the clock, Chrissy sped through Merlin. Beverly Walsh's house was located on the west side, a few blocks from Merlin High. The houses here showed the same slow decay, with the ones nearest the school boarded-up, derelict husks. The GPS told her she had reached her destination in one of the in-between neighborhoods, and she pulled the van over against the curb and checked the house number.

Beverly's house was an old craftsman style bungalow, small yet cozy, boasting a cheerful yellow paint job. The paint had begun to flake off in some areas, but the yard was a riot of colors, hundreds of blossoms adorning the place, lending it the appearance of an enchanted cottage. The narrow gate of the picket fence squealed as she went through, alerting the woman inside to her arrival.

The front door swung open as Chrissy made her way up the steps, revealing a beautiful, statuesque woman wearing a skirt made of handkerchiefs, each one a varying shade of yellow, down to her bare feet. Her head had been shaved down to the skin, and when she extended an arm to shake Chrissy's hand, an array of brightly colored bracelets clinked together, producing a melodic tinkling.

"You must be Chrissy," she said.

"That's me. It's so nice to meet you, Mrs. Walsh."

"Oh, please, call me Bev." Her smile was honeyed and welcoming. "Come on in, sugar."

Inside, the home possessed the same charm as the exterior. Quilted blankets were draped over the backs of two overstuffed armchairs. An equally overstuffed sofa sat against the wall under a large picture window that filled the room with natural light. Bookshelves lined two of the walls, every shelf so crammed with books Chrissy imagined adding just one more would cause the whole thing to collapse. On the wall opposite the window hung a tapestry, created from dozens of fabrics, all different shades and patterns, each piece fitting together to create a massive butterfly.

"Would you like some tea?"

"I'd love some."

Watching Bev from the archway that bridged the kitchen and the sitting room, she noted the elegance and fluidity in her movements as she went about preparing the tea — each motion deliberate and exuding confidence. A peaceful tranquility that

Chrissy hadn't felt in ages flowed through her, erasing some of the lingering fear left behind by her nightmares. When Bev returned with the tea, she set a steaming cup in front of her and settled down in one of the armchairs across from her.

"I'm so glad you got my message."

"So am I," Chrissy said, wrapping her fingers around the delicate teacup. "I'm sorry I didn't answer when you called. I haven't been sleeping too well."

Bev waved a hand in the air. "No need to apologize. This place tends to have that effect on people. The nightmares can be dreadful things."

Chrissy blinked back her surprise. "People complain about nightmares?"

"Oh yes. It's not just you." Bev raised her cup to her lips and took a small sip. "But that's not what you're here to talk about, is it?"

"No, it's not." She reached into her bag and pulled out the audio recorder. "Do you mind if I record this?"

"Go right ahead."

Placing the recorder down between them, Chrissy pressed record and took out her notebook. "I was hoping you might be able to tell me a little bit about Merlin High, what it was like before the fire, as well as some of your own experiences. You were a student there, right?"

"I was. I had just started my senior year when the fire happened." A bittersweet smile crossed her face. "It was shaping up to be a great year. The football team had won the homecoming game the night before, and we were all still flying pretty high on the win and the subsequent after parties. You know how it is."

"My school never won any of our football games, but we definitely had the after parties."

Bev chuckled. "Things were different back then. Nobody really minded if we were out all night. These days, if your kids aren't home, tucked in bed safe and sound by midnight, folks call the cops and send out a search party. Back then, stretches of time passed when I didn't see my parents for days at a time. Or, if I did, it was only in passing. We were left to our own devices, for the most part. But back then, Merlin was a much smaller place. Before the fire at the school, nobody thought anything bad would ever happen here."

"I can't imagine how it must have affected everyone. It was a terrible tragedy," Chrissy said. "You were one of the survivors, weren't you?"

Bev's lips drew down, her expression grave. "Yes, I was at the school the night of the fire."

"I'm so sorry."

"Don't be. I was one of the lucky ones. I had stepped out for a smoke," she said with a humorless laugh. "That damn cigarette saved my life. That's irony for you. Anyway, I stepped out with some friends to smoke around the back of the building when the first screams of fire came."

"That must have been terrifying."

"At first, we thought it was a prank, some kid screwing around and causing trouble. Once we understood what was happening, we did our best to help folks out through the back door of the gymnasium, but by then it was too late for most of them." She leaned back in her chair and ran a hand over her smooth scalp, looking pained.

"You couldn't have known," Chrissy said.

"Maybe not, but the school was abandoned after that night. A couple of months later they allowed us to go back to the undamaged sections to retrieve anything that had been left in our lockers, but almost nobody did. It was no longer a place for the living."

"Then you believe there are spirits that still reside in the school?"

"I don't just believe it, honey. I know there are, and they're not all friendly. Anyone who was here at the time can see it. The newer folks, the ones who don't have history here, they're the ones who refuse to acknowledge the truth of it, even when it's plain as day. The infection of it is right here in these neighborhoods."

"What do you mean?" Chrissy asked, shifting in her seat.

"You're a smart girl. I'm sure you've seen it."

"I think I have," she said slowly. "Are you talking about the homes?"

"Indeed I am." Bev nodded. "The people living right up against the school were the first to sense it. There's something dark in that school, and it's been moving out into the neighborhood. The nightmares and sounds of screaming in the night became unbearable for most of the folks around here. One by one, they just up and left."

"And you think the nightmares are caused by the spirits?"

"Could be the spirits. Could be the evil thing that happened that night."

"Do you mean the fire?" Chrissy asked, leaning forward. "You're the second person to say something like that. Before coming here, I was under the impression it was an accident."

"The fire was no accident."

"None of the reports I read said anything about it being set intentionally, though. One of them mentioned that some kid may have seen something, but since no other article brought it up, I just assumed it was a mistake. There's no evidence that the police were looking into it as a case of arson."

"I know what the reports all say, but not one of those reporters was there. They didn't see the Roach boy carrying around a gas can earlier that day, but I did. And the cops sure as hell didn't want to listen when I told them."

A cold dread spread through Chrissy's body. "I'm sorry, did you say 'roach boy?'"

"Derrick Roach. A troubled boy, that one."

She scribbled the name in her notebook and stared at it for a moment before looking up. "Who was he?"

Bev took a long sip of her tea. She studied Chrissy over her cup for a beat, then set it back down on the table. "He was an odd kid. Angry all the time. These days, they would have said he was the one most likely to become a school shooter. He had no friends, though Lord knows he tried. Went about it all wrong. He would scuttle from group to group in the cafeteria, snatching food off people's plates, laughing and joking about it. He thought it was hilarious, but it only pissed people off. That was how he was; he would try everything to get accepted into one clique or another but never figured out the right way to go about it."

"Sounds like a sad life."

"Must have been. Kids at that age can be terrible to each other."

"And you thought you saw him with a gas can the night of the homecoming dance?"

"I don't think I saw him. I did see him," Bev said, calm as could be. "So did a couple of my friends."

"Surely if you reported it, the police would have taken it seriously."

Bev laughed bitterly. “They might have if the others had survived the night. But one voice? One person pointing a finger at the son of the police chief?”

“The Roach kid was the son of the chief?” Chrissy’s voice rose to a near shout.

Bev gave a short nod and took another sip of tea.

Chrissy reeled from the onslaught of new information. So many pieces of the puzzle were trying to click together in her thoughts. When one of them finally did, her eyes snapped up to Bev.

“You were the source in that one article, the one who mentioned a student carrying a gas can.”

“No, that wasn’t me. I’m not sure who told them, but I never spoke to any of the reporters. A few called the house, but my mama gave them a real talking to. Told them they were ghouls to be pestering a young girl after such a traumatic experience.”

Chrissy sat back heavily and shook her head.

“You don’t believe me?”

“Oh, no,” she said quickly. “I believe you. It’s just...a lot to take in.”

They let the silence stretch out for a time, both lost in their own thoughts. Bev at last spoke, her voice hollow with regret. “I often wonder if the whole thing might have been prevented if we had all said something about Derrick as soon as we saw him. But we didn’t realize...”

Chrissy couldn't imagine the magnitude of the events that night, how it must have felt believing you might have been able to stop it. It was too heavy a burden, and her heart ached that this woman had been carrying it for so many years.

"Well, I guess you're interested in hearing about those spirits who are still present in the school," Bev said, standing and crossing the room to one of the walls lined with books.

"I am. Do you know anything about the girl in the bathroom?"

"The singing girl, you mean? Sure I do. She's one of the good ones."

"Do you have any idea who she was?"

Reaching up, Bev pulled out a narrow book and brought it over, setting it down on the coffee table. Chrissy shifted on the sofa, making room for her to sit beside her. The book was an old yearbook, the same one she had pored over at the library. She recognized the bold horizontal stripes slashed across the cover. It was a copy of the 1986 yearbook, but this one was full of students' signatures and well wishes for the summer.

Turning the pages, Bev opened it to the class of juniors and pointed to a photo of a girl with a mass of curls that somehow managed to look both wet and crunchy at once. Chrissy looked between the photo and the woman sitting beside her. Despite the drastic change of hairstyle, the 1986 version of Beverly Walsh possessed the same open smile and dark eyes that sparkled with joy.

"The amount of money I made my mama spend on mousse..." She chuckled and turned the page.

The smile on Chrissy's face froze as Bev pointed to another picture. High cloud of blonde hair, heart-shaped face — the girl from her nightmares stared up at her in black and white. How had she not recognized her sooner?

"Alorah," Chrissy whispered.

"That's right."

"Did you know her?"

"Everyone knew Alorah," Bev said. "We didn't run in the same circles, but she was always kind, always said hello. She even tried to befriend the Roach boy once."

"And you think it's her spirit who sings in the bathroom?"

Bev stood and moved back across the room, returning to the seat she occupied before. Chrissy raised her eyes from the yearbook and found Bev's appraising gaze locked on her. She appeared to be considering whether to say something more, so Chrissy remained silent and waited.

At last, she seemed to come to a decision. "I've spoken with her on occasion."

"You've been to the school since the fire?"

"No. I don't go near the place, not if I can help it. No, she comes to me. From the time I was a little girl, I've had certain gifts, I suppose you might say."

Chrissy's eyebrows shot up. "You're a psychic?"

Bev gave her a disparaging look. "I don't use that word. I can't predict the future, and I can't read your mind or give you next week's lotto numbers. I just have a special connection with the spirit world and sometimes I'm able to speak with some of those who have gone on before us."

"And you've spoken to Alorah?"

"Many times."

A list of questions as long as her arm popped into Chrissy's mind. Although she believed in the spirits and the afterlife, having had a handful of experiences as a child, something about self-proclaimed psychics rubbed her the wrong way. Since launching *Othersiders*, she had received dozens of emails from people who claimed to be psychic, saying they could feel the energies of the souls in the houses they investigated, that they had messages to deliver. Only, the activity in the houses in question was nothing more than Rodney's little tricks.

But Bev knew about the spirits in the school, and even pointed out Alorah as the singing girl, a detail that mirrored Chrissy's own dreams. There must be something to that.

"So why is she still at the school?"

Dark clouds were gathering in the east where Bev looked out the window, her fingers steepled in front of her. "There can be many reasons why the dead might linger. Being unable to let go of strong emotions, such as love or hatred, is the most common, in my experience. In this case, you've got both."

Chrissy was about to ask her what she meant when Bev abruptly stood with an apologetic smile.

"It has been lovely speaking with you, but I'm afraid I have an appointment I must get to."

Glancing at her watch, Chrissy was surprised to discover how much time had flown by. Retrieving the recorder from the table, she switched it off and tucked it away in her bag.

Halfway down the steps, she paused and turned on her heel to face Bev who still stood in the doorway. "You mentioned the nightmares earlier. Do you ever get them?"

"They're hard to escape when you live this close to the school."

"How do you stop them from happening?"

Bev's gaze turned reflective.

"You learn to navigate those dark corners," she said, her voice carrying the weight of experience. "It's not about avoiding the nightmares; it's about finding the strength to face them and choose a different path."

Seventeen

THE CLOUDS IN THE east crawled across the sky, covering most of Merlin, black and threatening. Chrissy left Bev's house, making a quick stop at the supermarket to pick up sandwiches, pasta salad, and a box of saltines for Bill. By the time she left the store, the clouds had broken, unleashing a torrent of rain. Darting across the parking lot, she shielded herself with a bag of groceries raised over her head. She sat in the van for a spell, listening to the television static sound of raindrops beating down all around her.

Her thoughts turned to Alorah. Even though the nightmare had grown fuzzy upon waking, the only clear part being the scratching, scrabbling legs of the cockroach digging in, she admonished herself for not recognizing her sooner.

And on the topic of roaches, what about the whole Roach boy thing? She couldn't shake that. It was far too coincidental, too intentional. If what Bev said was true, and she and her friends had seen him with a gas can only hours before the dance, then they couldn't ignore the possibility that he had set it intentionally. She claimed she wasn't the one who provided the information to the newspaper, and there was no reason to believe she was lying, but that would mean at least one of the other survivors had witnessed the same thing that day.

Chrissy shook her head, trying to clear the clutter of thoughts away. There were too many loose threads, too many coincidences, and no obvious answers. What she needed, she thought, was one more night in the school. Considering the last night had gone south, one more night seemed like more than a good idea. It was necessary.

Whipping out her phone, she brought up Sam Cleeves' number and hit dial, explaining the situation and asking about the possibility of going back for another night of investigation.

"I'm sorry to hear about your friend. Of course, you're all welcome to come back tonight. Could even drop by tomorrow night too, if you'd like. S'all the same to me. You've got the key. All I ask is you give me a holler if you plan on dropping by so I know it's you and not some trespassers come to poke around."

Chrissy thanked him, hung up the phone and peered out the window. The rain continued to beat down, forming small pools in the depressions of the asphalt. There were still a couple of hours to kill before she was supposed to meet with Donnie Melton, the only other person to return her call and agree to an interview. If she returned to the hotel and found that Bill was feeling better, she decided she would ask if he and Rodney would come with her down to the school to interview Donnie and set up for another night of investigating. The offer of not only one extra night at the school, but two, couldn't be passed up. They would have more footage for the show than they had ever gathered for an episode before, probably enough to make this case into a two-parter and go all out.

There was also the hope burning away in her chest that they would make contact with Alorah again. Chrissy had more questions than ever after talking to Bev, and she was convinced

Alorah held some of the answers she needed to figure out everything that was happening in the school.

Keying the ignition, the Ghostmobile roared to life, and Chrissy pulled out of the parking lot, making a slow path through the rain back to the hotel.

Upon returning, she knocked softly on Rodney and Bill's door. Rodney opened it, and she stepped into the room, giving Bill a once-over. He sat upright in the chair, still waxen and pale, but he gave her a weak, grateful smile as he accepted the saltines she brought him.

"Feeling any better?"

"A little," he said.

"Well, that's good news." Turning, she addressed Rodney. "Find anything interesting on the tapes?"

He shook his head. "Not on any of the stationary cameras. I couldn't find the audio from the bathroom, though. Did it get left in the van?"

"Oh." She rooted around in her bag and pulled out the recorder. "Yeah, sorry. I grabbed it for the interview."

She passed off the device and went to what she assumed was Rodney's bed, based on the amount of clothing strewn across it, dumping out the remaining contents of the grocery bag. Taking a small container of pasta salad for herself, she dug in and chowed down as she filled them in on her meeting with Beverly.

"She had a lot to say and dropped several major bombshells," she said through a mouthful of pasta. "One of them being the fact that she and a group of friends saw someone with a gas can the day of the fire."

Rodney looked up sharply. "Was she sure about that? It happened a long time ago. Do you think you can even trust her memory?"

Chrissy shrugged and glanced over at Bill, whose eyes bore holes into the back of her head. She squirmed, trapped between their intense stares, and drew herself to her full height. "I mean, she seemed pretty credible. A little unique, but not crazy or anything."

"Well, then why didn't anyone tell the police about it? Why didn't anyone investigate?"

"She was the only one who had seen it who survived the fire, and the cops were less than receptive."

Rodney didn't appear convinced, but his eyes softened around the edges. "I'm not sold on it, Chrissy. Someone would have investigated."

"I'm just telling you what she told me."

"Alright, well, did she say who she thought she saw with the gas?"

"She did. This is the wild part. Well, one of the wild parts. His name was Derrick Roach. Roach! And, get this: he was the son of the chief of police."

Bill made a small choking sound from the corner. When they looked over, he was trembling and had turned a ghastly shade of green.

"I think I'm going to be sick again," he muttered, struggling to his feet. He hurried into the bathroom, the door slamming behind him.

Rodney winced. "Guess the crackers didn't go down too well."

"Poor guy. I'll assume that means investigating tonight is out of the picture."

"Looks that way," he said. "So Roach, huh? I'll admit, it is a kind of weird coincidence."

Chrissy nodded and leaned forward. "I know, right? Bev told me the people who lived close to the school were more or less driven out by the nightmares. I wish some of them were still around so I could ask what their nightmares were about. Maybe they all featured a certain giant cockroach."

"The dude you're interviewing this afternoon might have some insights. He lives nearby, right?"

"Yup," she said, scraping the last stray onion up from the bottom of the container. "I should ask Sam about the dreams too. He lives down the street from the school."

"Good plan." Rodney reached over and grabbed a tightly wrapped sub sandwich, tearing the paper halfway off before sinking his teeth into it. Speaking around his food, he said, "You mentioned Roach is just one of the big bombshells. What else did this lady tell you?"

"Well, she told me who the girl in the bathroom is."

"Oh yeah? And how does she know that little tidbit?"

The smile on Chrissy's face faltered. She would have to choose her words carefully. Whatever she said might make Rodney less inclined to believe everything Bev told her. He was already skeptical when it came to spirits and the afterlife, and if she tried to explain things the wrong way, he would throw out all the information Bev had given her, calling it all a load of horseshit.

There was no way around it. Just rip it off like a Band-Aid. If he didn't want to believe, then fine. He just had to do the job.

"She spoke with her."

He stared at her blankly for a moment, then threw his head back with a bark of laughter.

"Oh, come on, Chrissy," he said once his laughter subsided. "You can't really believe that."

She raised a shoulder. "I do."

"But why?"

"Because..." Squaring her shoulders, she started again, gathering all the confidence she could muster. "Because she's the same girl from my nightmare. The one who told me to sing. And it's the same girl I saw in the yearbook. Alorah Smith."

Darkness swept over Rodney's face, as if a metal shutter dropped down, erasing the mirth that had been there moments ago. When he spoke, his tone was low and flat, each word edged with ice. "It sounds to me like she's a crazy woman who wants her fifteen minutes."

It was Chrissy's turn to laugh. "Fifteen minutes? On a tiny online ghost hunting show? Rodney, that's ridiculous."

"No. What's ridiculous is giving this woman a platform to make a mockery of a tragedy."

"She wasn't making a mockery," Chrissy said, struggling to keep calm as her cheeks heated. "She knew this Alorah girl, and she knows she saw Derrick Roach the day of the homecoming dance, carrying a gas can."

"That's just it," Rodney replied, his voice held all the warmth of a winter storm. "How can you believe her on the gas thing when she also thinks she can talk to ghosts? If I were you, I'd drop it."

Turning in his chair, he set his sandwich on the desk, grabbed his headphones, and turned his attention back to his laptop.

"Rodney."

"I have work to do."

She stared at his back in disbelief. She hadn't expected him to like the idea that Bev claimed to have spoken with the spirits at Merlin High, but she never expected him to shut down and ice her out.

"Fine," she said, raising her voice so she could be heard over his headphones. "If you want to be so closed minded, that's your business."

Grabbing her bag, she stormed across the room, yelling through the bathroom door as she left. "Hope you feel better soon, Bill."

Chrissy fumed as she paced the length of her room, leaving a trail of worn carpet fibers in her wake. How dare Rodney blow her off? There she was, going out and getting things done, finding things out that would only improve their chances of drawing out the spirits, and what had he been doing?

"Hardly anything," she muttered to herself.

The interview with Bev wasn't a waste of time, and she wouldn't drop it. In fact, she would use the information to capture evidence of the paranormal, as well as to bring justice to the families who lost their children and loved ones in the fire. If, that was, she found evidence that it had been set on purpose, a theory she was well on her way to believing. If she brought that story to light, the sheer volume of new subscribers to *Othersiders* would be enough to secure her future, at least for a while.

She huffed out a long breath. If Rodney wouldn't help, so be it. If he wanted to be a narrow-minded jerk, she would just have to take it upon herself to find proof Bev was right about everything.

But a hollowness sat in her gut. She needed someone to talk to, someone to be on her team. She had always been able to count on Rodney to be her sounding board, but as soon as they had found something real and tangible, something worth investigating, he was slipping away. Last night, she thought he might be starting to come around to her side of things. He had come face to face with the paranormal, something he couldn't argue away. Instead, he hadn't just pulled away; he shut her out completely, and that was far more painful.

Stopping in her tracks, she decided she couldn't spend any more time pacing the room like a caged tiger. Donnie wasn't supposed to arrive at the school for another hour or so, but the walls of her room were closing in, making her feel claustrophobic, trapping her in her own misery. She needed to get out.

She crossed the room and opened her bag, placing a camera, audio recorder, and clip mic inside. She even tossed in an EMF detector for good measure. A delicious shiver of exhilaration coursed through her. She had never gone into a place to investigate on her own, but if she left now, there should be enough time before Donnie arrived to have a little wander through the halls, conduct a mini solo investigation. Armed with the information she had gotten from Bev, who knew? Maybe Alorah would come out and talk to her.

The rain had slowed to a steady drizzle, though the air was heavy and charged with the promise of more to come. Dark clouds grumbled, the sky briefly illuminated by flashes of sheet lightning as Chrissy drove towards the school. The muted gray light washed out the building's facade, making it look sinister and cold, a stark contrast to how it had appeared on her first visit. While she sat in the van outside the gate, a chill settled into her bones as she realized she would soon be alone in the building with the ever-present darkness. Brushing that aside, she dashed off a text to Sam, informing him that she would be at the school for the next couple of hours. She slipped her phone into her pocket, grabbed the bag from the passenger seat, and sprinted through the rain and past the fence.

Inside the doorway, Chrissy shook the raindrops from her raincoat and scanned the halls, noting that the lighting was less than ideal. After setting the bag down, she pulled the hood of her slicker up over her head and stepped out into the gentle drizzle again to find a location with enough light for the interview.

The exterior of the right wing stood imposing and bleak, its empty windows staring out like eyeless sockets. All at once, she was gripped by the sensation that she was being watched from one of those windows, but she refused to look up, fearing they might not be quite so empty after all.

Rounding the corner, she found herself looking across the school's quad, a big square where grass had once grown, long since choked out by clots of tall weeds. A sizeable picnic table stood in the center, upended and towering over the space like a strange monolith. What appeared to have once been a pergola leaned drunkenly towards the school. A few tables and chairs still sat beneath it, and if not for the wooden beam, which had fallen at some point and was now balanced precariously on top of one of the tables, it would have been a perfect spot to sit and have lunch.

Chrissy approached the seating area and gingerly reached out to test the weight and balance of the beam, hoping she might be able to roll it off. With a small push, she soon realized that its position wasn't as precarious as it looked. It was wedged between two of the upright beams, held snugly in place.

The light in the courtyard still wasn't the best, but it seemed to be the only choice with the limited options available. Before the weather rolled in, Chrissy had planned to shoot the interviews inside the halls of the school, but the power had been shut off decades ago, and the storm clouds didn't allow enough sunlight to filter through the windows to cut through the darkness.

Drying her palms on her jeans, she reached out and gripped the beam in both hands, giving it a wiggle. The upright posts resisted, not wanting to release their hold, but with a little finesse, she was able to slide the downed beam out. No longer held in place, the uneven weight of the thing caused it to topple over and roll onto the ground with a bang that echoed off the walls of the school. She rolled it further away with her foot and stepped back to get a view of the shot. Satisfied, she made her way to the front of the building to have a quick look around.

As she came around the corner, a figure standing outside the gates of the school caught her attention. With hands shoved deep in their pockets, they stared up at the second-floor windows. They had pulled the hood of their raincoat up, casting their face in purple shadows. Chrissy was about to call out to the figure when another voice came from the opposite direction.

"Hello there!"

Her head snapped in the direction of the new voice. A thin man with a dark, bushy mustache waved from the school's entrance. She lifted an arm in greeting, and by the time she glanced back at the gate, the person outside the fence had already turned away, hurrying down the sidewalk, away from the building. Confused, she made her way towards the man with the mustache.

"Donnie Meltan?"

"That's me." The man beamed from beneath a mustache so full, Chrissy wondered if it might be fake. He was all smiles and handshakes, and something about the way he was put together reminded her of a math teacher.

"Thank you so much for coming out in this weather to do this," she said.

"Not at all. Happy to oblige. There's a lot of history here, and history is my specialty." He leaned forward, his yellow rain slicker making a pleasant whispery sound as he did so. "I teach history at the high school next town over."

"You still live in the area?"

He nodded and rocked back on his heels. "After finishing my degree, I came back to Merlin. Of course, it's changed quite a lot since I was a boy."

"I can imagine."

"Well then, where do you want me for my closeup?"

"Let's head around back." Ducking into the entryway, Chrissy scooped the bag from the floor and motioned for him to follow as she led the way around to the courtyard.

When they stepped into the area, Donnie let out a whistle. "What a mess. This used to be *the* place to have lunch. Well, if you were one of the kids who didn't have a car. The kids with cars would go off campus and eat at Tony's, the burger joint downtown."

Chrissy stood back, giving him space as he looked around, taking everything in with a vague nostalgic smile. When his eyes landed on the burnt-out shell of the gymnasium, his face fell. He made a soft tutting sound and wagged his head back and forth.

"Such a senseless tragedy," he muttered under his breath.

She waited, allowing him a few more moments to process. The rain had at last subsided, and not knowing how long they would have before it started back up, she stepped forward and pulled one of the least damaged chairs out from one of the tables. Using the sleeve of her coat, she brushed away the small puddle of rain that had collected on the seat and turned to Donnie with an apologetic smile.

"It might still be a little wet. Of course, you're welcome to stand, but the process can be a bit tiring."

He hopped over the wooden beam she had dislodged and eased himself down into the chair. "A little water never hurt anyone."

"Let's just hope there's no more of it for a while," Chrissy said, glancing up at the heavy clouds still hanging over the school. After clipping the small mic onto Donnie's shirt and wrestling the tripod and camera into position, she took a step back and hit record, the eyes of the school peering down at her as she began her questions.

Interview with Donnie Meltan

CR: So Donnie, you were a student here at Merlin High in 1987, correct?

DM: Sure was. Go Wizards!

CR: So you were a...junior the year of the fire?

DM: Sounds about right.

CR: What was Merlin High like back then?

DM: Oh, it was like any other high school, I suppose. We had our fair share of cliques; the jocks, the preps, the burnouts, the band kids, the losers, the nerds. That was me. I was king of the nerds. Suppose I still am. At least, the kids I teach these days sure think so.

CR: I'm sure that's not true.

DM: No, no. It's okay! Nothing wrong with being a nerd. In fact, it's probably what saved me that night.

CR: The night of the fire?

DM: That's right. The night of the homecoming dance.

CR: How do you think being a nerd saved you?

DM: Well, back in those days, being a nerd wasn't the same as it is today, you see. Used to be a social life death sentence. Oh, uh...poor choice of words, I'm afraid.

CR: That's alright. We can cut that part out.

DM: Appreciate it. Yes, well, being a nerd was not so good for the social life. But today, that's not the case. Some of my nerdiest students have girlfriends and are quite popular. Sure wish that was the case back when I was in high school. Being a nerd then was seriously uncool. Instead of doing things like going to dances or parties, we pretty much just kept to ourselves. As such, the night of the fire — the homecoming dance — I wasn't there. I was at home with some of my friends — I did have some of those, by the way — and we were messing around with the new computer my family had just gotten. Of course, now it's not that weird to skip out on parties to surf the web all day. But back then, not so much.

CR: So, you weren't at the school the night it burned down?

DM: Not that night, no. But I was there in the afternoon.

CR: What for?

DM: A.V. Club. We were setting up the sound equipment for the dance. Dances were always fun, even though we didn't attend most of them, because we got to mess around with the sound system.

CR: Did you see anything unusual?

DM: Unusual how?

CR: I read one newspaper article that mentioned the possibility of someone around that day with a gas can. A couple of other people have said something similar.

DM: Oh, yes. Well, that's a tricky subject. I didn't see anything personally, no, but I have heard that rumor.

CR: Do you think it's a possibility the fire was set by a student?

DM: I think it depends on who you ask. But since you're asking me...I wouldn't say it's outside the realm of possibilities.

CR: Why would someone want to do that?

DM: Sure beats me. People do all sorts of terrible things, especially when they're that age, you know? Brain's not fully developed yet. Some of the kids I teach, they get some downright terrible and dangerous ideas. Have you heard about that cinnamon challenge the kids are doing?

CR: Yeah, I've seen that one online.

DM: Pretty dumb, if you ask me.

CR: Well, I sure don't plan on doing it.

DM: Smart girl.

CR: Alright, let's move on to another rumor. People say there are still spirits roaming the halls of Merlin High. What's your take on that?

DM: Now, I'm not really a believer in the paranormal. Sorry, I know you were probably wishing I was. But I do believe that sometimes, events leave an imprint on the world. You can feel it when you enter a place where a momentous event has happened in history. I've felt it at Antietam and Valley Forge. You can feel it at Proctor's Ledge in Salem. While I've never seen a ghost, I have felt the weight of history. So, to answer your question...Do I believe there are ghosts here? No. But I do believe the events of October 2nd, 1987 have left an imprint on this place.

CR: That's really interesting. In the world of paranormal investigation, we believe there are two kinds of hauntings: intelligent and residual. Intelligent haunts are just that: intelligent. Residual haunts are more like spirits going about their lives as they would have when they were alive, walking up stairs that were long ago destroyed, going through walls where there had once been a door. What you're talking about sounds a lot like residual hauntings.

DM: It does sound similar. Though, again, I haven't seen any ghosts, residual or intelligent.

CR: You haven't had any experiences here since the fire? I've heard that the folks who lived nearby ended up leaving due to nightmares and hearing screams coming from the school in the middle of the night.

DM: Well...

CR: You seem hesitant to answer that.

DM: It was a long time ago is all. I don't even live near the school these days.

CR: What about when you were a student?

DM: I...didn't live too far, no.

CR: If this is making you uncomfortable, you don't have to answer.

DM: It was just so long ago, you see. I did have nightmares, but we all did. After sixty-seven of your classmates died, who wouldn't?

CR: You make a good point. Well, Donnie, thank you so much for coming out here on this rainy day to talk with me. It's been really fascinating to learn some more about the history of this place.

DM: Happy to do it. As a history buff, I'm always interested in making sure the past is well documented. Makes things easier for the historians of the future.

CR: That's very true.

DM: Hey now, I just had a thought. If you're interested in a little slice of life back at Merlin High, the A.V. Club made video yearbooks back then. One of my old club buddies recently dug them up and uploaded them to share with the guys. I'm sure I could find the files and email them to you. There's some really interesting stuff in them.

CR: That sounds amazing. Thank you. I'd love to check them out.

EIGHTEEN

WAVING FROM THE SCHOOL'S entryway, Chrissy watched Donnie hop into his battered blue sedan and drive off. Although she was disappointed by the fact he hadn't known anything about the spirits in the school, or had any more information about the person seen carrying the gas can, he did give her that little tidbit about the video yearbooks.

She turned back to the school and squared her shoulders, determined to go through with her plan to conduct a brief solo investigation. Camera in one hand, EMF detector in the other, she shouldered her way through the front doors and into the dim halls of Merlin High. The heavy door banged shut behind her, and she just about jumped out of her skin. With a nervous laugh, she forced her feet to take another step forward to prove, mostly to herself, that she wasn't afraid. When she came up with the idea, she had thought investigating during the daytime would be easy. The sunlight would dispel most of her anxiety. But now, with the overcast sky, the halls were almost as dark as they were in the middle of the night.

Throughout her childhood, Chrissy had heard things go bump in the night or seen shadows moving around her bedroom on many occasions. One particularly active night when she was six, she had drawn her blanket up over her head and cried for her mother.

"The old woman won't go away, Mama."

"Ahh, sweetheart. You don't have to worry. She isn't here to hurt you," her mother cooed, gathering Chrissy's small, trembling form against her. "None of them want to hurt you. They are only our loved ones who have already passed on."

"But why are they here? They're scaring me!" Chrissy sobbed, hot tears soaking into her mother's blouse.

"They're tied here because they love us so very much. They don't mean to scare you. They just can't speak to us the way they used to."

"I don't like the way they talk."

"I know, baby, but they're here to watch over you and keep you safe. Do you understand?"

Standing alone in the entryway, Chrissy repeated her mother's words like a mantra. Whatever spirits were here, there was no need to fear them.

But something had changed. Something was wrong. The oppressive weight that always settled in when she stepped into the school was now thicker. Heavier. Like the past was alive here, and it could reach out at any moment and grab hold of her. She tried to shake it off, feeling ridiculous for even thinking it, but the sensation clung to her and refused to be ignored.

"It's just because I'm alone," she said, hoping that hearing the words spoken aloud would be enough to convince herself. She was here, damn it, and she wasn't going to let this opportunity slip through her fingers. She would prove to Rodney, her parents, and the rest of the world that she knew what she was doing.

With renewed resolve, Chrissy made her way down the left wing. Everything had happened so fast the previous night, and there hadn't been a chance to investigate down this way before having to pack up and leave. The gymnasium was the one place, besides the ladies' room, that she was sure was ripe with paranormal energy. She headed that way now, towards the scene of the fire.

Fallen bits of plaster crunched underfoot, and the scent of old smoke grew stronger the closer she got to the doors of the gym. Once she reached them, she squinted through the weak light to where the edges had warped and twisted from the intense heat of the inferno.

Images of students trapped inside came unbidden to her mind, their last moments filled with pure terror and desperation. She brushed her fingertips over the door and drew her hand back with a gasp. It was searing hot. Tentatively, she reached forward again, inching her hand as close to the door as possible without actually touching, but no heat radiated from it now. Ready to pull back again, she breached the final distance, placing her palm against the door, but there was only the sensation of cool metal against skin.

"Well, that was weird," she said out loud. "Must have been my imagination."

Peering at the door, Chrissy kicked herself for not having thought to bring the thermal camera with her. She could picture where it was, too. She passed right over it when she was packing her bag. It was right there, sitting next to-

All of the hairs on the back of her neck suddenly rose, all of her thoughts dropping out through the bottom of her skull. She held her breath.

Footsteps.

Faint but unmistakable, coming down the hallway in her direction. She whipped around, staring wide-eyed down the corridor. She remembered the person she had seen standing outside the fence, and she desperately tried to remember whether she locked the gate after Donnie left. If that person had come back and found the place unlocked...she didn't want to finish the thought. She was scrappy and would fight like hell, but she was certain she would be no match for a man that size.

But as she scanned the dark halls, she found no hulking shape, no movement. The school looked the same as it always did. Still, the sound of footsteps continued, and they seemed to be getting louder.

Not wanting to startle whatever was making the noise, she slowly drew the EMF detector from her pocket and held it out in front of her.

"Hello? Is there someone here?" she asked, her voice sounding far more confident than she actually felt.

The footsteps picked up their pace. Whatever was moving in the hallway, it was advancing with rapid strides.

"Who's there?"

A flash of green startled her before she realized it was only the EMF detector registering a fluctuation. The steps drew closer, and the little green light blinked several more times before turning solid.

The footsteps were moving fast, at the pace of a jog. Chrissy tore her gaze away from the device, only to find an empty hallway stretching out in front of her.

Her breath hitched as from the corner of her eye, she saw the EMF flash up into yellow, then orange. A rapid flurry of beeps squealed from the box every time the lights jumped all the way up into the red zone.

Now, the footsteps were running, sprinting down the hall. Her eyes flickered between the EMF and empty corridor. The box continued its bursts of lights and beeps, finally settling into a steady, shrill whine as every single light flashed red.

Chrissy's knuckles turned white as she gripped the EMF detector, its plastic edges imprinting in her palms. A small squeak tried to escape, but stuck somewhere in her throat. The footsteps thundered towards her, right in front of her. She squeezed her eyes shut at the same time that whatever was coming crashed into her.

Her lungs seized up, paralyzed by cold fear, a blast of frigid air smashing into her like a freight train. The forceful blow left her breathless and uselessly gasping for air. The edges of her vision went black. On the edge of consciousness, she at last managed to draw a deep breath. Air rushed into her chest, leaving her head fuzzy and full of the droning of a million bees.

The footsteps were gone. The EMF fell silent. Her eyes were still screwed shut, but the way the light filtered warm and bright through her lids was unfamiliar. She opened her eyes to narrow slits and found herself staring down at freshly buffed linoleum. Confused, she forced her eyes wide, struggling to understand what she was seeing. A few feet ahead of her, balmy afternoon sunlight spilled across the dark green and white floor. Raising her head, she looked down at what appeared to be Merlin High's left wing.

The windows — each pane now intact — permitted the light to fill the hall and made the drab olive color of the lockers appear almost cheerful against the checkered floor. The walls were chalky white and smelled of fresh paint. Outside, the weedy clumps of dying grass and hardpan in front of the school had been replaced by a sprawling green lawn. Trees lined the street in vibrant reds and oranges, the ground beneath covered in leaves. The corner of the student parking lot was just visible, packed with boxy old cars Chrissy hadn't seen anywhere but in movies made decades ago.

She remained motionless, still unable to come to terms with what was happening. It was like being back in one of her dreams, but that wasn't possible. Unless she had passed out. Yes, she supposed that might be it. She had never passed out before in her life, but that didn't necessarily mean anything. There was a first time for everything.

The shrill sound of the class bell startled her from her thoughts, and she found herself pushed up against the doors of the gymnasium as classes let out and students flowed into the hallways.

A familiar heart-shaped face appeared amidst the sea of scrunchies, weaving its way through the crowd. Golden curls bobbed as she moved, defying the sheer volume of hairspray required to keep them in place. Sporting an acid washed Levis jacket, Alorah dodged students expertly, pausing to wave or smile as she passed by. She was moving away from the gym, and Chrissy rushed after her.

"Hey! Wait!"

Nobody seemed to notice Chrissy as she pushed her way through, but she could feel the brush of their sweaters, the press of bodies as she kept pace behind Alorah. The unmistakable perfume of hairspray and deodorant-tinged body odor permeated the halls, the signature scent of high schools everywhere.

Through a break in the backpacks and denim, she caught another glimpse of Alorah as she turned and headed up the stairs to the second floor. Chrissy hurried forward into the crush of students, trying not to lose sight of her, though she had a decent idea of where she was headed.

After shoving past several kids and calling out with no response, Chrissy was now almost certain nobody could see or feel her, so she stepped into the ladies' room just as the door was swinging shut.

Alorah stood in front of a mirror, her backpack resting in the basin of the sink. She reached into it, pulling out a brush and purple can of super-hold Aqua Net. A soft chuckle of disbelief escaped Chrissy's lips as she watched the girl proceed to backcomb her hair, somehow teasing it into an even fluffier style than it already was.

One of the bathroom stall doors opened, and a girl with a dark, glossy braid emerged. Alorah beamed at her through a haze of hairspray.

"Hey, Tiff! What's up?"

The dark-haired girl stepped up to the sink next to Alorah and began to wash her hands. "Not much. How about you?"

"You know, same old, same old," Alorah said brightly. She appraised herself in the mirror, gave one final spray, and then turned to Tiff. "You going to the homecoming dance?"

"Yeah. Tommy asked me, like, last week."

"That's so great! Tommy's a total babe," she said, tossing the can of Aqua Net into her backpack.

"Don't I know it. What about you? I bet you've had a date lined up for, like, ages."

Alorah shrugged her backpack up over one shoulder. "Well, at first, I wasn't sure I was going to be able to make it. My parents wanted me to babysit my little brother that night, but I talked them out of it last minute. I've totally been brushing people off for the last few weeks, but I'm sure someone will ask again."

"Oh, like, for sure."

"And if they don't, I can always go stag." She checked her hair in the mirror one more time, giving it a little fluff before turning. "Well, gotta jet. I'll see you at cheer practice."

Chrissy followed Alorah through the door and down the now-deserted hallway. She had a bounce to her step, which made her curls bob up and down cheerfully. Halfway down the hall, she stopped in front of a locker and spun the dial, popping the door open. She sang under her breath, and Chrissy recognized it as the melody she had been singing in her nightmare. Alorah's voice came out soft and sweet, and Chrissy couldn't help but smile at how carefree and happy she appeared to be.

"Hey, Alorah."

Alorah flinched at the grating, nasal voice. Keeping her head buried in her locker, she acted as though she hadn't heard anything. Chrissy turned to see who had spoken, and her stomach clenched like she had been socked in the gut. Somehow, without ever having seen the boy before, she knew exactly who he was. Two long, greasy strands of hair fell in front of his face like curtains, obscuring dark, sunken eyes. His head hung down between rounded shoulders, and he reeked of cigarettes and grease. He slammed a hand on the locker next to Alorah's, making both Chrissy and Alorah jump.

"I said, hey Alorah."

Alorah took a deep breath behind her locker's door before closing it and turning to face the boy.

"Hey Derrick."

Derrick leaned against the lockers, crossing his arms over a baggy Led Zeppelin tee that reached his knees. "What's up?"

"I'm heading to cheer practice."

"How 'bout you ditch and come hang with me? We can smoke out by the bleachers."

With a tight smile, she said, "Thanks, but I don't smoke."

She made a move to leave, but Derrick stepped in front of her, blocking her way. Chrissy's throat tightened, worried about where this interaction was heading.

"You don't gotta smoke. We can just make out a little." He licked his lips and let his eyes crawl up and down her body.

"Ugh. Don't make me ralph."

Anger flared across Derrick's face, and he took a menacing step towards Alorah. Striding forward, Chrissy tried putting herself between the two, but as soon as she was in his line of sight, a sick churning gripped her insides. Doubling over, she backed away, out of his gaze, and the nausea began to lift.

"Alright," she said to herself. "Won't be doing that again."

"Why do you gotta be such a mega bitch?"

Alorah glared at him. "Why do you have to be such a creep-azoid?"

Derrick took another quick step forward and grabbed Alorah by the shoulders. Her eyes went wide with fear for a moment before she regained its composure. Steeling herself beneath his grip, she glowered up into his face.

"If you don't let me go, I'm going to scream and tell Principle Engles. It'll be your third strike, and you'll be expelled."

He threw his head back and laughed, an empty, hollow sound. Instead of releasing her, he shoved her hard, slamming her into the lockers. He brought his head down, those oily strands almost brushing her cheeks, and grinned into her face, now white with terror.

"I don't give a flying fuck about Principle Engles, and I don't give a flying fuck about third strikes."

Chrissy tensed as the encounter played out in front of her. She wanted to scream, to tell Alorah to run, to call for help, to scratch and kick and fight, but there was nothing she could do to stop this. If this was a dream, or a vision of something that happened long ago, she didn't know. All she knew was she had no power to change these events.

Derrick leaned in even closer, his hot breath making Alorah cringe away. "How about you come with me to homecoming, huh, Alorah? Wanna be my date?"

"No."

Chrissy expected another outburst, but Derrick's voice remained terrifyingly calm and mawkish. "Aw, come on, baby. You know you want to."

He slid his hands from her shoulders and down her over arms. When he reached her wrists, he grabbed them hard, wrenching them up over her head and pinning her against the lockers. Alorah let out a distressed whimper, and once again, Chrissy tried stepping forward, reaching out to pull him away. She couldn't let this go any further. Although she had been able to physically feel the presence of the students earlier when they passed by, her fingers now simply passed through Derrick as though he was nothing more than vapor. Her own sound of distress echoed Alorah's.

"I'm telling you right now, Roach, let me go!" Though her voice trembled, she stared the boy directly in the eye.

He slammed her wrists against the lockers, her Swatch watch making a metallic thunk as it made contact with the locker door. His eyes burned into her with pure hatred. "Don't you *ever* call me that, bitch! I think you need to be taught some manners."

Desperate tears sprang to Chrissy's eyes. Afraid of what came next, she wished she could protect the young girl from all of it. And then, all at once, everything changed. Alorah's face darkened with determination. She brought a knee up fast and brutal between Derrick's legs, and he dropped like a stone, crumpling to his knees with a guttural roar. As soon as his grip fell away, Alorah took off at a sprint, leaving him writhing and groaning on the floor.

Tears now turning to ones of relief, Chrissy's entire body went weak. She glared over at Derrick, who had managed to struggle to his feet but stood hunched over, his hands hovering protectively over his injured crotch. His shoulders started to shake, and a small part of Chrissy rejoiced in the fact that Alorah quite literally brought the creep to his knees and made him cry.

But that joy turned sour in her stomach as she realized that no, he wasn't crying. He was laughing. He raised his head, glaring daggers in the direction Alorah had fled.

"You're gonna pay, bitch. You're gonna fucking pay."

Nineteen

DERRICK STAGGERED TOWARDS THE spot where Chrissy stood frozen. He turned his head and, for a moment, she was certain he could see her, but that wasn't possible. Nobody had been able to see or hear her since she stepped into this...what? Dream? Vision? Whatever it was, she had been undetectable. Still, she held her breath and wished herself invisible as his eyes locked on her and narrowed. A wave of that same nausea roiled in her gut. His jaw wrenched open wider than humanly feasible, and with a primal roar of untamed anger, he charged.

Another blast of cold air hit, slamming all the breath from her lungs and leaving her gasping once more. The stench of rancid hostility swept over her, making her already swimming stomach do another queasy flip.

Despair crashed over her, soaking down into the very marrow of her bones. She felt slick and slimy with it. Her whole body shook as she fought it, desperate to throw off the cloak of misery that smothered and tried to pull her further down. Thoughts that were not her own flashed in rapid succession.

You're worthless.

You should end it.

There's no point.

Just die already.

Her eyes flew open and she was back in the dilapidated Merlin High of the present, in front of the row of lockers where Alorah had been standing. The hallway, so alive moments ago, was now hollow and stale. Whatever it was that happened, it was over, and Roach was gone.

But for how long?

Panic flooded her veins with ice water, and she wanted nothing more than to get as far away from the building as fast as possible. She tore down the hall to the stairs, skipping steps as she flew down them, the EMF detector still clutched in a death grip. As soon as she hit the bottom of the stairs, she sprinted to the door, stooping to snatch her bag off the floor, and smashed through the front doors of the school.

Outside, she took in deep lungfuls of rain-sweetened air, desperate to rid herself of the stench Roach left behind. Had he passed through her the same way her own fingers passed right through him? The thought almost made her gag with disgust.

After she squeezed through the gate, she paused, for a moment, to lock it. She kept her eyes down, refusing to look at the building. With the gate now secured, she turned and jogged the rest of the way to where she had parked, practically throwing herself into the driver's seat of the van and slamming the keys into the ignition.

With the high school firmly in her rear-view mirror, the panic began to settle in. She drew in great, hiccupping sobs while her body shivered from head to toe. She didn't think she would ever stop shaking.

Everything her mother taught her about spirits was wrong. They weren't all here to keep us safe, and this one certainly *did* want to hurt her. None of her readings or studies about encounters with the dead ever mentioned anything like this happening. What this was, Chrissy had no clue. If it was a dream, then how did she end up on the second floor?

"I guess I could have developed sudden onset narcolepsy," she said to herself with a manic giggle.

The adrenaline began to wear off, little by little. The shakes slowed, and her body thrummed like she had jammed her finger into an electrical socket. She was shot. She wanted nothing more than to go back to the hotel, crawl under the blankets, and try to forget the entire thing, but as she drove, she kept replaying bits and pieces of the event.

When the footsteps rushed her and everything started up...had she turned on the camera at that point? She wracked her mind, but her memory was all jumbled. If she pressed record before it began, the tapes might be able to clear things up, like if she had passed out or not. More than that, it might have captured a voice, or apparition, or something. The tiniest shiver raced across her skin. She knew she shouldn't expect too much — she may not have hit record on the camera, after all, and more than likely, nothing would even show up — but there was a chance.

A quiet hope blossomed alongside the lingering fear, and she pressed her foot down on the gas.

It was just going on seven o'clock when she pulled up outside the hotel. Several missed calls from Rodney flashed on her phone, and she groaned, annoyed with herself for not having checked it sooner. He hadn't left any messages, so ignoring the calls for now, she stuffed the phone in her pocket, gathered up the equipment, and hurried up to the second floor. Despite her eagerness to go over the footage and see if anything had been picked up on camera, she knew she would have to check in with Rodney and Bill first. She dropped her bag in her own room, then knocked on their door.

The door flew open. One look at Rodney's irritated expression, and Chrissy's defenses shot up. The way he behaved earlier, he had no right to be pissed at her.

"Hey, Rodney. Sorry. My phone was on silent, and I-"

"Where the hell have you been?"

"I went to interview Donnie Meltan. I told you that."

"Yeah, but that was hours ago. You haven't been answering your phone."

"Like I said, I forgot to switch it from silent," she said, bristling at his accusatory tone. "I was just doing a little investigating on my own since I was out there. It was...well, it was super weird." She set the equipment down on the floor and looked around. "How's Bill? Still not feeling well?"

"That's what I was trying to call you about. I have no freaking clue where he is," Rodney said, his voice strained.

"What do you mean? Did he go for another walk?"

He threw his hands up and huffed in annoyance. "If he did, he's walking a damn marathon. He's been gone for hours, too."

"Okay, tell me exactly what happened."

"Right. So, after you left, I went over some tapes. Bill was just...sitting there. Staring. It was a little weird, but he's a weird dude, and he's not feeling so hot, so it's whatever. Anyway, about 30 minutes go by, and I have to take a piss. While I'm in there, I hear the door shut. I come out, Bill's not here. So, I figure he's gone to get some ice, or maybe he needed to throw up again while I was in the bathroom so he went to find another one. I don't know. But after an hour, he's not back."

"Did you try calling him?"

"Of course I did. He's not answering."

Chrissy sat down heavily on the bed. "He might have gone to find a doctor or something, but I'm sure he's fine. He's a grown man."

"I guess." He turned his phone over in his hands a few times before flipping it open to check for a message with a frown.

He was worried, that was easy enough to see, but she was surprised he was acting so normal, considering the circumstances. It was as though their little spat earlier never happened. Part of her wanted to stay mad at him, but her own feelings were beginning to thaw in the wake of everything that had gone down at the school.

"It's alright, Rodney. If he doesn't show up in the next hour, we'll go out and look for him."

"I don't even know, man," he said, tugging at the roots of his hair. "This whole thing has been so off. Your nightmares, Bill getting sick and wandering off, weird shit happening in the school. The vibes are just...sketch."

Chrissy snorted. "You're telling me."

He shook his head and raised his eyes. "Well, how did the interview go?"

"He didn't have a lot to say about the night of the fire. He wasn't there, but he did tell me that the A.V. Club made video yearbooks back then. One of the guys digitized them, and Donnie said he would send them over. I figured I'd give them a look, see if we could use some of the footage in our show if we can get permission."

"Huh, I had no idea they did that."

"Neither did I," she said. "My school definitely didn't."

Rodney's phone vibrated in his hand. He flipped the phone open and let out a long sigh. "It's Bill. He says he's fine and coming back now."

"Oh good. Did he mention where he was?"

"Nope. Asshole."

Chrissy laughed and stood, stretching her arms over her head. "I told you everything would be alright."

"I guess."

Once again, she was gripped by the anxiety to go check the footage from that afternoon's encounter. The need to know what might have been caught during the bizarre incident lodged in the pit of her stomach, but one look at Rodney's stressed-out, worn-down face, and she knew she couldn't leave him waiting for Bill all alone. She didn't think she could tell him about what happened, not yet. She was torn between the two and, sighing inwardly, turned to Rodney with a resigned smile.

"Do you want to see if Donnie sent over some of those yearbook videos and check them out?"

He rubbed the back of his neck, hesitating. "I don't know. I should probably finish going over the tapes I started on."

"Oh, come on. We can see what life was like in the 80s. You might even have fun."

"You are aware I was there for it, right? And so were you."

"Yeah, but I was only there for a few years." Reaching over, she snatched the laptop from the table and returned to the bed, swinging her legs up and stretching out. With her back against the headboard, she patted the spot beside her. "Come on. You look like you could use a break."

"Rude." He cast his eyes around the room for another excuse before relenting. "Alright. Fine."

Chrissy grinned with triumph and scooted to the side of the bed, making sure there was plenty of room for him. As soon as he settled in alongside her, she pulled up the browser and opened her email. To her surprise, a new message sat at the top of her inbox, with one attachment. Rodney read over her shoulder.

Here's the yearbook video I was telling you about. I was only able to find one of them, but hopefully, it helps.

-Donnie

When she double-clicked the attachment, the laptop's small speakers blared to life with a generic-sounding synth riff. Bright lights slashed across the black background, sweeping over each other to create a glowing neon box. Blocky letters spelled out "Merlin High Wizards" and zoomed into the frame of the box as a narrator began speaking in a very nine o'clock news voice.

"Merlin High School is proud to present: The Merlin High School Video Yearbook. Featuring memories from the 1985-1986 school year. Starring the students and faculty of Merlin High. Goooo Wizards!"

Chrissy smirked at how dated it was. It screamed 1980s with its retro-futuristic design and bright colors. She stole a quick glance at Rodney, who appeared to find the whole thing as hilarious as she did.

The video transitioned to a scene of a teenage boy in a pink, buttoned up Polo shirt pulling open a classroom door while grinning cheesily. He welcomed the person holding the camera into a room filled with students working in groups at several tables. The walls of the room were painted a garish yellow, with two thick purple stripes running around the top.

Chrissy gave an exaggerated shudder. "Things were too bright back then."

Rodney pointed to a kid wearing aviators on the screen. "That's why we always had to wear our shades, even inside."

They continued to watch clip after clip of teenagers in classrooms, eating at the cafeteria, goofing off and throwing arms around each other to the soundtrack of some generic 80's music. The scenes flashed to the football team running plays on the field. For every clip, a small graphic flew in, announcing the final scores of each game. The Merlin High Wizards appeared to be a totally average team, ending the season with six wins out of their ten games.

Rodney gradually began to relax beside her as the video played, even nodding his head along with the cheesy, upbeat music, until all of a sudden, he went still. She had been staring at him from the corner of her eye when this happened, and quickly shifted her gaze to see what had caused his reaction. A stand of bleachers packed with students filled the screen, and a line of cheerleaders waved their pompoms in the air in front of them. She scanned the crowd, but nothing seemed out of the ordinary.

"You alright?" She asked.

His gaze was fixed on the screen, and his shoulders crept up towards his ears. "Hmm?"

"You seem tense. Did you see something?"

He shook his head. Only when the scene switched to a clip of the drama club did his expression soften, the tension draining away.

The video kept playing, switching from theater performances to the choir and debate teams, though the amount of camera time spent on those programs was considerably less. It shifted scenes; a group of students goofing off in the hallways, a couple leaning against a set of lockers, laughing. Chrissy's eyes widened as the hallway came into view, looking exactly as it did when she was at the school, the hunter green and white tiles, the drab green lockers, the bright white walls, all identical to her flashback, as she had decided to call it.

The next shot showed a pair of girls, matching in red striped sweaters and fluffed up bangs, grinning up at the camera from a table in the middle of the cafeteria. In the background, a lanky, dark-haired boy stood watching the two girls. Chrissy sat up with a gasp, startling Rodney and almost throwing the laptop across the room.

"What it is?" he asked, alarmed.

Scrambling to grab the laptop, she hit pause and backed the video up a few frames to make sure she wasn't seeing things. But there, right on screen, was Derrick Roach in the flesh, just as he had looked at the school. All she could to was jab a finger at the spot where he stood.

He took the laptop and glanced at the grainy image. "What? Do you know this kid?"

She nodded, eyes round with alarm. "That's Roach."

Rodney leaned forward and squinted. "Who?"

"Roach, the kid Beverly Walsh saw with the gas can before the homecoming dance."

He raised an eyebrow. "Okay...so?"

Taking a deep breath, she turned to face him. "So, I know he did it."

She watched the walls come up again, and Rodney's face grew stony. He started to shake his head, but she reached out, placing a hand on his arm to stop him from saying anything.

"Please, you need to listen. Something happened at the school today."

"What do you mean? Are you okay?"

"I'm fine," she assured him. "You're not going to believe me when I tell you, but something did happen, and it was...well, it was so..." She trailed off, struggling with how to explain what had occurred when she didn't quite understand it herself.

Rodney's expression softened. "I'll believe you, Chrissy."

She gave a short, dry laugh. "You probably won't once you hear it."

"Try me."

Aware that the small amount of progress made towards normal might come crashing down, she told him about everything she experienced in the halls of Merlin High, from the sound of footsteps rushing her, to the attack on Alorah, and Derrick's final threat. When she finished, she kept her eyes down, waiting for the laughter, but instead was met with silence. Maybe he wouldn't laugh, she thought. Maybe he would just have her committed.

At last she lifted her gaze to find him staring, slack-jawed, and pale as the moon. She searched his eyes for some hint as to what he was thinking, hoping it wasn't that she had lost her mind. She reached out to touch his hand, which shook violently.

"Rodney?"

He cleared his throat. "Um..."

"I know it sounds crazy. I know-"

"No. Well, yes. But, um..." He cleared his throat again. "Listen, I haven't been completely honest with you."

"What do you mean?" she asked.

"I already know the whole history of Merlin High. I...um...I grew up here."

He got up from the bed and crossed to the window, looking out into the gathering dusk. Chrissy stared at his back in shock.

No wonder he had been so reluctant to come out here. Doing the math, she figured he would have been about 10 years old when the school burned down. It must have been a terrifying event for someone that young to process.

"Actually, I was supposed to go to Merlin High," he continued. "I couldn't wait. I saw how much fun my sister had there. She was crazy popular. I wouldn't have said this to anyone back then, but I wanted to be just like her. When you started talking about her, I wasn't sure what to do. I thought I could push through, leave it alone. Nobody would need to know. But then the other night, when you were singing..."

A jolt of realization hit, and Chrissy's stomach went into a freefall.

"Your sister?"

He turned to face her, a mask of grief, hidden for decades and now ripped open and raw, covered his face. "Alorah."

Unable to bear the sight of him standing there so broken and fragile, so consumed by sorrow, her own heart shattered. She rushed across the room and wrapped her arms around him. She expected him to resist, and at first, his body tensed at the contact, but he soon surrendered and collapsed into her.

"I'm so sorry, Rodney," she whispered. "I had no idea. I would never have..."

She bit her lip, not sure that what she wanted to say held any truth. Would she have turned the opportunity down if she had known? She couldn't say, but it didn't matter now. Now, her priority would be to figure out how to finish the investigation without inflicting any more pain.

"I should have told you. I didn't want to ruin it for you. I couldn't. You needed this so badly."

Choking up, she shook her head. "Not at your expense. I would never do anything to hurt you, Rodney. I care about you too much."

He pulled back, his eyes desperate and searching. Behind them was so much pain, and something else. Before she knew it, his lips crushed against hers. Strong arms circled her waist, clinging to her as though he was downing in his sadness, and she was the only way out. Her head swam. This was a terrible idea. She tried to make herself pull away, to put a stop to it before it went any further, but she couldn't make herself do it. She wanted it as much as he seemed to.

Ignoring the relentless warning bells going off in her head, she gave in, returning his kiss with equal intensity, her hands moving around to his back and pressing herself against him. He responded with a rumble from deep in his chest and moved a hand up, tangling his fingers in her dark curls.

He took a small step backwards, and for a moment, Chrissy thought he was doing what she should have done in the first place and putting an end to it. Instead, he cupped her face in his palms, eyes swimming with a mixture of grief and need, and brought his lips to hers once more. It didn't have the same frantic desperation of the first kiss. This one was sweet, gentle as her heart beat a slow bass drum rhythm in her chest.

She slipped her hands under his shirt, the heat of him radiating through her. Pulling him close again, she let her fingers wander, brushing over his skin and tugging his shirt higher. He reached down and pulled his shirt up over his head, tossing it to the floor. Bending slightly, he wrapped his arms around the backs of her thighs and scooped her up. Legs around his waist, arms linked behind his neck, her pulse thundered.

His eyes searched hers. With her nod of encouragement, he took a step towards the bed just as the door to the room flew open with a bang, and a huge, dark figure stepped into the room.

TWENTY

CHRISSY LET OUT A short scream as the figure stepped inside, the hood of his jacket falling away.

Bill stared at them for a few awkward moments, then raised a soggy white paper bag clutched in his fist.

"You scared the shit outta me, dude!" Rodney set Chrissy down gently and turned to Bill. "Where the hell have you been?"

Bill lifted the bag a little higher and nodded his head towards it. "Went to get some medicine."

"For five hours?"

He shrugged and stood in the center of the room, water dripping from his rain drenched coat. Chrissy's eyes darted from one man to the other, words deserting her in the face of the uncomfortable silence sitting between them. Bitter disappointment flooded her, leaving her confused and disjointed. She was glad Bill had returned — of course she was — but as Rodney retrieved his shirt from the floor and tugged it over his head, she couldn't help but wish he walked just a bit slower.

Clearing her throat, she gathered her laptop and rushed towards the door. "I've got some work to do. If you guys need anything, I'll be in my room."

She stole a quick glance back at Rodney. When he didn't meet her gaze, she fled, shamefaced, out the door.

Holed back up in the safety of her own room, she dropped into the chair beside the table with a groan. Letting her head drop back, she closed her eyes, willing the burning in her cheeks and chest to disappear. Quiet filled the room, broken only by the faint hum of electricity sputtering from the bedside lamp. She pressed her cold fingers against her face and took a deep breath.

She needed a distraction.

Reaching for the laptop, she flipped it open and pulled up the video yearbook again. When Rodney kissed her, every other thought scattered like dandelion seeds in a puff of wind, but now, the bombshell that he dropped came rushing back to her. Alorah was Rodney's sister. She still couldn't wrap her mind around it. If the spirit in the school was Alorah, which Chrissy was now certain of, then what did that mean for Rodney? What did it mean for the investigation?

Every time he popped into her thoughts, she couldn't help but replay the kiss, the interruption, and worst of all, the way he hadn't even glanced in her direction when she left. Embarrassment welled up in her throat, threatening to choke her. Could you die from humiliation, she wondered?

Putting him out of her mind, she focused on a new task. Roach appeared at least once in the video yearbook. That meant there was a possibility he might be in some more shots in the second half of the video she hadn't watched. Just the sight of him made her squirm, but she still hoped to find more footage.

As she worked her way through the video, she came to the spot where Rodney had tensed up. She paid close attention to the images, and as the cameraman panned to the line of cheerleaders, she spotted Alorah and her unmistakable halo of golden curls.

The rest of the clips rolled by with nothing of note; no Alorah and no Roach. Scenes of everyday high school life unfolded, giving up no clues or hints until she reached the clip from the cafeteria. She slowed the playback, scrutinizing every frame. Roach slid into the shot and out again, his expression dark as he stared at the two striped sweater girls, but the footage revealed nothing new about the boy. She went on, studying each scene in the hopes of catching a flash of greasy hair or the outline of that baggy tee.

The video switched to a clip she hadn't seen yet; girls in ruffles and puffy dresses of hot pink and turquoise flitted across the screen, hanging on the arms of gawky boys in pale-colored tuxedos. The awkward charm of a high school dance played out before her, all smiling faces and a sea of blue eyeshadow.

A couple standing two feet apart, the boy's hands placed nervously at the girl's waist, hers on his shoulders, swayed back and forth, serenaded by Journey's *Faithfully*. The couple noticed the camera, and the girl turned away while the boy stuck his tongue out. Caught up in the moment, Chrissy almost missed Roach's appearance in the shadows of the background. She looped the section back, keeping an eye on the area where he would soon appear. The video, grainy and dark, made it difficult to make out at first, but she could tell it was him by the oily hair that hung over his face.

She paused the video and leaned back, wondering what he had been doing at a school dance. He wasn't dressed for it, not exactly. He had foregone the traditional tuxedo in favor of a tuxedo tee-shirt paired with black cargo pants. She gave him props for at least skipping the baggy band tee.

He looked to be speaking with someone out of frame, laughing and shaking his head as his eyes crawled over the couples on the dancefloor with an expression of contempt.

"What are you looking at?" she muttered under her breath.

Moving forward frame by frame, she followed the trajectory of his gaze until the object of his disdain came into focus. Not at all surprising, it was Alorah, adorned in a poofy, knee-length dress in a shimmery pale pink. She was the image of an 80s beauty queen, from her oversized fashion earrings down to the matching pink silk gloves that ran all the way up to her elbows.

Roach seemed to still be engaged with whoever sat off screen, but his eyes never left Alorah as she moved between groups. The camera panned right, whisking her out of frame and revealing the person next to Roach. Chrissy squinted, trying to make out the grainy shape as part of it slipped into the shot. It was a boy, and he acted friendly with Roach, if not actual friends. If she could get a clear enough image of this kid, she could use it to compare with yearbook photos, then track him down if he still lived in the area. That was a lot of ifs, she knew, but she was eager to know if this person might have some vital piece of information about the events surrounding the fire.

As soon as the figure came into view, the scene switched to a different school event. Chrissy cursed out loud and skipped it back to the last shots of the dance. Before it cut away again, all she was able to make out was an extremely long pair of legs and bent over torso. Whoever he was, he appeared to be quite tall and skinny. No matter how long or hard she studied the image, she couldn't make out any other features.

Pressing play, she kept an eye out to see if Roach or his mysterious friend made any more appearances, but neither one showed up again. Frustration mounted as the video came to an end, and she set the laptop aside. It felt as though a crucial piece of the puzzle hovered right in front of her, just out of reach. There was no doubt in her mind that Roach's friend would provide some key piece of information she needed, but once again, she found herself up against a wall.

With nothing more she could do that night, she decided she might as well have an early night and try to sleep. Switching off the lamp, the room at last fell silent. Lying in bed, enveloped in the darkness, she thought about the skinny boy with the long legs and wondered if he might be connected to the fire too.

As she began to drift off, her mind turned away from the investigation to Rodney and the way he kissed her. A warm giddiness spread through her, casting a glow over her fading consciousness. But as soon as she recalled the way he avoided her gaze, she went cold, like a bucket of ice water thrown over her, extinguishing any excitement she felt. They'd made a huge mistake. Things could never go back to how they were before. The dynamics had shifted, and uncertainty and doubt pressed in on her.

Now restless and wide awake, she flipped over and shoved all thoughts of Rodney, the passionate kiss, and his perfect body into a box and pushed them into the back of her mind to collect dust alongside all her other troubles.

Twenty-One

It was the first night since arriving in Merlin that Chrissy hadn't been plagued by nightmares. At some point in the evening, the weather broke, the sun burning away the last remnants of the storm. She went about her morning routine with a half-smile on her face. Even the moments when her thoughts went rogue and settled on the kiss she shared with Rodney, she easily put them back in their box. No panic spirals. No self-doubt. Just straight in the box and filed away.

After showering and dressing, she snatched the camera she used at the school, and uploaded the footage to her laptop. The events of the night left her too flustered to try to go over it, but now, she was crawling out of her skin with anticipation. Finally, she would have some insight as to what had happened to her.

Once the file finished loading, she opened it and pressed play, cranking the volume as high as it went. The dim light of the hallway appeared, shaky, as she moved down towards the gymnasium. She heard her own breath, the sound of her gasp as she yanked her hand away from the door.

"Well, that was weird. Must have been my imagination." Her words echoed through the halls.

There was nothing but the sounds of her own movements as the camera angle spun away from the door and down the hall.

Her own voice called out, asking if anyone was there. Straining her ears, she listened for anything in the silence, the hint of a footstep, but came up empty. The camera hadn't captured it.

Disappointed, she continued to watch. It may not have caught the footsteps, but from the way her breaths turned shallow as she stared into the dim hallway, she knew the moment when things shifted had arrived.

Past Chrissy gasped.

The image shook violently.

The video stopped.

"What the hell?"

She moved the cursor over the playback controls and discovered the video cut off after only five minutes and thirty-two seconds of filming. When the invisible force slammed into her in the halls, it had affected the camera, bringing the recording to an abrupt end.

So much for figuring out what happened to her.

Her expectations going into it had been low anyway. Oh, she had hoped, but she wouldn't let this minor disappointment throw off her day. Closing the laptop, she glanced around the room. This would be the final night of their investigation. When Bill came in the night before, he had looked terrible, but Chrissy didn't want to delay another day. If he was still sick, she and Rodney were perfectly capable of covering the night themselves. Rodney knew a little of how to operate the big camera, and Bill could run over the ins and outs with him again before they headed out. The shots wouldn't be quite as professional, but it would be better than nothing.

Before any of that could happen, though, Chrissy needed to do a bit more digging. Grabbing her phone, she sent a text to

Bev. If anyone would be able to identify the tall, lanky kid from the video yearbook, it would be her.

After asking if she had a moment to answer a few more questions and pushing send, she stared at the phone. The moments ticked by, and she drummed her fingers against the case, willing a reply to come through. When none came, she decided to occupy herself with a heaping plate of hotel waffles, followed by another visit to the library.

Stepping out of her room, checking to be sure it locked behind her, she turned to head down the hall and stopped short. Outside the door to the next room stood Bill, stock still and staring at the floor. His lips moved quickly as he muttered incoherently under his breath. Every now and then, the fingers on his right hand gave a little twitch, as if to shoo an annoying fly. She watched him for a moment before giving a little wave. Not wanting to intrude, she started towards the stairs.

"Chrissy, wait."

She swiveled, concerned by the roughness of his voice.

Head bowed, eyes glued to the floor, he remained eerily still.

"Morning, Bill. How are you feeling today?"

He raised one shoulder. "Not great."

"That's too bad," she said. "Listen, if you're not up to going to the school tonight, Rodney and I-"

"I'll be okay."

With a tilt of his head, he gave her what she supposed was an attempt at a smile, but came across more sneer-like than anything. His complexion, previously waxy and pale, was now downright ashen, and with his lips drawn back in that grimace of a smile, he looked like a dead man walking. She felt the lightness that had carried her through the morning falter.

"Are you sure? I'm not trying to be rude, but you look really sick. I don't want you to feel like you have to come tonight if you're not up to it. Rodney and I should be able to handle it by ourselves."

Bill seemed to consider it. When he opened his mouth to respond, the hall light next to him flickered a handful of times, making his shadow dance wildly against the wall. His body twitched in response, and he dropped his head down to his chest again.

"I'll be there," he said. "I just need some more rest first."

He turned and began a slow, shuffling retreat to his room, his hand continuing that odd flicking motion. Chrissy thought she should follow him and make sure he was alright, but seeing Rodney right then was sure to kill off what was left of her good mood. Going in there now would send her into overdrive. She'd be analyzing every word he said, every glance in her direction. Besides, she had far too many things to get done, and she couldn't risk the distraction when she had yet another mystery to unravel.

Down at the continental breakfast, she made herself a Belgian waffle, filled a small Styrofoam cup to the brim with coffee, and sat down to think. Last night, Rodney said that everything about this place, this investigation, seemed off from the start. Though Chrissy hated to admit it, he was right, and now that she was aware of his ties to the town, to one of the spirits here, she had to wonder if it was wrong to keep moving forward with the investigation. Before, it had only been a tragic event that would make a fantastic episode, but now that Rodney was tied into the story, it felt almost too personal.

It had always been personal for him, she reminded herself. Right from the beginning, he tried to express his feelings, telling her it wasn't a good idea, but she was stubborn. She pushed. She pushed and he caved, like she knew he would. Would she still have pushed if she knew then what she did now? The question had been rattling around in her head all day. Was she the type of person who would exploit someone's pain for their own benefit? She didn't think so, but...

Part of her still screamed for her to keep going with it. She needed to finish the investigation, see the story through to the end. If only they could uncover the true cause of the fire.

She shook her head. In the event they discovered Roach did set the fire, there was no way they could put that in the show. At least, not his name. Too many liabilities. Even if they couldn't use it in the show, perhaps simply knowing the truth of what happened on homecoming night would help bring closure, to Rodney and to Alorah.

An idea began to take shape and claw its way to the front of her mind. The goal of *Othersiders* had always been to gather evidence of a life after death, but maybe it was time for a pivot. Bev claimed to have the gift of speaking with those who had passed. If they asked her to come along to speak with Alorah, she may be able to help her cross over. It would be a new approach, helping the spirits they encountered to move on. If Bev wasn't able or willing to do it herself, Chrissy was certain she would know of someone who would. And perhaps if Alorah was able to move on and find peace, Rodney would be able to find some too.

Sandalwood and lavender washed over Chrissy, soothing her nerves as soon as she stepped into Bev's home. The text she sent earlier only said she had a few more questions to ask, hoping it would be harder for her to say no to Chrissy's request in person.

Bev ushered her into the sitting room, where the yearbook already sat open on the coffee table, along with a pot of mint tea and two mugs. She settled down into the sofa, nodding her thanks as Bev filled her cup.

"So, you said you've got some more questions for me?" she asked.

"I do. Yesterday, during an interview with another former student, I learned that the A.V. Club made a handful of video yearbooks. He sent one of them over for us to check out."

Bev nodded. "I remember those."

"Well, as I was watching it last night, I spotted this." Chrissy removed a folded piece of paper from her notebook. On it was a printout she had made earlier in the hotel's business center of a still from the video of Derrick and the tall boy he sat next to. She slid the image across the table to show Bev, who brought it up to her face. "Do you happen to know the boy Derrick is talking to here? You said he didn't have friends, but these two seem to be pretty close."

Bev tilted her head to the side, narrowing her eyes as she thought. "Well now, it's a bit difficult to see. It's not a very good picture."

"I know. It's the only time this kid is shown on camera. I can't make out anything besides the fact that he's got to be about six-foot-six and kind of skinny."

Inspecting the photo for a beat, she set it back on the table with a shake of her head. "No, I can't quite make it out. I'm sorry."

Chrissy folded the paper back up and slid it between the pages of her notebook. The photo had been a long shot, but she had to at least try. “Can you think of anyone from back then who matches this description? Really tall? Skinny?”

She shook her head again. “Not that I can recall, but I got out the yearbook, like you asked. You’re welcome to take a peek.”

Chrissy pulled the yearbook closer as Bev came around and sat beside her on the sofa. Diving back into the snapshots of the past, they flipped through page after page, searching for anyone who might have been the boy with Roach. Hope faded as they neared the back of the book, until Bev stuck a hand out, stopping Chrissy from turning the page.

“Wait a minute. This boy.” She pointed a perfectly manicured finger at one of the headshots in the freshman class spread. “This boy right here.”

Chrissy peered down into the pimply face of a boy with sad, Basset Hound eyes hidden behind thick rimmed aviator glasses. In the sea of smiling faces, he stood out with his sullen expression. His hair was cut into a terrible mullet, parted down the middle, and a faint darkness above his upper lip hinted at the beginnings of a patchy mustache. It was impossible for Chrissy to tell how tall he was from a single headshot, but the way his tee-shirt hung on his frame made it obvious the kid was thin. She looked at the bottom of the page, finding the name that paired with the photo.

“Gary Maslon?”

“I don’t remember the name, but I believe he showed up about halfway through the school year. Tall, bean-pole of a kid. I didn’t think of him before, since he was just a freshman, and I hardly ever saw him around back then.”

“Did you ever see him hanging around with Roach?”

“Oh, honey, that was ages ago. I didn’t even remember this boy existed until now.”

Understandable, Chrissy thought. She doubted if she would be able to recognize any of the freshmen from when she was a senior, and that had only been a few years ago. But now she had a name, Gary Maslon, and she jotted it down in her notebook.

They leafed through the last pages of the yearbook, but it provided no other leads. Bev stood and went to the bookshelf, slotting the book back into place before returning to her easy chair.

"I've been thinking about what you told me, about how you've spoken to the spirits at Merlin High," Chrissy began, working her way up to the other reason she had come to speak with Bev. "I was wondering, have you ever helped any of them cross over?"

She arched an eyebrow and sat back in her chair, appraising Chrissy from across the room. After a moment, she gave a slow nod. "I have."

"At the school, or...?"

"A few at the school. A few elsewhere."

"But not Alorah?"

"Not Alorah."

Chrissy leaned forward, brows knitted together. "Why not?"

"There are things keeping her tied here."

"What kind of things?" she asked.

"I couldn't say."

"But you've spoken to her."

Bev sighed. "Yes, but it's not that simple."

The room grew quiet as Chrissy tried to keep herself from peppering the woman with too many questions. She was more confused than ever, but she didn't want to annoy her and risk being thrown out before she'd had a chance to ask the big question.

"Would you be willing to come with us tonight to try and help her move on?"

"No." She shook her head emphatically. "I'm sorry. I've done my best to help, but she's not ready. Besides, it isn't only Alorah who's left behind. The other soul in the school, well...I want nothing to do with him."

"Other spirits are in the school?" Chrissy frowned. Other than the encounter in the ladies' room, the tapes showed no evidence of any other activity in the building. If other spirits *were* in the school, they had been awfully quiet, not counting the running footsteps that led to the flashback. The tape hadn't picked those up before going black.

"You think Alorah is the source of all the nightmares?"

"I thought they were just...I don't know. I've been reading about the fire and deaths for the last three weeks. I figured it had all gotten into my head."

"Hmm. And what about everyone else's nightmares?" Bev snorted and shot her a look of pure disappointment. "I told you before, it's not only you. Do you remember what I said when you were here last time? That both love and hate resided in the school?"

Chrissy nodded.

"Alorah is the one kept there by love."

"Then who's kept there by hate?"

"I thought it was obvious." Bev said. "It's Derrick Roach."

How hadn't she put the pieces together sooner? She replayed the events surrounding the school and her dreams, each one now illuminated by the revelation that Roach had never left Merlin High.

"He's still in the school too," she said.

"Mm-hmm. He's still tied there by his hatred and anger."

"Oh no." Chrissy gasped. "He's in there with Alorah. She's trapped with that...psycho? Why does she stay? Why would she stick around with him?"

"Like I said, she can't go yet. Something is tying her here."

"But what?"

"You should go ask her yourself." Bev rose and headed towards the door, signaling that she was done with the conversation.

Chrissy followed, reeling from the heavy weight of this new information and all the questions it spawned. Stepping out into the warmth of a late-summer morning, she turned to Bev once more.

"Would you please reconsider coming out with us tonight? I think it's possible we can help Alorah. One of the people on my team...he's her brother."

Bev gave her a hard look. "Alorah's brother is here?"

Chrissy nodded, gulping down the concern she might have betrayed Rodney's confidence by telling her. What other choice did she have? They needed her help, more so now she knew Alorah was trapped in that school with her tormentor and possible killer.

"His name is Rodney. If everything you've told me is true, we owe it to her to help her leave that place and get away from Roach once and for all. I think if you'd come along and do whatever it is you do, we can get her to move on."

Bev gazed past Chrissy, conflict warring in her expression. She didn't say a word. A bird started up, its song piercing the tense silence. Realizing there would be no help, Chrissy retreated down the steps. As soon as she hit the end of the walkway, Bev's voice cut through the birdsong.

"I'll come. Tomorrow, though. I'll need to prepare."

With a gentle click, the door closed on Chrissy, leaving her to figure out what she would tell Rodney.

TWENTY-TWO

IN THE FRONT SEAT of the Ghostmobile outside Bev's house, Chrissy pulled up the internet browser on her phone and punched in the name Gary Maslon. The search turned up dozens of pages, most of them for law firms. Though it was entirely possible the Gary she was looking for went on to become a lawyer, none of the photos of the Gary Maslon in question were the right age or build. She skimmed through all the results that popped up on social media, but again, no luck.

A text from Rodney flashed on the screen, providing a much-needed break from the exercise in frustration, but her stomach dropped when she read the message.

Come to the school ASAP

Why? What's going on?

Without waiting for a response, she keyed the Ghostmobile to life and headed to the school, anxiety following her like a shadow. Merlin High was only a few blocks from Bev's house, and within minutes, she was pulling over outside the fence.

Throwing the van into park, she surveyed the area, finding no sign of Rodney anywhere.

She hopped down from the drivers' seat and walked towards the building, keeping a cautious eye on her surroundings. Someone had unlocked the gate, rolling it back far enough to allow a person through. Last night, she left the keys to the gate on the bedside table in Rodney's room, but she couldn't think of a single reason he would have come here on his own, or why he sent her the urgent message to join him.

She slipped through the opening in the fence, casting a glance up at the face of the school. Bright summer light bounced off the bricks, but despite the warm glow, the school's cold empty windows glared down, making her shiver. Squinting against the brightness, she scanned the length of the building, searching for an indication of where Rodney might have gone. Nothing moved in the windows, and she thought nothing appeared to be out of place until her gaze landed on the front door. It stood wide open.

She approached the doors and poked her head through when a hand shot out from the open door and gripped her wrist. A sharp exhale whooshed out of her as Rodney's face materialized in the doorway, a finger held up to his lips, urging her to stay quiet.

"Sorry," he whispered as he stepped through the entrance and into the sunlight.

"What are you doing?" she hissed.

"I followed Bill here. He left right after you this morning. Wouldn't tell me where he was going, so I decided to follow him."

"And he came here? Why?"

Rodney glanced over his shoulder through the open doors and shrugged. "No freaking clue. He's been banging stuff around in there, opening lockers and classrooms and talking to himself. Something is seriously wrong with the dude."

Chrissy listened for a moment, and sure enough, the sound of lockers being slammed came from somewhere deep inside the school. "Should we go talk to him?"

"I don't know if it would do any good. When I tried talking to him this morning, he kind of acted like I wasn't there."

An icy darkness seeped out from the school's entry, and she took a step back. Bill's behavior troubled her. He was still extremely sick, and it was possible he spiked a fever and was now wandering the halls in a delirious state. If that was the case, they needed to get him out of the building and to a doctor fast.

"Roach!"

Bill's voice boomed through the hallways, making both Rodney and Chrissy turn. The sound of pacing echoed through the school, followed by another loud clang of a locker being slammed.

"I know you're here, dammit. Where is it?"

"Where is what?" Chrissy mouthed silently at Rodney, who only shrugged.

With a swift motion, she gripped Rodney's hand and pulled him down the steps and along the outside of the left wing, stooping so as not to be seen through the shattered windows. She slowed where the footsteps sounded loudest and pressed herself up against the brick wall. Rodney followed her lead, easing up to the wall next to her. They could hear Bill breathing, ragged and raspy, as he continued to pace back and forth in the hallway. Every so often, the pacing was broken by another locker being torn open and slammed shut, locks rattling.

"You think this is funny?" Bill shouted. The sound of a boot hitting the lockers followed.

The animosity that laced his voice sent a shock of fear through Chrissy. She had never known him to be a violent man. He had never said an angry word, never so much as raised his voice around her, and this new side of him put her on edge. A quick look at Rodney told her he was having the same thoughts.

Footsteps started up inside the building again as Bill moved further down the hallway towards the gymnasium. Giving a signal, Chrissy crouched down and trailed the sound until it came to an abrupt stop once more.

"This where you like to hang out now, Roach? Too scared to come out from the gym?" A high-pitched bark, more animal than human, floated from the hallway. "Does she have you stuck in here? Not allowed to come out and play?"

At risk of being spotted, Chrissy peeked through the nearest window. With both fists raised, Bill beat on the twisted metal doors to the gymnasium. He yanked his hands back with a hiss and clutched them to his chest.

"Well, that's a neat little trick. You think this is funny?" His voice ramped up to an actual scream on the last word. From this distance, Chrissy could see the spittle flying and she dropped down below the window frame. "I'll show you funny."

Strides thundered through the hallway. Rodney pulled her to her feet and set off after him. Hunched down, they ran around the side of the building and out of view just as Bill kicked the doors of the school closed with a bang. Gravel crunched under his enormous boots as he stormed away from the school.

Craning her neck, Chrissy peered around the corner of the building to find him forcing his mass through the gate's narrow opening. Once through, he turned and yanked the gate shut.

With the hood of his coat pulled up, casting his face in deep shadows, recognition turned her blood to ice. She kept an eye on his bulky form as he stalked away, now certain he had been the dark figure lurking outside the school the day before.

"What in the name of hell was that about?" Rodney slumped against the building. When she didn't respond, he glanced over. Noticing the confusion and fear on her face, he pushed himself off the wall and took her by the shoulders, turning her to meet his gaze. "Hey, are you okay?"

She peered up at him, the warmth of his hands thawing the chill in her veins. "He was here yesterday."

"Who was? Bill?"

"Yeah," she said. "It was him. I'm positive. Just now, standing outside the gate, he looked exactly like the person hanging around during my interview with Donnie."

Lines of worry creased his face. "You didn't tell me someone was lurking around."

"It wasn't a big deal."

"I mean, it kind of is. You could have been hurt."

"But I wasn't."

He held her gaze, concern flickering in his eyes before he glanced away. "Okay, so are we thinking that Bill's been coming to the school every time he's run off the last few days?"

"It looks like it."

"But why? It sounded like he was looking for something, but what? And, again, why?"

"I don't know, but if it has to do with Roach, it can't be anything pleasant."

Chrissy glanced up, noticing how close they were to the exposed portion of the gym. Where they stood, she could see the windows closest to the fire's center were marked with streaks of black soot where the smoke made its escape. Once more, it struck her as odd that none of her digging unearthed any statements from the investigators pinpointing the exact cause of the inferno. Considering the scale of the fire and the significant loss of life, it seemed only natural that there would have been an investigation.

"Come on," he said. "Let's get out of here."

Casting one final glance back at the collapsed gym, Chrissy reluctantly nodded. She wanted nothing more than to stay, to try and figure out what Bill had been searching for inside. But as Rodney's hand slipped into her own, this time his grip tender, she turned away from the charred remains of Merlin High.

Instead of returning to the hotel, Rodney guided the Ghostmobile along a series of meandering back roads, each landmark he pointed out brightening his mood. Since revealing the truth about his connection to Merlin High, he seemed much lighter and unburdened, acting more like his old self. She felt her own spirits lifting the more he rattled on about this house, or that tree, and she found herself laughing at all his ridiculous childhood stories.

"That's where my old friend Tommy lived. I broke my leg right on that lawn," he said, almost wistfully.

At some point during the drive, his hand drifted over and settled on top of hers, only leaving to gesture at some spot that played a pivotal role in his upbringing. Unsure what they were or what might happen between them, she tried to just live in the moment, enjoying knowing the kiss hadn't ruined anything.

A massive hurdle still lay ahead; she would have to tell him about her plan to have Bev help move Alorah on. The mere thought of that conversation filled her with trepidation, but deep down, she had no doubts that helping his sister cross over was the right thing to do. Not only did she have to deal with that whole situation, she also had Bill's strange behavior to figure out. This case continued to throw obstacle after obstacle into her path.

"How'd you break it?"

"I jumped off his roof," he said as Tommy's house flew past.

"Idiot."

"I was," he laughed.

They turned down a few more neighborhood roads, ending up on a street crammed with cars and dripping with traffic lights. Strip malls spread out in each direction, and nestled in the center of it all stood a sprawling building with neon lights spelling out Merlin Plaza. Rodney squeezed the hulking van into a parking spot and turned to Chrissy with an excited gleam in his eye.

"A mall?" she asked, looking around dubiously.

"Not just a mall. *The* mall!" He jumped out of the van and beckoned her with a quick jerk of his head. At a brisk, almost skipping pace, he headed to the entrance, forcing her to break into a jog to keep up.

The cold blast of air conditioning hit first, followed by the conflicting riffs of soft pop music filtering out from the different storefronts. Foot traffic was sparse, and one or two of the shops in this area were shuttered and dark. A bored employee sat at a jewelry kiosk in the middle of the hall, poking at his phone screen.

Rodney let out a small sound of disappointment.

"This place has changed a lot."

"Did you expect there to still be a RadioShack?" Chrissy teased, giving him a bump with her shoulder.

He gave a self-conscious smile. "I guess not, but this used to be *the* spot to hang out. It's so dead now."

Only a handful of people milled around, window shopping. Two old ladies decked out in matching plum velour tracksuits power walked the lengths of the corridors in an endless circuit of fitness.

"Well, it is the middle of the day on a Thursday," Chrissy said.

"True. Still...I used to cut school all the time to come here. There used to be an arcade right where that boutique is." He pointed towards a shop displaying racks of graphic tees and skinny jeans up front. "That's kind of a bummer. I wanted to take you there to play Space Invaders."

"Sorry it's all changed."

"It's cool." His eyes lit up as he shifted his gaze in the opposite direction. "Let's go see if Mario's is still here."

Chrissy followed as he trotted towards a bright, open area where the smells of several different cuisines mingled, creating a strangely pleasant mix. Like the rest of the mall, only one or two patrons populated the seating area, but every counter was manned, and the food displays were filled with an array of offerings. The mall may be dead, but the food court still lived.

With a whoop of joy, Rodney approached a counter with a massive blinking red neon sign hanging above it. The menu board behind the disinterested cashier was old, the plastic shielding yellowed and shot through with a spiderweb of cracks. Pieces of paper showing updated prices had been taped over the original prices printed on the menu beneath.

After ordering and paying for two huge slices of greasy pepperoni and two large drinks, he scooped up the sagging paper plates while Chrissy grabbed the drinks, and they settled down at one of the tables in the seating area.

"Cost a lot less when I used to come here."

Chrissy laughed and brought her slice up to her mouth. "When was the last time you were here?"

"I guess it was right before Alorah..." His expression grew somber. "We moved away after the fire. My parents couldn't handle it."

"I'm so sorry, Rodney."

He shrugged. "It happened a long time ago. I'm over it."

The easy chatter died away, and they focused on their pizza, the air thick with stifled emotion. She couldn't shake the feeling that his walls were coming back up, that he was withdrawing into himself. If he was going to start shutting down again, she figured she might as well rip the bandage off and tell him her plan. She hated doing it and spoiling the afternoon, but whatever closeness had built between them, it was already crumbling.

"So," she said, wiping grease from her lips with a napkin, "I have to talk to you about something."

Rodney's eyes flicked up from his pizza, and he gave her a guarded look. "Okay."

"I've asked Bev to come with us on the investigation tonight."

Eyes narrow, he said nothing.

"I'm hoping she can help Alorah move on."

He stopped chewing. His face froze, fixing her with a solid stare. Uncomfortable under his gaze, she shifted in her seat, but she wasn't going to back down. This was important and needed to be said. When he at last moved, it was to reach out and grab his drink. His hand flexed around it once, causing the paper cup to crease.

"I don't know how to respond to that."

"She's trapped, Rodney. Trapped with him. After what he did to her-"

"What are you talking about?"

"I'm talking about what I saw at the school. I told you, Roach attacked Alorah in the hall, and she-"

"Stop."

His voice was ice.

Chrissy twisted her napkin in her hands. The small muscle in his jaw worked, and he swallowed hard. Searching his face for any hint of what he was thinking, she found nothing. The wall was up, and she was out.

"Why would you do something like this?" he asked quietly.

"I want to help her. I want to help you." She reached out for his hand, and he pulled it out of reach.

"I know this investigation is important to you," he said, the strain in his voice apparent. "I get that you've put your entire future on this, but I thought once you knew about my connection to this place — to Alorah — I thought you might, I don't know, back off just a little bit. But now you're talking about crazy visions and bringing in a psychic."

"She's not a psychic. She..." The words died on her tongue as he shook his head in disbelief.

Abruptly, he stood and dug into his pockets, tossing the keys to the van onto the table. The clatter as they hit the laminate tabletop filled the desolate food court.

"I have to go."

"Rodney, wait. I'm not doing this for the show." How could she make him understand? "I'm doing this to help your sister.

She's been stuck in that school with Roach for the last twenty-two years, and I can't stand the thought of her being there for another minute."

Desperation flickered in her eyes as she tried to catch his gaze, but he refused to even look at her, shock and hurt etched deep into his face. When she reached out for him once more, he took another step back.

"I thought we were friends, Chrissy. I thought we were going to be..." His eyes locked on hers for a moment before breaking away. "Shit."

A lead ball sunk through her chest and into the pit of her stomach as he strode away, leaving her alone with a half-eaten slice of pizza. Her eyes prickled with the threat of oncoming tears, and she squeezed them shut in an attempt to keep them at bay.

They came anyway.

Twenty-Three

Chrissy took one of the crumpled brown napkins from the table and wiped the smudges of eyeliner beneath her eyes. Two half eaten slices of pizza and her untouched soda sat in front of her, a depressing reminder of her situation. A peal of laughter cut through the gentle murmur and general din of shoppers going about their business. Blinking away the last of her tears, she gazed out across the seating area to find the crowd had grown substantially over the past twenty minutes. After lunch on a Thursday struck her as an odd time for there to be a rush on the mall.

With a sniff, she reached for her drink to wash away the salty aftertaste of tears. Drawing the cup towards her, she peeled the paper wrapper from a straw and stabbed it into the lid, which emitted a cringe-inducing squawk.

Rolling the cup between her hands, she worked her current problem over in her mind. Somehow, she needed to figure out a way to convince Rodney that her idea to bring Bev in had nothing to do with boosting views, and everything to do with helping him and Alorah move on.

The noise in the food court ramped up as an influx of mall-goers seemed to appear out of nowhere, filling the tables. Chair legs squealed against the tile floors, food frying behind counters growing to a loud hiss as dozens of conversations swirled and mingled together.

Her gaze casually drifted over the clusters of people gathered at the tables around her, and she raised her drink to her lips to take a sip. A couple of girls walked past, arms linked, donning matching high-waisted jorts. It always fascinated her the way fashion trends had a way of coming back around. The memory of the head-to-toe denim looks of her pre-teen idols came to mind, and she dreaded the day when the Tennessee tuxedo made a return.

Across from her, a group of teenage boys in muscle tees and leather jackets converged at the table. Even in the heat of a Midwest summer, teenagers would rather melt than give up their image. But on closer inspection, she realized that there was something strange about them. It was almost like watching a 3D movie without the glasses, distorted and doubled. She blinked several times, trying to clear the remnant of tears away, to bring the group into sharper focus, but the haziness remained.

She brought a hand up and took a swipe at one eye, then the other. Distracted by the influx of people and attempting to clear whatever blurred her vision, she had forgotten her lips were still wrapped around the straw. She took a sip, but nothing came up. Her eyes flicked down to her drink, and she gave it a shake, hoping to dislodge the bit of ice that must have gotten trapped. When she looked up, her vision cleared, and everything came into sharp focus.

She bent to take a sip of her soda, her throat now parched, but the blockage remained wedged tight. In an attempt to force the small pebble of ice up, she sucked harder and shook the cup at the same time. A sign above one of the stores drew her attention as she shook her cup again. The blocky red font lined in yellow proclaimed the store to be "Tape World."

Tape World? Chrissy frowned around the straw. Those went out of business long ago. If one had survived out here in the middle of Merlin, were there really enough people around who still listened to cassette tapes?

As she mulled it over, the obstruction at last gave way and started making its way up the straw.

Her eyes moved to the store next to Tape World, her frown deepening. Wicks 'N' Sticks. An old memory surfaced of frequent trips with her mother to the mall near her house growing up. They always made a stop at the shop filled with candles and home goods whenever her mother took her shopping for back-to-school clothes. Every visit Chrissy begged to buy one of their unicorn candles, but her mother always told her "maybe next time." Though she never got one of her own, she loved visiting them in the store, giving each one its own special name. When the company declared bankruptcy, her mother had been heartbroken. One day, she came home with a massive bag of bric-a-brac she picked up at their going out of business sale.

There was no way...

The obstruction in the straw worked its way to the top, but instead of cold, sweet relief, she felt an odd tickling sensation on the tip of her tongue. She froze. Tickling soon became scratching. Tiny hooks grappled onto her mouth. Jerking away from the cup, the ticklish scratching continued scraping against her lower lip. Raw, instinctive fear bubbled up inside her and she spat frantically. Swiping a hand over her mouth, she dislodged a massive, many-legged thing, flinging it across the table.

Scrambling backwards out of the chair, she stared down at her drink in horror. Two more segmented legs poked up through the straw's opening, jabbing at the air, looking for purchase. Another fat, black spider hauled itself up and out, landing with a sickening plop on the plastic lid.

"No, no, no, no, no," Chrissy moaned, shaking her head, as though she could shake the image in front of her away. It wasn't possible. Something that size couldn't fit inside a straw. It couldn't. *It couldn't.*

The spider she had swept onto the table scuttered towards her, soon joined by the second as it began its descent down the side of the cup. Paralyzed with fear, her eyes bulged as she saw more movement in the straw. It twitched once...twice. She wanted to look away, but terror kept her eyes trained on the revolting scene unfolding before her. The acid in her stomach surged and burned its way up her throat.

When hundreds of tiny spiders erupted from the straw, pouring over the lid, down the cup, and covering the top of the table, Chrissy's brain finally kicked into gear. A blood-curdling scream wrenched itself from her constricted chest. Turning, she sprinted from the food court as fast as her legs could carry her.

As she reached the edge of the area, she shot a glance behind her, checking if anyone else had made a run for it, only to find the space deserted. How had that many people escaped so fast? Whipping her head forward, she rounded the corner and barreled straight into a massive object. With the wind knocked out of her, she fell back and curled over in a standing fetal position.

A pair of enormous black boots appeared in front of her.

"Sorry." She choked out an apology to the person she had slammed into, still struggling to catch her breath. "I didn't see you there."

The feet didn't move, and the owner didn't respond. Chrissy uncurled her body, bringing herself up to her full height, only to find none other than Bill looming over her. She took a tiny step away from him. The rage-filled screams that filled the school only hours ago were still fresh in her mind.

"Oh! Bill. Hey. What are you doing here?"

He towered over her, but his eyes were fixed just behind where she stood. A quick glance over her shoulder, following his gaze, revealed nothing besides an empty corridor.

"Um, are you alright?"

He locked onto her with unfocused eyes. "Hi, Chrissy."

"What are you doing here?" she tried again, trying to sound as casual as possible. The way his voice came out, flat and far away, made her uneasy.

He gave a slow blink. "Same as you. Grabbing a bite to eat."

"Oh. Nice." She took another small step backwards.

"Did you like the pizza?" He shifted his attention back to the spot over her shoulder.

"Uh, yeah. It was good."

Bill continued to stand there, unmoving, eyes still hovering. Being alone with him was making her uncomfortable, though she couldn't say why. He hadn't done anything other than stand there, but something about his eyes and the way he stared off at nothing creeped her out.

Chrissy realized she could hear the ambient music filtering through the hall and became all too aware of the fact that they were the only two people in that section of the mall. All of a sudden, she didn't want to be there. She toyed with the idea of running back to the safety of the crowds in the food court, but thought of the hordes of spiders back there, lying in wait... In that moment, she would rather face the spiders.

"Well, I was just about to head back," she said, taking yet another step, increasing the distance between herself and Bill. "I'll see you back at the hotel."

His dull and lifeless eyes slid to her face. "Not if I see you first," he said, a mirthless smile curling his lips.

She turned away from him and walked down the hall, measuring her steps and trying not to let her fear take over. Whatever was going on with Bill, she couldn't deal with it now, and she didn't want him to know that he had her spooked.

As soon as she was around the corner, she broke into a jog. The food court opened up before her. It appeared exactly as it had when she and Rodney arrived, with only one or two people sitting at the tables, bored workers posted behind the counters. She slowed and glanced over to where she sat moments ago. Two pieces of half-eaten pizza and a large drink still sat on the table. Nothing had been disturbed. No signs of a spider infestation. Of the people seated in the area, none looked alarmed or like they had just witnessed the birth of a thousand spiders from a soda cup. So, where had all those other people gone?

The tiny hairs on the back of her neck stood up and her muscles went rigid as the feeling of being watched crept over her. She wondered if Bill had followed her, then remembered he said he came here to grab lunch. Forcing herself to relax and appear as though she was casually looking in the storefronts, she continued towards the exit. Her steps faltered when she reached the spot where Wicks 'N' Sticks had been. Only now, the sign said Blue Elephant Toyshop. Thinking she must have gotten turned around somehow, she searched for the bright Tape World sign, but it was nowhere to be found. None of this made sense. The food court was the same, but the stores were all different.

That feeling of being watched became almost unbearable, and she couldn't stop herself from checking over her shoulder. Sure enough, at the opposite end of the food court, arms folded over his chest, stood Bill. His head hung down, his eyes fixed on the floor. He wasn't the one watching her.

A figure beside him leaned in, speaking into his ear, a wicked grin lighting up its face. The greasy hair hanging in curtains and baggy Dio tee shirt sent Chrissy's heart into overdrive as it slammed against her rib cage. Roach raised a hand and twiddled his fingers in a little wave.

Chrissy spun and ran for the door.

Twenty-Four

The Ghostmobile stood like a shining beacon of safety as Chrissy sprinted through the parking lot, crashing into the side of the van and scrambling to unlock the door. She cursed the van's old age as she scraped paint a handful of times before at last succeeding in getting the key in the lock. Door thrown open, she clambered up into the drivers' seat, tossed her bag into the passenger's side, and slammed the door behind her. Keying the ignition, the engine roared to life, and she hit the gas, tires squealing with indignation, having never been asked to participate in a getaway before.

Only once the mall shrunk to a speck in the rear-view mirror did she allow herself to think about what just happened, not that any of it made sense. The neat little boxes she tried to sort it all into were of no use. Too many things had been shoved in there, all stacked on top of one another: her home, Rodney, the spiders, Bill and Roach, Alorah. Now, all of them were toppling over and spilling across her thoughts.

Reaching over the gap, she fumbled in her bag for her phone and dialed Rodney's number. It rang several times before it sent her to voicemail.

"Oh, come on." She smashed the end call button with her thumb. He was mad at her. She understood that, even though he had the wrong idea, but to ignore her calls? Anxiety mounted as she pressed redial. It only rang once before being rejected and sent to voicemail.

"Dammit, Rodney."

Her foot jammed down hard on the accelerator, and she had to pull herself back, focusing on easing her tension. The last thing she needed was to get picked up for speeding. As soon as she opened her mouth everything would come bubbling out, and they'd cart her off.

With Rodney rejecting her calls and Bill acting like a full-on weirdo, she had no idea who to turn to. Tears welled up once again, and she swiped an angry palm over her eyes. It was all too much. The investigation had been wrong from the start, but she had been too stubborn, too eager to grow their audience, too determined to prove that encounters with spirits were real. She choked on a bitter laugh at the irony. The fact was, those real encounters were causing the team to splinter and fall apart in a spectacular fashion.

Unfamiliar streets flew by as she drove, uncertain of where she was headed or what she should do next. Going back to the hotel was her first thought, but Rodney would most likely ignore her knocks as he had her phone calls, and if Bill came back while she was standing alone in the hallway, she wasn't sure what she would do, especially if Roach showed up with him.

With desperation crawling in, she searched her contacts and called the one person she thought might be able to help. She crossed her fingers and gripped the steering wheel, silently begging them to pick up.

"Hello?"

"Bev? It's Chrissy."

"You alright?"

The concern in her voice was the feather touch the dam inside her needed, and the tears came flooding out.

"Not really. I need your help."

Water running and a clattering of dishes filled the background as she spoke. "Come over."

Chrissy thanked her through sniffles and ended the call.

By the time she pulled up to the yellow house, Bev stood at the gate, the front door of her house propped open, welcoming her.

"I'm sorry to bother you again today, but thank you for letting me come," Chrissy said. The tears stopped flowing by that point, but she swiped at her cheeks, which she was sure were streaked with mascara.

"Come on inside, honey. I've got a fresh cup of tea with your name on it." Bev held the gate open for her and guided her up the steps, a reassuring hand resting on her back.

She led Chrissy into the cozy living room, where a cup of tea waited on the coffee table as promised. She brought it up, inhaling the sweet herbal aroma of honeyed lavender. Bev perched on the arm of her chair, watching her over her own cup, waiting for her to speak.

"Something really weird is happening," Chrissy started. Hot tea spilled over the side of the cup and onto her hands as they began to shake. "I'm not sure what's going on, but I think one of the members of my team is being possessed. Maybe I am too."

"What makes you think that?"

Leaning forward, Chrissy set her cup down and pressed a hand to her forehead. "I don't know. I've been seeing strange things. Things I can't explain at all."

"Tell me what you've seen."

"It sounds crazy. I sound crazy."

"It won't sound crazy to me."

She paused for a long moment before beginning.

"I think I saw into the past. Yesterday, at the school, something rushed at me. One minute I closed my eyes, and when I opened them, it was like I was back in the 80s. There were kids in the halls, and I saw Alorah. Then, Roach turned up. He tried to attack her, but she ran away. He said he was going to teach her a lesson, and then it all just disappeared."

"This happened yesterday? Why didn't you tell me all this when you were here earlier?"

"I didn't think it was important then," Chrissy said, her voice small.

"But you do now. So what happened in the last couple of hours to make you change your mind?"

"I think it happened again, but it was a lot shorter this time. More...personal? At the school, it was like I was being shown something, but at the mall, it was almost like it was targeted at me. The food court was empty, and then it wasn't. And the stores were different, places that haven't been around for years. Then, there were the spiders." Her subconscious brought a hand to her lips, wiping at the memory of those hairy, scratching legs. "It was disgusting. They were everywhere, and then they weren't. None of this makes any sense."

Chrissy looked up, her eyes begging the woman for answers.

"Why did you get into paranormal investigation?"

"Well," she paused, thrown for a moment by the question. "I've always been interested in it. I used to hear voices talking to me or moving around my room when I was a little girl. My dad thought I was nuts, but my mom explained it was the spirits of loved ones who passed on, so I guess I just wanted to learn more."

Bev nodded. “People like us do tend to have very active childhoods.”

“People like us?”

“Chrissy, I believe you have a gift that allows you to interact more freely with the other side than most. The spirits can sense you are closer to the veil, so they’re more likely to reach out to you. It would explain why you’ve been experiencing the things you have.”

Chrissy sputtered a few times then stopped trying all together. This was crazy. This woman was crazy. She wasn’t like Bev; she couldn’t speak with spirits. True, there were things she couldn’t explain from when she was a young girl, but she hadn’t experienced anything more than a strange knocking or sounds of footsteps since. If she possessed an ability to communicate with the dead, why had she never captured a single thing in the hours of footage they filmed for *Othersiders*? Why was it only happening now?

“That doesn’t make sense. I haven’t been communicating with anyone. It’s only been nightmares and weird flashes of the past.”

“Not everyone experiences these things the in same way. Some folks see the spirits as they were in life. Some only get vague feelings from them. My own gift allows me to converse with them like you and I are right now. You appear to have the ability to glimpse into their own times.”

The explanation did nothing to clear things up. She always believed in the afterlife, in capturing proof, but this was uncharted territory. She wanted evidence, not to become a conduit.

“But it can’t just be me. I’m not the only one weird things are happening to. A member of the team has been acting odd ever since our first night in the school. He's not been himself at all. Like I said earlier, I'm worried he might be possessed."

"Possession is incredibly rare," Bev said, looking doubtful.

"Well, I can't think of any other reason he's being so..." Her hand fluttered in the air, trying to find the right words, trailing off when they wouldn't come. "He's just being weird, and he was at the mall at the same time the spider thing happened. Not only that, but I could have sworn Roach was with him."

The corners of Bev's lips drew down. "Well, that explains the spiders," she muttered.

"What?"

"If Roach was there, it explains why you caught a glimpse of things as they were when he was alive. The spiders were probably some nasty trick of his."

"But why me?"

"I told you, they can tell you're closer to them than most other folks. It's like being in a place where nobody speaks your language. As soon as someone shows up who understands you, you're going to try to talk to them."

"Okay, but why is he making horrible stuff happen? Why is this all starting now? Not once has a spirit tried to reach out to me, and I've been actively searching for them."

Bev rubbed her temples. "I can't tell you why it's starting now. These things don't always make sense. As for Roach, he was awful in life, so of course he's still going to be awful after. Dying doesn't change the core of a person."

Chrissy tried to take it all in. Her brain felt soggy and over-saturated with everything Bev was telling her. It gave her a headache. Cradling her head in her hands, she inhaled deeply.

"I'm worried about my team," she said.

"Well, you can put aside your fears of possession. Roach may have some strength, but it's not enough to take over your friend's body."

"Then what's happening to him?"

"It seems, for whatever reason, Roach has attached himself to your friend. Why, I don't know."

"Can we unattach him?"

"We can try, but first, you need to figure out why he's drawn to your friend. There's got to be some reason Roach specifically chose him to cling to."

Searching through her cluttered mind for anything that might link Bill and Roach, she came up empty. How much did she actually know about Bill Weston? Never one to open up and share his life story, all Chrissy knew about the man was that he lived alone somewhere in Westlake, was a great cameraman, and seemed to be a nice enough guy the last year they worked together. It dawned on her that she had no idea who Bill was.

"To be honest, I don't know him all that well. He did mention he was bullied when he was in school. That might be something."

"Could be." Bev took a sip of her tea. "Could be Roach found himself another outcast, someone he thought he could torment after all these years."

"Someone besides me, you mean," Chrissy scoffed.

"It gives us a place to start at least." She set her cup down. "I don't know how this is all going to go down tomorrow. It could be a bit tricky now that Roach has a new plaything. He might not be as easy to move on."

"Should I be worried? Can he hurt us?" Chrissy thought of the way the spiders scratched her lips, how the smoke choked her in her room that night. What else was he capable of?

"Roach can't. It's your friend who worries me."

"Bill? He wouldn't hurt a fly. He's never..." She stopped herself. Before, she would never have entertained the idea that Bill was capable of violence, but the anger in his voice at the school forced her to rethink.

"You just be sure you've got everyone there tomorrow night. For now, you should get some rest. It's going to be exhausting for all of us."

Twenty-Five

Chrissy tried to follow Bev's advice and went straight to the hotel from her house, but the room was too hot, too stuffy, and she couldn't shut her brain off long enough to fall asleep. Taking on Roach would be a massive challenge, if she believed Bev, which she struggled with at the moment. The thing she said about Chrissy having a so-called gift to communicate with the deceased was absurd. Was she supposed to take it at face value and call herself a psychic now?

No matter how much she wanted to disregard everything Bev said, she couldn't do it. Even though it was crazy, she trusted the woman. Perhaps that was naïve, but her gut told her Bev was their best chance at helping the spirits in the school move on. It wasn't going to be easy, though. She wasn't even sure she could get Rodney and Bill to come down to the school with her.

Giving up on sleep, she shot Rodney a text asking if they could talk. Her nerves had her fingers drumming the screen as she waited for a reply, each second dragging on forever. Just as she was ready to give up and go to his room to confront him, a soft knock came at her door. With a quick glance through the peephole, a sense of relief washed over her when she saw Rodney standing there with his hands stuffed in his pockets.

"Hey," she said, opening the door. "Come in?"

He hesitated, then stepped into her room.

"Look, I-"

"I'm sorry about leaving-"

She offered a self-conscious smile as they spoke over each other. "Sorry. You go ahead."

"I wanted to say I'm sorry for leaving you at the mall today. That was super lame of me."

"At least you left me the Ghostmobile," she said.

"Well, yeah," he said, a touch of indignation in his tone. "I wouldn't abandon you in a strange place with no way to get home."

They lapsed into an awkward silence.

"What did you want to talk about?" Rodney asked.

"Oh. I also wanted to apologize. I didn't mean to upset you earlier. Truly, I didn't."

He held her gaze for a moment, his expression unreadable. When he didn't fill the silence, she pressed on.

"Something weird is going on here. I think you know that. After you left, I ran into Bill at the mall."

Rodney's brows furrowed. "Bill was at the mall?"

Chrissy nodded. "And I had another weird episode in the food court. I saw stores that don't exist anymore, and then the spiders....I don't want to talk about them. But as I was leaving, I saw Bill standing with that Roach kid."

"He was with someone?"

"Not just someone. It was Roach. I'm positive."

He ran a hand through his hair, frowning. "I don't understand. You saw Bill with a ghost. At the mall. How did he even get there?"

"Beats me, but I went to see Bev after. Don't look at me like that. I needed to talk to someone, and you were rejecting all my calls. Anyway, among other things, she told me she thinks Roach has attached himself to Bill for some reason. That's why he's been acting so weird. She agreed to help us, but she needs all of us to be at the school tomorrow night."

Rodney shook his head. "This is insane."

"I know how it sounds," Chrissy said. Hell, she felt the same, though for different reasons. "But something's not right here. You said so yourself. My nightmares, the episode at the school yesterday, the mall today, your sister singing in the bathroom. I know you heard it. At this point, I don't care about the show. I care about your sister, I care about Bill, even if he is acting super sketchy, and I care about you. I don't want Alorah to be stuck in there with that creep for another minute, but I can't help her without you. Please, Rodney. I need you."

His expression softened as she spoke, and he reached out and brushed a tear she hadn't noticed off her cheek.

"If we do this, will you promise me one thing?"

"Anything," Chrissy said.

"No cameras."

Her stomach dropped. When she said she didn't care about the show, she meant it. Or so she thought. But no cameras?

Biting back disappointment, she nodded again. "No cameras."

"Alright, then I'm in. What do we have to do?"

"Honestly? I have no idea."

Seated across from each other on the beds, she filled him in on all the details of the events at the mall after he left, as well as her discussion with Bev. She wanted to leave out the part about her own apparent abilities, since she wasn't sure where she stood on the subject. There was also the possibility Rodney would flip out over it. In the end, she told him everything, and as expected, he was skeptical, but to his credit, he kept his mouth mostly shut. Once she finished, he rested his chin on his clasped hands, his gaze shifting to the window as he mulled over the information.

"Jeez, dude. That's a lot to wrap my head around."

"I know," she said, chewing the inside of her bottom lip.

He released a long breath. "Putting the, uh, powers aside... She thinks this Roach kid is somehow influencing Bill to, what? Just be a weirdo?"

"There has to be more to it than that. Bev said we needed to figure out what his motivation is. I thought it might be because he was bullied as a kid. Maybe Roach can sense that and is just doing what bullies do?"

"I don't think that's it. I got picked on too, remember? He hasn't screwed with me at all."

"Well, you're Alorah's brother. It's possible he doesn't want to because of that."

Rodney gave her a dubious look but shrugged and moved on. "So, how are we supposed to get Bill to come with us tomorrow? The way he keeps disappearing, we've got to come up with a plan so he's not AWOL when we need him."

"That's a good question. I'm hoping if we frame it like it's just the last night of investigation, he'll come along with no issue. Has he come back yet?"

"He hadn't before I came in here. I could go check," he said, though he made no effort to move.

Chrissy considered going to see if he had returned, but quickly decided against it. "Do you think he's gone back to the school to keep looking through those lockers?"

"I mean, it's possible. What was that all about, anyway?"

"No clue. What would he even be searching for?"

"Maybe the ghosts stole his wallet."

Chrissy grabbed a pillow from the bed and tossed it at him. "I'm serious," she said with a laugh.

"Well, why don't we go down there now? We can check it out, see if that's where Bill went. If he's not around, we can try to figure out what he was looking for."

It wasn't a bad idea, but the thought of running into Bill at the school was entirely unappealing. Until now, she had thought of him as a giant teddy bear of a man, but there was something about seeing a man that size ranting and raging that made him seem more like a grizzly ready to rip her limb from limb. Rodney would be with her, but she wasn't certain the two of them combined would be able to fend off someone as large as Bill should he decide to turn grizzly on them.

"Alright, let's go. But if he is down there acting weird, can we agree to leave and come back here? I don't want to confront him if he's kicking lockers and screaming again."

"Works for me," Rodney said, his crooked grin making an appearance. "I'm a lover, not a fighter."

The school loomed ahead at the end of the street, giving no hints as to whether Bill was inside. Rodney pulled over against the sidewalk a block away and killed the engine. Neither of them moved. They simply sat, staring at the building.

Rodney broke the silence.

"Well, we won't be able to tell anything from here."

He popped open his door and slid out, sneakers landing on the pavement with a quiet thud. She gripped the door handle and left the relative safety of the Ghostmobile, moving to Rodney's side in front of the van's grille, heat radiating from the engine.

"Ready?" He cast a sidelong glance at her. "I promise I won't run off screaming if we come across anything weird."

Chrissy gave a short snort of a laugh. "Everything that happens here is weird."

The evening had grown warm and heavy. Leaves on the trees were still, begging for even a slight breeze to come through and lift the oppressive air that settled in. They approached the building, slowing as they neared.

The gate had been rolled back a couple of feet, and Chrissy's steps faltered as she turned to Rodney.

"Did we shut the gate earlier?"

He shook his head. "I'm not sure. I don't think I closed it. Did you?"

She shrugged, unable to recall. With everything that happened over the past several hours, the events of the morning felt as though they were decades ago.

"I don't remember if I did or not, but Bill still has the key," she said.

They glanced back up at the school, peering through the windows from a distance. The stillness of the day amplified every sound, but the building remained silent.

After listening for a few more beats, Rodney took a step forward. "I don't think he's inside. We would have heard him by now."

Giving it one last distrustful look, Chrissy followed him up the steps and into the school. Inside, the hallways stretched out on either side, dark and still. No banging, no screaming. The place was dead quiet.

"Where should we start?" she asked.

He jerked his head towards the left-wing corridor. "I guess down that way. That's where Bill was earlier."

Leading the way to the end of the hallway, he stepped up to the first set of lockers. Several were impossible to access, sealed off with clunky combination locks, the faces caked with soot and grime. Chrissy moved to the end of the row and reached out, gingerly taking the latch of the first unlocked locker door between her fingers and lifting. At first it didn't want to budge, but she gave it a little wiggle and the latch lifted, the locker swinging open with a metallic groan.

Empty.

When the first row yielded nothing, they moved on to the next. A handful of lockers in, and Rodney slapped a palm against his forehead.

"Dude, I'm an idiot."

Chrissy cocked an eyebrow.

"Bill already went through these. He didn't find whatever he was looking for here, so why would we?"

"Should we try upstairs?" she asked.

"Might as well."

Heading up the stairs, they moved down the second-floor hallway to where she had seen Alorah during her episode the day before. Worry she might at any moment slip into another one of those flashbacks set her on edge, every step echoing in her ears and amplifying her tension. If it happened now, she thought, at least Rodney would be there to witness it.

Although she couldn't pinpoint Alorah's exact locker, she had an idea of the general area. From there, it would only be a matter of searching until they found the right one. She wasn't sure what she would find, or if it would have anything to do with what Bill was looking for, but she was here now, and she wanted to see if anything was in there. It seemed as good a place to start as any.

The lockers on this floor had far more smoke damage, which made deciphering the numbers almost impossible. Most of the unsecured lockers were empty or contained only a blackened textbook or two. A thin layer of filth from decades of neglect covered the entire place, and Chrissy could feel the grime seeping into her pores.

"Whoa. Chrissy, you gotta come see this."

"Did you find something?"

"I found *something*, alright," Rodney laughed.

Abandoning the locker she had just pulled open, she went over to Rodney, who stood grinning like an idiot with one hand on a locker door. As she got closer, he flung it open so she could see in.

At first, she didn't know what had worked him up. Inside were a few books, an old Trapper Keeper, and a rather impressive collection of old lipstick tubes scattered around the bottom. Then, she spotted the inside of the door. It was covered from top to bottom in photos carefully cut from magazines, their edges curling in. Through a scrim of soot, a young Rob Lowe was the main focus of this 80s heartthrob shrine. A few images of Jon Bon Jovi and Prince were added throughout, creating a masterful collage. As she looked closer, she could make out old smears of bright pink kiss marks on one or two of the photos, and she burst into laughter.

"I don't know why you're laughing," Rodney said, trying to keep a straight face. "I bet your locker looked exactly the same when you were in high school."

"I was too cool for a locker."

"Uh huh, sure you were."

Grinning, she went back to resume her search. They continued down the hallway, encountering more empty lockers. By the time they finished with the third set and came up with nothing, she began to wonder how she had gotten it so wrong.

"Should we call it a day?" Rodney asked. "We haven't found anything more interesting than a lipstick-smeared Rob Lowe."

Chrissy glanced around the hallway, frustrated but not willing to give up quite yet. "Let's try one more row. If we don't find anything, then we can head out."

Every unoccupied locker chipped away at her enthusiasm. Drawing near the center, with only a few lockers remaining between them, she raised her gaze to the next one. The smoke wasn't as bad this far down the hall, and the numbers were easier to make out. She hesitated, hand pausing mid-air as she read the number.

2,433.

Something about the number nudged and poked at her memory, like she knew it from somewhere. Those four silver numbers had her searching for their meaning, for whatever connection her subconscious was attempting to make. Lifting the locker's latch, she expected it wouldn't budge, but it came easily, and she pulled the door open.

On the top shelf was a rusty old white can, exclaiming "extra super hold" underneath the hot pink Aqua Net label. Beneath it hung an acid wash denim jacket Chrissy immediately recognized.

Warm breath against her ear made her jump. Rodney stood beside her, his gaze fixed on the jacket in the locker. He raised a hand to reach for it, then stopped, letting his arm drop at his side.

"Is it..."

"Alorah's," he said, more to himself.

They stared into the locker. A few notebooks and other items peeked out from behind the denim, and Chrissy leaned forward, looking to Rodney for permission. He gave a tight nod, and she pulled out the jacket, revealing some old notepads and folders, along with a small makeup bag. She passed the jacket to him and took out one of the spiral bound notebooks, leafing through pages filled with math equations. Rodney stood behind her, staring over her shoulder at his sister's handwriting while clutching her jacket in his hands.

Noise at the end of the hall drew Chrissy's attention. She spun towards the sound, and her breath caught in anticipation as she strained to hear if it would repeat.

"What was that?" she asked over the pounding in her chest.

"I didn't hear anything."

Tilting her head, she listened for a long while, expecting the sound of footsteps to come rushing at her, but there was nothing other than her pulse hammering in her ears. With a sense of unease gnawing at her, she turned back to Alorah's locker.

Lines of class notes filled the rest of the notebooks, and Chrissy gently placed them back inside. She reached up to the top shelf to where a battered novel lay on its side next to the empty can of hairspray. Careful not to damage the old book, she brought it down and peered at the weathered cover, the blood-drenched face of a girl staring back up at her.

"Your sister liked Stephen King?" she asked.

"She was obsessed. Carrie was her favorite. I always wondered where her copy went. When we moved, I helped pack all her things up. It was too hard for my parents. I searched for this for days."

Chrissy turned the book over in her hands. This copy had been well loved, the spine sporting multiple cracks, the edges of the cover rounded and smooth and bearing a handful of creases. Thumbing through the pages, a slip of paper fluttered from the book onto the floor. Rodney stooped to pick it up. Holding it close to his face to read the time-faded writing, his expression darkened.

"What is it?" she asked.

The confusion creasing his brown suddenly smoothed. Tearing his eyes away from the page, he looked at her wide-eyed. "I think this is it."

"What do you mean?"

"I think this is what..." He trailed off. His face turned a sickly shade of white as his gaze moved past her, settling somewhere down the hall.

Goosebumps erupted all over her skin as every hair on her body stood at attention, an icy chill filling the school as the temperature plummeted. The voice inside her head screamed at her, telling her not to turn around. She forced her feet to move. To turn. To face whatever lurked in the hall behind her.

Twenty-Six

A DARK, STOOPING FIGURE stood at the top of the stairs. Hidden in the depths of the shadows, it was difficult to make out their identity, let alone if they were corporeal or not. Silent and unmoving, they regarded Chrissy and Rodney.

"Hello?" Chrissy forced out, hating how small and squeaky she sounded.

The figure remained rooted to the spot.

"Hey, man, the place is closed," Rodney called out. "You're going to have to leave."

The figure cocked its head to the side at the sound of Rodney's voice and began to straighten to a remarkable height. They stepped forward, bringing themselves out of the deepest shadows. Chrissy's hand flew to her throat as soon as the dark pools of the man's eyes came into view.

"Holy cow, dude. You've got to stop doing this," Rodney said.

Bill paused and fixed his eyes on the pair, standing wordlessly in the middle of the hallway. His eyes moved from Chrissy to Rodney, then down, focusing on the jacket draped over Rodney's arm then over to the piece of paper in his hand.

"I'm going to need that," Bill said.

Rodney stared back, confused. "What?"

Bill jerked his head towards the note. "I need that paper."

"I heard you. But why do you need it?"

"Is it what you were searching for earlier?" Chrissy asked.

Bills eyes landed on her and darted back to Rodney. "It doesn't concern either of you."

Tension simmered between the two men, and Chrissy reached out, placing a hand on Rodney's arm.

"What do you mean, doesn't concern us? It doesn't concern you. What are you even doing here, Bill? Why were you looking for my sister's stuff?"

Surprise flashed across Bill's face, softening his features and making him look more like the man they knew. He opened his mouth to say something but froze. The light around him shifted ever so slightly. Chrissy squinted, but whatever it had been disappeared before she could make it out. When she looked back at Bill, his expression had changed back to the waxy, hard-lined one from before, all traces of warmth erased.

"I said it doesn't concern you. There's things you two don't understand. You don't need to understand. You just need to give me the note."

He took a step towards them, and Chrissy shrank back against Rodney. With mounting panic, it registered that Bill was blocking the only exit, and it didn't seem likely he would let them leave with the note. She scrambled for an idea of how she could get them out of this mess.

"Why do you want this? Do you know this," Rodney raised the paper and glanced at it, "Gary kid?"

Chrissy threw a startled look at him, the name landing like a punch in the gut. "Gary?"

"That's who signed the note."

She snatched the paper from Rodney's hand and read it over, her pounding heart seeming to rise into her throat with each word. Rodney continued questioning Bill about why he was at the school and what he knew about his sister as she read the note over again.

Once she finished, she raised her head and met Bill's gaze. He stared back, eyes burning dark with...what? Anger? Hatred? Guilt? Most likely a mix of all three, she thought.

"You're Gary," she said, more a statement than question.

The strange flickering returned all around him, and his eyes turned to flint. She nudged Rodney, bringing his attention to the shifting shadows.

"What the hell?"

Bill's whole body tensed as his eyes rolled back in his head. Chrissy stuffed the note into her pocket and searched for Rodney's hand, clutching it in a vice grip.

The entire area behind Bill's left shoulder seemed to waver in and out, a formless, inky darkness growing and shrinking in on itself. The temperature of the hallway plummeted further, and Chrissy began to shiver. A deep thrumming reverberated in her skull, making the fillings in her teeth hurt. The noise mounted and her teeth chattered, and she was certain if it didn't stop soon, she would go mad.

"Cut it out!"

A high-pitched voice sliced through the sound, effectively cutting it off. Chrissy spun, and Rodney dropped her hand as he spotted the speaker the same moment she did. A teenage girl, curls blowing out from her face, stood in the hallway behind the pair.

Alorah.

Rodney let out a choked gasp, but the girl didn't acknowledge their presence. She moved swiftly past them towards Bill and the dark mass, which at some point had taken the shape of a person. As she neared, Bill started trembling from head to foot, and the black mass began to break up around the edges, losing some of its shape.

"You let him go, Roach. Right now." Alorah was beautiful in her radiant anger.

The shadow wavered, and Bill shook more violently. Chrissy pressed a hand to her mouth, terrified and flooded with concern. It looked like he was having a seizure. The temperature dropped a few more degrees, and the dark shadow seemed to suck the energy from the room into itself, solidifying once again.

Alorah's face became a mask of pure rage. Her jaw stretched wide and the sound that came out of her filled the entire school.

"LEAVE HIM ALONE!"

The scream reverberated through the halls, and both Rodney and Chrissy clamped their hands over their ears against the deafening wail. The mass behind Bill wavered then broke up, shattered by the force of it.

Bill's eyes were still rolled far back in his head, but the violent trembling subsided. Alorah looked up into his face, her terrible expression turning to one of pity as she reached up and placed a light hand on his shoulder.

"It's alright, Gary," she said softly.

Bill's eyes fluttered open. Face to face with Alorah, his face crumpled.

"I'm sorry. I'm so, so sorry."

She smiled up into his face and turned away. Her eyes filled with a profound sadness when they landed on Rodney. He stared, open-mouthed, at his long-deceased sister. If not for the oddly washed-out complexion, it would be easy to believe she was a solid, living person. He reached out, but Alorah shook her head.

"Not now, Roddy. You have to leave."

"Leave? But I just found you. How am I supposed to leave?"

"There's no time now. You need to get Gary away from here."

"Gary? You mean Bill? What is going on?"

"Go now. Roach won't stay away for long. You have to leave before he comes back."

Struggle and conflict played over Rodney's face, keeping him stuck in place. Seeing that he wouldn't be able to move on his own, Chrissy grabbed hold of his arm and pulled him towards the stairs. He offered little resistance but moved as though made of wood. As they approached Bill, she used her other hand to give him a shove in the direction of the exit. Stumbling on unsteady feet, he continued forward. At the top of the stairs, she cast one final glance behind her. The young girl was beginning to fade, but her lips formed a soundless *thank you* before slipping away.

Hurried footsteps echoed off the walls of the stairwell as they descended. The air was electric. It felt to Chrissy like the building was holding its breath, waiting to exhale and unleash something sinister. She pushed them forward, not eager to face whatever that something might be.

Rodney reached the doors first, crashing into them with his shoulder, sending them flying open. Bill stumbled out after him, feet kicking up dust and gravel as he half-shuffled across the lot. Chrissy followed as they squeezed through the narrow gap in the fence and spilled out onto the sidewalk. Jogging down the block to where they left the Ghostmobile, a soft thud came from behind her, followed by a muffled groan. She whipped around to find Bill doubled over, clutching his stomach. Rodney stood over him, clenched fist raised in the air.

"What's going on?" Chrissy asked, trying to catch her breath as a stitch formed in her side.

"That's what I want to know," Rodney said, the muscle in his jaw twitching. "What were you doing in there? Who the fuck are you?"

Still doubled over, Bill lifted a hand, signaling for them to wait a moment. After a few unsteady breaths, he straightened, keeping his eyes low.

"I understand you're upset with me."

"Upset?" Rodney yelled. "I'm so far beyond upset, Bill. Or Gary. Whoever you are."

"I know, but please hear me out. I never meant for things to end up like this. I had no idea he would still be here. Or Alorah, for that matter. I-"

Rodney moved as if to throw another punch, causing Bill to flinch away. Chrissy shot a hand out, grabbing Rodney by the arm.

"Not now, guys. There's a lot we have to talk about, but I don't think we're safe out here. We need to get away from this place."

"I don't think anywhere is safe with this asshole around. You saw how that black thing was attached to him. You said yourself he was with that creepy kid's ghost at the mall."

"He's not here now," Bill mumbled. "Whatever your sister did, it scared him off."

"Don't fucking talk about my sister."

"Rodney," Chrissy warned.

"How do we know we'll be safe with him, Chrissy? That thing could come back and possess him again at any moment."

She shook her head. "He's not being possessed."

"It sure as hell looked like he was possessed to me."

"Bev said Roach doesn't have that kind of power. But he is influencing you, Bill."

Eyes still downcast, Bill nodded.

"Come on," Chrissy said. "We need to talk, but it can't be here."

With a huff, Rodney stormed off towards the van.

"I'm sorry, Chrissy." Unable to meet her eyes, Bill dragged his feet, following after Rodney.

As the one with the calmest mind at the moment, Chrissy took the driver's seat. Starting the engine, she turned on the heater. Despite the lingering heat of the summer evening, the chill from inside the school had seeped down into her bones. She eased the van onto the roads and drove away from Merlin High, keeping one eye on the road and one on Bill in the rear-view mirror.

They drove until they reached a sign announcing they had left Merlin, please come again soon. No one said a word.

When they passed the city limits, Chrissy pulled the van over on the gravel shoulder and turned in her seat to look back at Bill. He sat slumped over, hands clasped in front of him.

"Alright, Bill. Talk."

He took a deep breath, his shoulders riding up before letting it out in a long whoosh. "I don't even know where to begin."

"At the beginning, asshole."

"Rodney, let him talk," she said. "You keep your mouth shut."

He glared at the floor but kept his mouth shut.

With a nod, she signaled Bill to continue.

"Okay. Well, like Rodney, I lived in Merlin. I didn't grow up there, though, just moved there when I was 14. It was the middle of the school year when I came. Everyone already had their little groups, and I had a hard time making friends."

"Oh, boo freaking hoo."

Chrissy glared at Rodney across the cup holders and turned back to Bill. "Go on."

"There was only one person in the school who paid any attention to me. He was kind of weird, but he was always pretty nice to me, and he was a senior. So, I started hanging out with him more and more. He wasn't a great kid, but hell, neither was I. We got up to some stuff, little things at first, nothing major. Just pranks. But things escalated. Soon enough, I found myself taking money from my mom's purse, stealing cassettes from Tape World, keying the principal's car."

"The Eagle?" Rodney asked, momentarily forgetting to be angry.

Bill nodded. "That's the one. Anyway, it was a difficult time for me. We moved to Merlin because my parents had gotten a divorce. My mom took me away from all my friends and expected I'd be fine. But it was rough, and I was pissed. I'll admit, I let Roach talk me into things I never would have done before. That's on me. But I was vulnerable, and I thought they were harmless at the time. They were only pranks. Until one day, they weren't."

He paused, his face twisting as he grappled with whatever emotions his past brought up.

Rodney began to speak, and Chrissy reached out to silence him before they went too off track. Bill had to work through this one on his own, and it would do no good to have Rodney pushing him.

"One day, he came to me, talking about how every one of the stuck-up kids at Merlin High needed to be taught a lesson. He was fuming. I tried to get him to tell me what happened, but he would only say that we needed to show them that they couldn't get away with treating us like garbage. I couldn't tell you what set him off that time, but I agreed with him. While I hadn't been around Merlin as long as he had, hadn't experienced a fraction of the torment, I'd had my share. The way kids treat you when you're different...it's not right."

Anger started to build in his voice, but he shook his head as if to clear it away, and he continued.

"When he told me the plan, I didn't think he was serious. It wasn't until he showed me the gas can that I realized he meant to go through with it. I didn't want to." At this, he raised his eyes to Chrissy's first, then to Rodney's, his expression pained and desperate. "Honestly, I didn't want to go through with it. You have to believe me."

"If that were true, you should have told someone what he was planning on doing," Rodney said. "Don't give me this bullshit about not wanting to do it. You did it, Bill. You're responsible for the deaths of sixty-seven people."

Bill sagged and brought his hands to cover his face. Disgusted, Rodney turned away from him.

Chrissy stared out the window. Trees lined this part of the highway, lush and green, shadows thickening in the evening light. A bright russet ribbon stretched out on the horizon, touched with flecks of orange, setting the sky on fire. She didn't blame Rodney for his reaction. That Bill went along with Roach's plan, allowing himself to be dragged into something so evil, forced her to question everything about his character. How was it possible for a person to commit horrible deeds but appear so normal? So decent? And how had she missed it?

"What's you real name, Bill?" she asked.

"Gary. Gary Maslon."

"Did you know who Rodney was when we first met?"

Bill's shook his head with force. "I had no idea, swear to God. I only connected the dots when he said something about his sister back at the school. I would never have come here with you if I had known."

"What happened that night?" Chrissy asked, cutting Rodney off before he could hurl more deserved vitriol at Bill. "You have to tell us everything."

"I can't-"

"You have to," Rodney said, his voice tight.

"I've relived that night so many times in my head, trying to think of how else I could have gotten her to listen to me. Please don't make me go over it again."

"Gotten who to listen?" Chrissy asked.

Bill risked a glance at Rodney. "Alorah."

"Tell us what happened," she said.

Defeated, he slumped back into the seat.

"We went to the school that afternoon, before the dance. Roach took me around and showed me where he planned to start the fire. The spot was right next to the emergency exit, behind the bleachers. He had all this old paper and oily rags he took from the auto shop. At first, it seemed like he was telling the truth; it would be a small fire, mostly smoke. It was only supposed to scare them and ruin their night. Someone would see the smoke, and everyone would get out before anyone got hurt. But then he told me he was going to lock the gym doors."

Chrissy gasped at the confession. The doors had been locked on purpose. That wasn't a prank. That was flat out murder. And Bill — soft spoken, kind Bill — had a hand in it.

"I asked him why," he continued. "He said he wanted them all to suffer as much as he had. He was pissed off at all of them, but especially at your sister. I guess she humiliated him one time too many."

Rodney lunged into the back from his seat, straining against his seatbelt. Chrissy hesitated, a fleeting impulse urging her to let this play out. Hell, he deserved it. But she shoved Rodney back into his seat and nailed Bill with a piercing glare.

"Alorah didn't humiliate him. He tried to attack her in the hallway, and she defended herself."

"I'm just telling you what Roach told me," he said, putting his hands up in defense. "He didn't tell me what exactly happened, only that he wanted all of them to suffer, her most of all."

He paused then, picking at the loose stitching of the seat. When he spoke, his voice was far away, distant.

"I couldn't let it happen. I loved your sister."

Rodney stiffened, his eyes swimming with rage. Once more, Chrissy had to place a calming hand on him, pushing him back. She could see how much dredging up the past upset him, but the truth had to come out. These things demanded exposure, to face the light of day, lest they continue to fester, to rot inside each one of them.

"She barely knew I existed, but...well, she was the girl. I think everybody was a little bit in love with her. She was gorgeous and smart, but most of all, she was kind. Like I said, everyone was kind of awful to me, but not her. She would smile at me in the halls.

"When Roach told me his plan, I couldn't believe he would want to hurt Alorah. I knew he didn't like her, but hurt her? I just couldn't believe it. At first, I wasn't too worried, because she wasn't supposed to be there. I overheard her telling someone she had to babysit her little brother that night."

Bill's gaze shifted to Rodney, who looked ill.

"But to be safe, I left a note in her locker. I told her to stay away from the homecoming dance. I don't know if she saw it, or maybe she didn't pay any attention to it. Either way, it didn't work.

"When the dance started, everything began to fall apart. Roach and I were hiding in the back. I was watching people come in, keeping an eye out, while he was getting things ready. That's when I saw her come in. I panicked. She wasn't supposed to be there. I knew I had to warn her, so I told him I needed to use the bathroom, and I slipped away to find her, to warn her. But Roach found her first."

Twenty-Seven

"What do you mean 'Roach found her first?'" Rodney asked. Nylon dug into his palms, turning them white as he gripped the seatbelt.

Night had crept in, only a faint slip of gold remained against the deep blue sky. Bill fidgeted in his seat as they waited. Chrissy had never heard the man speak so much in one shot, and his voice was beginning to grow rough. With use or regret, she wasn't sure.

What she was sure of, amidst all this chaos, was that this had turned into something much bigger than she expected. All she ever wanted was to prove spirits were real, but her relentless pursuit only seemed to create a whole heap of problems. Her boyfriend left her (good riddance), her relationship with her parents was strained, she would likely lose her home, and she uncovered the truth that one of her friends was a murderer. At what point did it stop being worth it?

Bill resumed plucking at the loose stitching and picked up his tale.

"I looked for Alorah all over the place until a chaperone spotted me and asked to see my ticket. I tried to make some excuse, but they threw me out. By the time I was able to sneak back in, Roach had found her and... Well, I don't know exactly what he did, but I found her in the hallway outside the bathroom. She had been crying. I told her she needed to leave, that something bad was going to happen. She smiled at me. I remember that so clearly, her red, puffy eyes and that sweet, sad smile. She told me it was alright, that she'd already dealt with it. I didn't know what she meant. I begged her to go. She said she would think about it. I begged some more, and I finally thought I got through to her. She said the night couldn't be salvaged anyway, so she might as well go home. I watched her head towards the exit. I thought she left."

"But she didn't," Chrissy said.

Bill shook his head and stared out the window. "No. I don't know if she just said what I wanted to hear, or if she changed her mind. Doesn't matter. She went back in, and I..."

He twisted his fingers into tight knots in his lap, the popping of knuckles filling the heavy silence. Chrissy watched Rodney from the corner of her eye, noting the rigid lines etched into his face as he grappled with these new bombshells. Each word from Bill's mouth hit him like a sledgehammer, striking one devastating blow after another. The truth of Bill's role in the fire shook her to the core, but it was nothing compared to the torment Rodney must be going through.

"I was pissed off," Bill said. "When I made my way back into the gym and saw his smug face, I knew he had done something to her, so I confronted him. He laughed in my face. He knew she would be there, he said, that that was the whole point. Then, he called me a stupid, lovesick puppy, that she would never give me the time of day.

"I didn't say anything. I had gotten her to leave the school. She would be safe, and afterward, she would thank me for saving her life. I was still pissed, but I kept quiet. I realized he was no better than the rest of them. So when he said it was time, I decided he needed to learn a lesson, too. And I did something that has haunted me every single day of my life."

"What did you do?" Chrissy asked, her stomach sinking as the horrible truth started falling into place.

"I was supposed to go and lock the doors to the gym, leaving him to light the fire and leave through the emergency exit. The toggles on the main doors had already been flipped and would lock as soon as I shut them. But when I slipped out through the emergency exit, I barricaded it so he wouldn't be able to escape either."

"You what?" Rodney exploded, unable to contain his outrage any longer. "You're the reason so few people made it out. All their deaths are on you, you piece of shit!"

"Don't you think I know that?" Bill sobbed. "I was so focused on getting back at Roach for hurting Alorah, I wasn't thinking straight."

"Why didn't you stop him? You could have stopped him," Rodney said, trembling with rage.

"No one would have listened to me, and he was my friend. If I turned him in, I would have nobody."

Time stretched on for what felt like ages. Tension and grief soured the air. Rodney was pulled so tight, he was almost vibrating. She wanted to do something, anything, to help, but there was nothing she could do to take away the pain and betrayal.

A sharp ache filled her chest. Everything had fallen apart. Her team — her future — was crumbling right in front of her. She needed to keep it together, keep everything in control, because it was obvious neither Rodney or Bill were in any shape to. Right then, she wanted to shove it all into one of her precious little boxes and push it away, not have to think about it, but that strategy wasn't working any more. There were too many boxes and not enough space. Still, she wished someone else would take over so she wouldn't have to deal with any of this.

Her phone rang, snapping her out of her little pity party. She moved to silence it but saw Bev's name on the screen.

"It's Bev." She accepted the call. "Hello?"

"Chrissy, what happened? Is everyone alright?" Concern laced her words.

"Not really," Chrissy said, unable to hide her surprise. "How did you know?"

"I had a strange interaction with Alorah. It was difficult to understand her, but she made it clear that I should call you."

"There was another...incident at the school." Her eyes darted up to glance at Bill in the rear-view mirror.

"What kind of incident?"

The van was a tinderbox. Unsure of how much to reveal with everyone on the verge of igniting, she opted for less. "Um, Roach was there. And Alorah. She told us to run."

Bev made a *tsk*ing sound on the other end. "I think I need to hear more about this incident. It might give me a better idea of what we're going up against. Can you and your team come to my house and tell me what happened? It's late, but if we're going to do this, I need to understand what Roach is capable of. We can decide where to go from there."

"We'll be there in twenty."

Chrissy ended the call and sank back into the threadbare seat. For a moment, she paused, drawing in deep, steadying breaths to anchor herself. She could feel Rodney and Bill's expectant gazes on her, but she didn't speak. With a deft twist of the keys, the familiar growl of the engine filled the cabin, and she flipped the Ghostmobile around, pointing it back towards Merlin.

"Well?" Rodney asked.

"We're going to Bev's." Her eyes settled on Bill in the rear-view mirror once more. "She needs to know everything."

The small living room felt extra crowded with the whole team inside. They were joined by Sam Cleeves, who Bev had asked to be present. The warm light from the lamps enveloped the space, shielding them from the darkness outside. The atmosphere was uneasy, with curious glances cast between them.

"Sam knows everything about the school," Bev explained once everyone had found a place to sit. "He has a unique connection to the building, and I believe his expertise will come in handy."

Sam offered a bashful smile. "Bev here has gone ahead and filled me in on some of the things you kids have been dealing with. I gotta say, I'm very sorry about the whole thing. If I'd had any idea...but then, I don't spend all that much time inside the place these days."

"You don't need to apologize," Chrissy said, eyeing the members of her team, irritation playing across her features. "You didn't know we had so many personal connections here."

"I'd say not. I still can't believe it," Sam chuckled. "Little Roddy Smith. Your father and I were friends long ago. You sure have grown up. And Gary, I apologize for not recognizing you. I don't believe I knew you too well back then, I'm afraid."

Bill gave a small shrug, keeping his head down. "No, sir."

"Sam," Chrissy said, steering the conversation back to the purpose at hand, "you've been living near the school ever since it burned down, right? Why were you never affected by the nightmares?"

"I can answer that," Bev cut in. "I've explained to Chrissy the attachments that the spirits have to the school, about how strong emotional ties have kept them bound there. Emotions are an extremely powerful force. I've always believed the nightmares never affected Sam because of the love he has for the school."

"And here I thought it was because of my insomnia."

Bev indulged him with a smile before focusing to the other three in the room.

"Now, I'm going to need you to tell me what happened tonight, without leaving out a single detail. My approach to this process hinges on knowing as much about the individual spirits as possible, so if we want to be successful, I need to know everything they're capable of."

All eyes settled on Chrissy. Rubbing her palms on her thighs, she launched into what she knew, going over every event in meticulous detail, from her own nightmares, to the team's experiences with Alorah and Roach, to discovering the contents of Alorah's locker. She paused, allowing space for Bill to jump in and explain his own part of the story and the role he played in the fire, but his eyes didn't budge from where they were boring holes in his own shoes. When he showed no sign of speaking up, Chrissy recounted everything Bill revealed to them in the van, sparing no detail. She came to the end, and it felt as though all the air had been sucked from the room. Attention shifted to Bill, who remained hunched under the weight of his own guilt.

"Is this true?" Sam asked, betrayal evident in his voice.

Bill's silence was his only answer.

A shadow crossed Bev's face, and her eyes narrowed to twin daggers, landing on the top of his lowered head. "We'll deal with you later. For now, we have to decide how to proceed with Alorah and Roach. Now that we know Roach is tied not only to the building, but also to Bill, it will be much more difficult to talk him into leaving."

"Forgive me for asking, but how is this all supposed to go down?" Rodney broke his silence. After having to endure the story of his sister's last hours for a second time, he sounded stripped bare, raw and exhausted. "I just don't understand what it is you can do to convince ghosts to leave."

"What your sister and Roach did tonight, making themselves visible, takes vast amounts of energy. It's only possible for short periods and leaves the spirits weak, but they don't need to draw as much energy with people like me. I can hear them without the aid of any gadgets. I'm able to have longer conversations with them and relay messages between our side and theirs."

"Like a translator," Sam said.

Rodney's brows furrowed. "So, we're going to waltz into the school and, what? Talk the ghosts into leaving? And you expect me to trust that whatever comes out of your mouth is coming from my sister?"

"How can you be so stubborn?" Chrissy asked. "After everything you've seen, everything I've told you-"

"Just because you've bought into whatever crap this lady has told you doesn't mean I have to. She may have convinced you that you're psychic, but it's a bridge too far for me."

Stung by his remarks, Chrissy launched to her feet and opened her mouth to defend herself, to defend Bev, when the other woman put up a hand.

"It's alright, honey. He has every right. You don't have to believe me, Rodney, but your sister is tied here, and we need to figure out why. The only way we'll be able to do that is if we speak with her. Whatever is keeping her here, she needs to let go. I've asked her to in the past, but she wasn't ready. However, if she speaks to you, I think we might be able to get to the bottom of it and help her move on."

Chrissy watched Rodney with a mix of anticipation and unease, her gaze tracing the subtle shifts in his expression as he eyed Bev. After what seemed like an eternity, he offered a grudging nod. A small sigh of relief slipped from Chrissy's lips, but she still bristled at his complete lack of faith in her. Even now, after everything he had seen, he remained skeptical about the things she experienced, and it hurt.

"Now, Alorah will be the easy part," Bev continued, addressing the group once again. "Roach is a whole other matter. That boy is a font of deep anger, and he's using that anger to influence Bill, the same as he used it when he was alive. Somehow, the bond between the two of them needs to be severed."

"How do we do that?" Chrissy asked.

"That depends on Bill."

Snapping his head up, Bill stared with saucer-wide eyes at her. "Depends on me how?"

"You're going to have to have it out with him. You need to break the hold he has on you. I can't tell you how; that's on you to figure out. But he'll never move on if he thinks he still has an ally here."

"I'm not sure I can do that," Bill mumbled.

"Well, you're going to have to." Bev's face was stern and unwavering. "What you did is inexcusable. If we didn't need you to get rid of Roach, I'd have carted you down to the police station by now. As it stands, you have to try to make some atonement for what you've done. Severing ties is the first step."

"What's the next step?" Chrissy asked.

"Once all connections are severed, it will be on me to talk him into going. Without any physical ties, and without Alorah to torment, I may be able to convince him there's nothing left for him here. If I'm successful and he chooses to leave peacefully, it's only a matter of cleansing and healing the space. That's where Sam comes in."

"And if you're not successful?" Rodney interjected, his tone still weaved with doubt.

"There are some banishment rituals I can try, and if all else fails, I can call in some help. I have some connections who have experience with stubborn entities. Normally, they deal with demonic forces, but as I said, that would be the worst-case scenario."

Chrissy's stomach tightened, squeezing into a hard ball. She couldn't shake the nagging doubts gnawing at her, wondering if they were equipped to handle the task at hand. True, Bev claimed she knew what she was doing and would guide them through it, but there was always a chance it wouldn't work, especially since they had to rely on Bill to cut ties with Roach. She wasn't sure he could do it. She wasn't even sure he was sorry about the hand he played in the deaths of all those students. When he relayed his story, his remorse had seemed genuine at first. But the way he spoke about Alorah, about how grateful she would be that he had saved her, didn't sit well, and she was beginning to have doubts.

In addition, he had barricaded the doors in order to punish Roach. If he could do that to his only friend, what was to stop him from turning on them? She tried to reconcile the two versions of Bill — the strange, angry boy who willingly participated in a heinous act, and the shy, quiet man who never said an unkind word — and found she couldn't do it.

"If we're all in agreement," Bev said, "let's plan on meeting at the school tomorrow, late afternoon. Does that work for you, Sam?"

The old man, who had quietly been staring at Bill with a frown, turned his attention to Bev. "Late afternoon it is."

With a nod that settled the matter, Bev stood, her eyes drifting over each member of the party before landing once more on Bill.

"Get some sleep. We're all going to need it."

TWENY-EIGHT

THEY HAD A PLAN. Chrissy tried to find some comfort in that, but the task ahead bogged her down as their little trio made their way back to the van. So much of this plan depended on others: Bill's ability to cut ties, Alorah's willingness to move on, how Roach would react to everything. She had no control over any of it. And what was *her* role? A bitter thought came to her. If the rest of them went to the school without her, the outcome would be the same as if she was with them. She couldn't even be in charge of filming the encounter, since she promised Rodney there would be no cameras. She felt a little lost and a lot useless.

Inside the van, Rodney faced Chrissy. "Now what?"

"I guess we do what Bev said and try to get some rest," she replied, exhaustion dulling her voice.

"Yeah, but what do we do about him?" He jerked his head towards the back where Bill sat.

"What do you mean?"

"Well, we can't just leave him alone. Who's to say he's not going to run off or something?"

Chrissy half turned in her seat. "He wouldn't do something like that. Would you, Bill?"

"He had no issue running away after murdering a bunch of kids," Rodney said before Bill could reply.

Nobody spoke. Instead, Chrissy started the van and pointed it in the direction of the hotel. As the homes sped past, illuminated by the sodium glow of the streetlights, she asked herself what they were going to do about Bill. No way could they let this go without reporting it to someone. She didn't know what consequences he would face, if there was a statute of limitations on something like that, but she didn't imagine he'd be a free man for much longer.

Though they had only been working together for a year, she had come to see Bill as part of her family. Could she really turn him in? Of course, she would have to. While he hadn't set the fire himself, he was the one to lock the doors, making it impossible for most of the students to escape in time. She didn't want to think of him as a murderer, but it wasn't too far from the truth.

Bill wrenched the door of the van open as soon as they pulled into the parking lot of the hotel, jumping out before it was in park. Chrissy and Rodney watched him trudge towards the entrance.

"I can't believe I have to stay in the same room as him," Rodney said.

"It's not going to be easy, but we need to keep an eye on him until tomorrow. Once Alorah and Roach have moved on, we'll go talk to the police."

"You mean the ones who brushed the whole thing under the rug?"

"It was twenty-two years ago. I doubt anyone from back then is still on the force." Chrissy reached out and hesitantly took one of Rodney's hands, giving it a gentle squeeze. "I know this is hard for you. Is there anything I can do?"

"I just want it to be over with," he said, letting his hand rest in hers a moment longer before sighing and scrubbing at his face. "I'd better head up and make sure he hasn't ducked out on us."

He opened the door and hopped out. He gave a small jerk of his head, and she jumped down, coming around to his side of the van. Taking her hand in his own, they made their way to the second floor.

Outside Chrissy's room, he stopped and turned to face her. The toll of the last few days was written on every contour of his face. The planes seemed harsher, the lines around his eyes deeper. A few days' worth of scruff covered his jawline. Even his eyes, normally so playful and vibrant, appeared sunken and dull. It was the first time since she had met him that he looked his age.

"Listen, Chrissy, I don't know what's going to happen tomorrow. I'm still not sure I believe Bev will be able to talk to Alorah and help her move on. Hell, I'm not sure I believe everything that's happened, and I've seen it with my own two eyes. No, don't say anything, let me finish. Whatever *does* go down tomorrow, I want to make sure we're on the same page regarding Bill. He has to pay for what he did to my sister and all those other kids. I know he's our friend — *was* our friend — but we can't let him get away with what he did, no matter how many years ago it happened. I need you to be on my side here."

"I am. I swear, the moment we wrap up at the school, we'll take Bill straight to the police station."

Rodney studied her face. "Why are you doing this?"

"What do you mean?"

"I mean, there isn't going to be a camera rolling, no footage for the show. You never knew Alorah. You don't have any reason to be so invested."

Chrissy furrowed her brow, the corners of her mouth drawn down. "You really think I'd give up on this because I couldn't use it in the show?"

"Kinda? Not that I'd blame you," he rushed on. "You've got a lot riding on this. But you've been so focused on the show, I kind of thought you'd lose interest if you couldn't get anything out of it."

"Well, shows what you know." She took a step back and moved to swipe her key card, but he placed a hand on her wrist, stopping her.

"That came out wrong. I'm just dealing with a hell of a lot right now. We all are, I know, but I don't even believe in this ghost crap, and now I'm seeing my dead sister who I haven't thought of in years, and people are telling me I need to talk to her so she can leave me again, and the guy I thought was one of my good friends turns out to be responsible for her death."

He stopped, exhaling sharply through his nose.

"I know. It's not fair, and I wish it didn't have to be this way. But as to why I'm still going through with this? I care about your sister. Maybe it sounds weird, but I do. I want to help her, and...I want to help you."

A smile she hadn't seen in what felt like ages appeared on his face. "You're a good kid, Chris."

Chrissy rolled her eyes and gave his shoulder a playful shove. "I'm not a kid."

"No. You're not."

A flush spread across Chrissy's cheeks and she turned away, flipping the key card over in her hand. "We'd better rest up. You've got to make sure Bill stays put and figures out his part."

"Don't remind me."

Swiping her key, she met his gaze. "Night, Rodney."

With a quick step forward, he closed the gap between them, pressing his lips to hers. A fluttering sensation shot up from her stomach and into her chest, the gentle pressure of his lips on hers somehow simultaneously quieting her thoughts and flooding her brain with a rush of emotions. They stayed that way for several moments until he broke away.

"Night, Chrissy. See you tomorrow."

She kept her eyes on him as he walked the few steps to his adjacent room and disappeared inside. With so many uncertainties, she didn't know what tomorrow would bring, but she held on to a flicker of hope. Ducking into her own room, she fell asleep, concerns about the show not crossing her mind once.

Twenty-Nine

A deep, guttural roar echoed through the darkness, followed by a series of loud pops and crackles. Heat radiated from every direction, and Chrissy tossed and turned, trying to find some relief from the raising temperature. At last, she managed to pry her eyes open, only to discover she was surrounded by flames. The heat was excruciating. It felt as though her skin was roasting, peeling away from her flesh as it bubbled up into great oozing blisters. Sweat poured down her face and neck. Her hair stuck to her skin. The acrid scent of burning wood and plastic filled her nostrils, forcing the air from her lungs in whooping coughs.

Keeping to the center of the bed, she scrambled to her knees and searched for a way out. The room was engulfed in flames, the walls and ceiling nothing more than smoldering embers. Everywhere she looked, the inferno raged on, consuming everything in its path. But as the fire licked hungrily at the edges of the mattress, something chipped away at her fear. Something was wrong.

A sudden, loud popping drew her attention. Her eyes darted up, certain the sound was one of the load-bearing walls buckling. Soon, the roof would crash through the ceiling and crush her to a pulp. But the walls were still standing, the ceiling intact.

She circled her thoughts back to what felt so wrong about the situation when it suddenly hit her. *Nothing had changed.* Despite the overwhelming heat, the flames did no more than lap at the edges of her bed, like waves on the beach. The sheets bore no scorch marks, the comforter hadn't ignited into a toxic fireball of synthetic batting and polyester.

Once the realization clicked into place, her breathing came easier. Her pulse slowed, and she squinted her eyes against the white-hot inferno, trying to see through it.

"It isn't real," she muttered to herself.

As if on cue, all the heat drained out of the room as the flames snuffed out, revealing everything just as it had been hours ago when she fell asleep.

"Nice try, Roach," she said to the empty room. Although everything seemed to be normal, she was rattled and it came through in her voice. "Really cool trick, but it's not going to work."

The sheer curtains drawn across the window flew away from the wall, snapping into the room. The temperature plummeted, chilling Chrissy's sweat-drenched skin. A shiver crawled up her back.

"You can't scare me off. Tomorrow, we're going to deal with your sorry ass."

The curtains snapped once more before falling limp against the window. She peered around the room, trembling as the adrenaline began to wear off. Her eye caught on the desk on the other side of the room. On top sat one of the audio recorders. She leapt from the bed and crossed the room, snatching the recorder. The air still carried a chill that sent her exposed flesh into goosebumps, and she hurried back to the bed, wrapping herself in the warmth of the blankets.

After hitting the record button, she set the device on the bedside table next to her and settled against the headboard. The small red light of the recorder glared brightly in the dark room, an unblinking eye keeping watch.

Audio Transcript

[00:04] CHRISSY: I see you're having a bit of trouble keeping it up, Roach. Your little tricks taking too much energy?

[00:04] [STATIC]

[00:05] CHRISSY: You just keep it up, douchebag. We all know who you are and what you are.

[00:05] [Loud knocking]

[00:05] CHRISSY: Oh, I'm so scared.

[00:07] CHRISSY: What the hell...

[00:08] [Sound of footsteps]

[00:09] CHRISSY: Nope. Not going to work, Roach.

[00:10] UNKNOWN MALE: [Unintelligible]

[00:12] CHRISSY: Have you given up? Going to let me get some sleep now?

[00:12] CHRISSY: Great. Thank you.

[00:34] [High-pitched audio feedback]

[00:34] CHRISSY: [Screaming]

[00:34] CHRISSY: Holy crap, that was loud.

[00:35] CHRISSY: Alright, note to whoever listens to this: Um, the audio recorder just woke me up with some crazy feedback. It's never done that before. So, uh...yeah. I don't know if that was another one of his weird tricks, or if the device malfunctioned, but...yeah, like I said, it's never done anything like that before. Anyway...I'm going to try to get some sleep again.

[00:37] UNKNOWN MALE: ...all the same...

[00:38] CHRISSY: Goodnight, Roach.

[00:38] UNKNOWN MALE: Fuck you.

[01:06] UNKNOWN MALE: Get out.

[01:29] UNKNOWN MALE: [Screaming]

[01:51] UNKNOWN MALE: Get...out.

[02:15] [Sound of footsteps]

[02:28] CHRISSY: [Moans]

[02:28] UNKNOWN MALE: [Unintelligible] Alorah.

[03:03] UNKNOWN MALE: All you bitches...

[03:05] UNKNOWN MALE: Gonna pay.

[03:05] AUDIO ENDS

THIRTY

SOMEONE WAS POUNDING ON Chrissy's door.

"Knock it off, Roach." She yanked the covers over her head.

The pounding didn't stop. Throwing the blanket off, she looked around the room with sleep-heavy lids. The muted light filtering through the sheer curtains told her the sun was just beginning to rise. It couldn't be any later than six, and the person at her door still wouldn't let up.

"I said knock it off!" she yelled.

"Chrissy, it's me. Open up."

The sound of Rodney's voice set her in motion, and she spilled out of bed, getting tangled in the sheets as she stumbled for the door and pulled it open. An extremely pissed off Rodney greeted her.

"Bill's fucking gone. Again."

He stormed into the room and began pacing up and down, his lips pressed into a white line. Chrissy followed his movements with a blank expression, not sure she'd heard him correctly.

"He's gone? What do you mean *he's gone*?"

"I tried to stay awake all night to make sure he didn't pull a vanishing act, but I passed out. Sometime in the last," he glanced at his watch, "two hours, the bastard snuck out and left."

"No. He wouldn't. He wouldn't do that. He promised he wouldn't." Chrissy was rambling, but she couldn't seem to stop. They'd had it all planned. They were about to end this whole thing, and now, the most important part of the plan had wandered off. Again.

"Well, he did."

"Did you check everywhere?" She pushed past him out into the hall, her head whipping back and forth as she searched for Bill. She went to the adjacent room, rushing inside as soon as Rodney unlocked the door. She pulled open the bathroom door, even throwing the shower curtain aside to see if he might be hiding behind it. Finding nothing, she sank onto the bed and dropped her head into her hands.

He really was gone.

Heavy breaths followed Rodney across the room as he resumed his pacing. She tried to conjure up the same anger inside herself, but all she felt was overwhelming despair. They had one shot at ending this, and Bill had up and disappeared, destroying their chance to set things right.

"Maybe he went for another walk?" she suggested, not at all believing it.

"I doubt it. If you were caught after twenty-odd years and someone forced you to face your past, knowing it would land you in jail, would you just let it happen? No. He bolted. It's all my fault. I knew I shouldn't have gone to sleep." He slammed a hand on the desk.

"Stop. You can't blame yourself for this. You were exhausted. We both expected him to do the right thing, but I guess the Bill we thought we knew, the one who would have done the right thing, doesn't actually exist."

Rodney stopped pacing and dropped onto the bed beside Chrissy, the mattress creaking under him. They sat, each absorbed in their own thoughts, the old air conditioning unit humming in the background. Her gaze wandered aimlessly around the room before landing on the watercolor ducks on the wall, tracing the curve of the wings as the reality of the situation sank in.

"Well, shit," Rodney finally said.

"I guess we could drive around looking for him," she offered half-heartedly. "I mean, I don't think we'd find him, but it might be worth a try."

"Nah. Wherever he went, he's going to be impossible to find. I say we go straight to the police and tell them everything that's happened."

"We don't have any proof," she said. "Besides, if we bring in the cops now, we'll probably be there all day, and we don't have time for that. We still need to go to the school and try to move Alorah on, with or without Bill's help."

"What's the point? I mean, listen, if what Bev says is true — and it's a big if — then it's possible my sister is somehow keeping this Roach guy from getting too out of control. If she goes and Roach doesn't, what will happen to this place? Maybe it's better for everyone if we just leave Alorah here."

Chrissy stared at him, eyes wide with disbelief. He refused to meet her gaze.

"You wouldn't do that to your own sister. You can't."

He raked his fingers through his hair. "No, I wouldn't. I've spent too long running from her. I'm going to have to deal with it eventually, so might as well be now. But it's going to suck, dude. Big time."

"I know." She took his hand, running her thumb across the rough skin of his knuckles. "But right now, we need to decide what we're going to do about Bill."

"Well, I'm not going to be able to get any more sleep with him God knows where. Might as well try driving around, see if we can find him. It's better than sitting around the room all day."

Chrissy agreed and got to her feet, pulling Rodney up with her. "Sounds like a plan. And I can tell you all about the visitor I had in my room last night."

"Wait, wait, wait. You're telling me that freaking kid is going after you now?"

Chrissy finished filling Rodney in on the noises and dreams she dealt with during the night. White lines on the pavement blurred past in a slow, hypnotic rhythm as the van traveled aimlessly through the neighborhoods surrounding Merlin High. They'd been driving for the last hour, scanning the area for any sign of Bill, to no avail.

"Kid's got balls, I'll give him that. But what does it all mean? Do you think he was messing with Bill last night, too? Maybe that's why he ran off. Roach convinced him to leave."

Chrissy shrugged and came to a stop at an intersection, checked both directions for oncoming traffic, and made a left turn.

"It's possible. All I know is it got so bad last night, I set up a recorder to see if it would catch any of what was going on. I'm a little nervous to listen to it, to be honest."

"I'll listen to it with you, if you want."

Chrissy offered him a grateful smile. "That would be great. Who knows, maybe he said something on the recording that might help us track down Bill, or anything in general that will help us get rid of him."

Rodney slung his arm out the open window and tapped a beat against the side of the door as they circled the neighborhood. Houses flashed past, but there was still no sign of Bill.

"This is pointless," he said after several more minutes. "I bet he's already left town or is holed up somewhere. We're not going to find him out here."

Reluctantly, Chrissy nodded and pulled over to the side of the narrow road they had been heading down, making a U-turn to head back towards the heart of Merlin.

"So what are we going to do?"

She adjusted the rear-view mirror. "What do you mean?"

"When we get to the school. What are we going to tell Bev? Do you think she'll want to call it off? She made it pretty clear we needed Bill to make the whole thing work."

"I don't know."

"Maybe we should call her and tell her what happened."

"I'd rather not." Chrissy paused. "I'm still hopeful Bill will turn up before we have to head over there this afternoon."

Rodney snorted but didn't say anything more on the subject.

The morning had grown warm and muggy. Chrissy turned the air conditioning knob on and was met with a blast of hot, dust-scented air. She fiddled with the settings. When it continued blowing hot, she gave up and cranked her window down.

"Will you tell me about Alorah?" she asked as a warm gust blew across the cab.

Rodney shifted in his seat and stared out at the passing scenery.

"What's there to tell? She was my sister. I was ten when the fire happened. I don't have too many memories of her."

"Why have you never mentioned her before?"

He raised a shoulder. "Like I said, I didn't really know her that well."

"Rodney, you have to talk about this. Bev is going to make you dig into it in a few hours. You can't pretend that it's nothing. It won't help Alorah," Chrissy said as gently as possible.

"I know." He took a deep breath. "I've been pretending it's nothing almost my whole life. But the truth is, I've always blamed myself for what happened to her. Pretty sure my parents do too."

Taking her eyes off the road for a moment, she cast a sidelong glance at him. "Why do you say that?"

"She was supposed to be watching me. When our parents told her she couldn't go to the homecoming dance because she had to babysit me, she was pissed. She begged them to let her go, but they couldn't change their plans. I wasn't happy about it either. I threw an absolute fit over it. I didn't think I needed a babysitter; I was ten years old. I could take care of myself.

"The night of the dance, my parents were trying to head out the door and I flipped out. I mean, I was a complete little shit. I screamed at them, saying I wouldn't let Alorah babysit me. I'd wreck the house, I'd make their life a living hell. Like I said, complete little shit. When they gave in, I think it was more to shut me up so they could get on the road on time. They said as long as she came home by ten o'clock, she could go to the dance, and I could watch myself." Leaning forward, he dug his palms into his eyes. "I played *Crystal Castles* on the Atari while my sister burned."

"Jesus, Rodney."

"So, yeah, that's why I don't like to talk about her."

She had no idea what to say, how to respond to something like that. For him to have carried so much guilt for so long...

"I'm so sorry," she said at last, knowing how pathetic and inadequate her words were. "But it's not your fault. You didn't know what was going to happen. You couldn't have known."

"Yeah."

The heavy burden he had been carrying settled on her own shoulders as she drove. Neighborhoods were replaced by office parks and chain restaurants as they neared the city's center. It was critical, now more than ever, for them to go to the school and help Alorah move on, not just for Alorah's sake, but for Rodney's, too. He couldn't continue living life feeling responsible for his sister's death. She refused to let that be his future, and she silently vowed she would find a way to end everything at Merlin High that afternoon.

As she turned down the road their hotel was on, Rodney slapped his hand repeatedly against the side of the van, yelling at her to stop. He threw the door open, and she slammed on the breaks with a startled yelp.

"What the hell? What are you-"

He fumbled with his seatbelt, swearing as he tried to unlatch it, and finally spilled out of the van. Shifting into park, Chrissy stared as he ran full tilt down the sidewalk. Her eyes darted further up the block in the direction of where he was running, and her heart did a little flip in her chest as she realized what had set him off. Scrambling out of her own seat, she took off after him, hoping she would be able to stop him before he beat the living hell out of Bill.

Thirty-One

"RODNEY!" CHRISSY YELLED, HER lungs burning as she sprinted down the street. "Don't hurt him! Don't kill him!"

The scene before her unfolded in an odd mixture of slow motion and jumps. Bill turned, and the look of surprise on his face would have been comical if not for the fact that Rodney was bearing down on him with murderous rage. One moment, he was sprinting full force, the next, his arms were thrown around Bill's broad torso, causing him to stagger backwards. Chrissy's legs churned beneath her, the sound of her sneakers slapping the pavement echoing off the surrounding buildings, as she raced to stop the two men from seriously injuring each other.

Rodney's fist flew first, catching Bill at the base of his jaw. Teeth snapped together with a sickening *clack* as his head shot back. He stumbled, hands raised in defense as Rodney landed another attack, this time sending a fist directly into Bill's stomach. All the wind rushed out of the large man, and he curled over on himself. As Rodney reeled back for another blow, Chrissy gripped him by the arm and pulled him away.

"Stop it! Stop it!" Her voice was a thin scream that Rodney didn't seem to register.

She tried dragging him away, but it was like touching a live wire. He was all anger and rage, jerking every which way, eyes laser focused on Bill, who was still doubled over, trying to catch his breath.

Keeping her grip on his arm, Chrissy stepped in front of Rodney, putting herself between him and Bill. Raising her other hand, she snapped in front of Rodney's face several times until he brought his attention down to her. Once his eyes locked on her, she recoiled, the intensity of his rage now directed at her for a fraction on a second. Straightening, she shoved a finger in his face.

"Rodney, now is *not* the time."

"Let me go," he said through clenched teeth.

"Not until I know you're not going to hurt him."

"Of course I'm going to hurt him! He tried to leave."

Bill opened his mouth to speak, but all that came out was a choked wheeze of a cough. Keeping her eyes trained on Rodney, she tilted her head and raised her voice. "What was that, Bill?"

"I wasn't...leaving."

"Like hell you weren't," Rodney snapped.

"I was...coming back."

"Coming back from where?" Chrissy asked.

Pressing his palms against his thighs, Bill pushed himself up, reaching up to gingerly touch his jaw. With a wince, he pulled his fingers away and replied, "I was trying to figure out what I'm supposed to do, how I'm supposed to be of any use. I was up all night trying to figure it out. It came to me this morning, but I needed to put some things in place to make it work."

Chrissy's grip on Rodney's arm loosened, and she turned to face Bill. "You came up with an idea?"

Bill nodded.

"Well, what is it?"

"I can't tell you."

Rodney started towards Bill again, but Chrissy tightened her grip.

"What do you mean you can't?" she asked. "Did Roach come back? Is he making you do something?"

"No, it's nothing like that."

"How can we be sure?" Rodney asked. "He was messing with Chrissy all night. Who's to say he didn't tell you to do something that's going to mess everything up?"

Bill's face blanched as he looked to Chrissy. "He was in your room last night?"

"Yeah. Rodney and I were on our way back to the hotel to listen to the audio I recorded after things kicked up."

"I didn't hear anything at all last night, I swear."

"How would you even know?" Rodney asked.

"I've felt him with me from the moment I set foot back in Merlin. Believe me, I know what it feels like when he's around." Bill furrowed his brow. "But I don't know what he would be doing in your room, Chrissy. Why would he go after you when I was right next door?"

"I don't know." She felt some of the tension in Rodney's arm relax, and she released her hold on him. "Right now, that doesn't matter. We don't have a whole lot of time before we need to get to the school, and we've got to figure out our next move. Is there any way I can convince you to tell us what you have planned?"

Bill hesitated then shook his head sheepishly. "It's better if I don't."

"Fine," she said. "In that case, let's all just head back to the hotel and try to make as much of a plan as we can."

He nodded and started walking up the block towards the hotel.

"You get the van," Rodney said, staring at Bill's receding back. "I'm going to follow him, make sure he doesn't run off again."

Chewing on her lip, Chrissy's gaze darted between the two men. "Go on. Just don't hurt him."

Rodney flashed her a grim smile. "No promises there."

Jogging after Bill, he left Chrissy with the van and an uneasy feeling she couldn't shake.

By the time afternoon rolled around, Chrissy was a bundle of nerves. Rodney refused to let Bill out of his sight, so the team spent the day crammed into one room full of awkward silence and bad feelings.

They went over the audio recorded the night before. The first time Roach's voice came through, it was faint, almost muffled. Rodney turned the volume up, immediately regretting the decision when the high-pitched feedback squealed from the speakers.

"What the hell was that?" Rodney moved his jaw back and forth as he rubbed the inside of his ear.

"I couldn't figure it out last night, either. I've never had one of these recorders make a sound like that before."

They played through the rest of the audio until it shut off with a clack.

Rodney stared at her with a horrified expression. "That was going on all night."

"I didn't hear any of it, only the knocking sounds and the feedback."

"I'm not super stoked he was in there with you all night."

"Hey, neither am I."

"What did he say at the end?" Bill asked. He had stayed quiet since they returned, keeping mostly to the chair in the corner. The wood creaked under his weight as he shifted forward.

Rodney shot him a dirty look from the edge of the desk where he perched, then went back to ignoring him.

Chrissy couldn't help but feel for Bill. Yes, he had done something heinous, but he had also come back. He claimed to have a plan of some sort to help put an end to Roach's reign of terror. He knew what his future held, but he didn't run away. It seemed he was willing to try and face his past and the consequences that followed.

As she observed him, his head lowered and hands clasped in front of him, the last year together flashed through her mind. The team had been so solid. They were going places. It was a struggle at times, sure, but they were all so committed to making *Othersiders* a success. After today, there would be no more *Othersiders*.

She tried to push the negativity aside, but the fact was, nothing would be the same after that afternoon. They would be returning home one member short, with no funds to find a cameraman half as good as Bill, and to top it all off, they would have no usable footage for the show. The entire trip had been one giant disaster. Oh, how she wished she had listened to Rodney in the first place and never come to Merlin.

But was that the truth? If they hadn't come, Rodney would never have been given the chance to say goodbye to his sister. Nobody would know the truth about the fire, and they wouldn't be able to heal from the scars the past left behind.

Also, she thought, allowing a small smile to cross her lips for the first time that afternoon, she wouldn't have realized how deeply she cared about Rodney.

A soft *ping* broke through her muddled thoughts, and she looked down at her phone.

"Bev says it's time," she said after reading the text message.

Rodney slapped his knees and stood. "Well then, let's get this over with."

Anticipation and anxiety hung in the air so thick, Chrissy could almost taste it. Her pulse thrummed in her veins and her temples pounded. Rodney gripped the steering wheel in both hands, laser-focused on the road as they sped towards the school.

It was entirely possible they would fail. Chrissy was all too aware of the fact. Alorah may not be ready to cross over. Worse, she might be willing to go, but Roach might not. Without Alorah to keep him in check, he could go on to wreak even greater havoc in the community.

She tapped her foot against the crusty floormats and shut those thoughts down. She couldn't afford to think that way, not now. Everything they were about to do would work. It had to.

When they arrived at the school, Bev and Sam were already waiting outside the fence. As they approached, Sam reached out and shook hands with Chrissy, then Rodney. Bill hung back, and the older man did not acknowledge his presence. The cheerful spark in his eyes held in each prior meeting was gone. There were no smiles or jovialities this time.

Bev gave a solemn nod. "I'm glad to see you all made it," she said, putting a slight emphasis on the word all that was impossible to miss. "I think we'd best get started soon. I've only been here a few minutes, but already, things are starting to feel strange."

Chrissy shot a nervous glance up at the building, its charred and broken windows staring back at the group with malice. "Strange how?"

"It's difficult to explain. The closest I can get is like when you walk into a room after an argument has taken place. There's a heaviness, a feeling you should turn around and go."

"Then maybe we *should* go," Rodney muttered under his breath.

Ignoring his comment, Chrissy turned back to Bev. "I've felt that every time we've come here."

"That makes sense. You're close to the veil, like I've said. Once we're in there, you may experience things more strongly than the rest of your team."

Chrissy lifted her chin and gathered all the confidence she could muster. "I'm ready. What's the plan?"

"First thing we'll do is contact Alorah." Her sympathetic gaze landed on Rodney. "It'll be up to you to help her make peace. Things will get heavy once we begin, I have no doubt. There's some unresolved trauma I believe the two of you need to work through before she can move on. You're going to have to let go of hurts you've held on to for too long. Do you think you can do this?"

Rodney opened his mouth, about to make a snarky comment, Chrissy was certain, but he seemed to reconsider. "If it'll help, I guess so."

Her tone lost its warmth and grew sharp as she addressed Bill. "And have you figured out what your role here is?"

"Yes."

The group stared at him, expecting him to go into detail. When he showed no signs of doing so, Sam broke the silence. "Care to elaborate, son?"

"No."

Rodney threw up his hands. "Damnit, Bill. Why the fuck not?"

"I just think it's best if I take care of it myself."

Frustration radiated from Rodney in angry waves, and Chrissy took a cautionary step forward, positioning herself between the two.

"That's fine," Bev said. "Whatever this plan is, do you believe it will help move Roach on?"

Bill let out a long breath. "I think so."

"Then we'll have to trust you'll go through with it. Remember, you won't be alone through this. I'll be facilitating the conversation between the living and the departed. As I've said, it takes a great amount of energy for a spirit to manifest to the point where we can see or even hear them. I don't believe we'll be seeing or hearing much of either Alorah or Roach themselves. Instead, I'll be relaying any words they have for Rodney or Bill."

"What if they don't want to speak with us?" Chrissy asked. "Will we still be able to move them on?"

"I'm quite certain Alorah will come through. She was rather insistent last night. She knows her brother is here, and she's eager to talk to him. The real trick will be Roach." Bev pushed her sleeves up her arms and gazed up at the building. "But we'll do what we can."

Uncertainty began to creep over Chrissy. She felt it spreading out, twisting through her brain, convincing her their plan wasn't going to turn out how any of them expected.

"What if it fails?" she asked. "Or what if we can move Alorah on but Roach won't leave? Won't that just make things worse?"

"It might," Bev conceded. "But we won't think about that yet. You have to have faith in the process, honey. If it comes down to it, I'll call up that friend of mine, and he can exorcise the place."

"Whoa, whoa, whoa," Rodney said. "We're talking about exorcisms now?"

"I'm sure it won't come to that," Sam said soothingly.

"I'm sure it won't," Bev agreed.

Chrissy gazed up into the face of the school. The heaviness was there, staring back down at her. Despite the brightness of the afternoon sunlight, the windows remained dark, like sunken, hollow eyes taking in their every movement.

"Alright," Bev said, "let's get started."

THIRTY-TWO

THE BUILDING, WITH ITS doors thrown open like a gaping mouth, looked surprised to see them. Or maybe it was screaming, Chrissy thought. Poking her head through the entrance, she peered down the hallway. She didn't know what she expected to find, but the place was the same as always. Nothing moved in the shadows, no classroom doors were open, nothing made a sound.

"Where did you see Alorah before?" Bev asked, leading the group deeper into the school.

"Upstairs. Outside the ladies' room," Chrissy replied.

"Then that's where we'll start."

Bev moved towards the staircase, and the rest fell in line behind her with Bill bringing up the rear. Chrissy caught Rodney glancing over his shoulder to the back, making sure Bill was still with them and hadn't run off again. She wasn't worried. Bill had come this far and claimed to have a plan. Though curious about what that entailed, she wasn't going to press the matter. They would all find out soon enough.

Upon reaching the top of the stairs, Bev led them towards the ladies' room. She placed a palm against the door. Her lips moved, forming soundless words, and Chrissy watched with fascination as the woman recited something she couldn't make out. Once she finished, she pushed the door open and entered.

The warm sunlight that filtered through the empty windows into the hallway was snuffed out as soon as the door swung back on its hinges. Their footsteps filled the room, bouncing off the tiled floor and walls, making it sound as if their number had tripled. Chrissy's gaze swept across the dimly lit space, straining to make out the shapes of her team. Once her eyes adjusted, she could just make out their vague silhouettes. She counted them, trying to remember the order in which they had filed into the room and placing a name to each figure. The longer she stared at their outlines, the more of them there seemed to be. Squeezing her eyes shut, she tried to convince herself it was a trick of the light or her mind playing tricks.

Her head swam. She pressed her fingers into her temples to alleviate the sensation, but that only made it worse.

Sneakers squeaked out in the hall.

Her eyes flew open.

Halogen lights flared overhead, causing her to blink several times against the harsh light that seared her eyes and made them water.

"Hey, I thought the power didn't work."

No one replied.

Blinking again, she gazed around. The room was empty.

"Rodney?"

Rushing to the first bathroom stall, she shoved at the door, and it crashed open with a bang.

"Bev? Bill?

In quick succession, she moved down the line of stalls, throwing each one open. All empty.

The lights stuttered once and resumed their steady drone. Crashing through the room, she fell against the swinging door and stumbled into the hallway. Whoever she had heard moving in the halls a moment ago was nowhere to be found.

She ran to the windows, once more intact, and peered out, her breath fogging the cold glass. The sky was painted in deep shades of purple and blue as night crawled over the horizon. A car turned into the parking lot, its headlights sweeping over several small clusters of students, all dressed to the nines. Music pumped up from the stairwell, muted and obscured by the raucous laughter of a handful of teens as they entered the building.

Chrissy staggered away from the window. It was happening again. Another flashback. Why now? And where was her team? Where was Bev? Or Sam? Her brain felt fuzzy, and she needed to sit down.

But someone was coming.

Pressing herself against the wall of lockers, she trained her eyes on the top of the stairs. Having no idea what to expect, she kept as still as possible, her breaths shallow.

The ruffled hem of a pale blue dress appeared.

"No, go in without me. I've gotta grab something from my locker, but I'll be there in a sec."

Alorah rounded the corner, a vision in blue. She passed by Chrissy, satin pumps tapping a delicate cadence as she moved gracefully down the hall. Stopping at her locker, she popped it open and began to rummage around inside. With the locker open, all Chrissy could see was the voluminous ruffle on the shoulder of her dress.

Another squeak of rubber soled shoes came from behind Chrissy. Before she could turn around, Roach was there, creeping up behind Alorah. He snatched her around the waist, eliciting a startled scream.

Pressing his lips against her ear, his words come out in a hiss. "Hey, baby. You made it."

She writhed in his grasp, struggling to break his hold. "Get out of my life, creep."

He made a grotesque kissing noise and pulled back, crushing her against him.

"Get off!"

He laughed as she tried kicking at his shins and missed. "You know, you're a real pain in the ass. Everyone around here thinks you're so amazing, but I know the truth. You're nothing but a stuck-up brat who thinks she's better than everyone else."

"If you don't let go of me right now, I swear I will-"

"What? Huh? Gonna run and tell the principal on me? Like I give a shit." He lunged forward in one massive stride, driving her face into the lockers and pinning her between the cold metal and his own body. His face was right next to hers, and Chrissy recoiled, almost able to smell his hot breath herself. Alorah had gone rigid, terror flooding her eyes.

"I could do anything I wanted right now. You know that?"

She whimpered.

Grabbing the oversized ruffle of her sleeve, he tore it from the dress, a sadistic smirk spreading across his face as she emitted another soft whimper. His thick, red tongue darted out from between his lips, and he ran it up her cheek, leaving a wet trail behind.

"I could do anything I want any time I feel like it. You just remember that."

With a sudden movement, he released his grip, smashing her face into the locker as he shoved himself off her.

Alorah remained pressed against the locker. Her body trembled so violently, it caused the metal to rattle. Once the footsteps faded, she slid to the floor with a deep, gut-wrenching sob. The torn ruffle lay lifeless at her side.

Chrissy tried to move forward to go to the girl's side, but the hallway warped and blurred with each step.

"No, no, no, no, wait. Alorah!"

The girl vanished. The hall went black.

Someone gripped her shoulder.

"What's wrong with her?"

"Chrissy?"

"What the hell is going on? Chrissy, talk to me."

As soon as Rodney's hand clamped down on her shoulder, Chrissy felt as though a bucket of ice water had been dumped over her. She drew in a noisy gulp of air and spun, almost knocking Rodney down in the process.

"Easy!" He gripped her other shoulder and held her still. "It's just me."

The sound of his voice finally registered, and she realized she was back. She locked her arms around Rodney, breathing him in to anchor herself in the present. They were all there, standing in the dark restroom of an abandoned Merlin High.

"What was that all about?" Rodney asked, stroking her hair as she clung to him. "You went all stiff and started making some super freaky sounds."

"I went back again. I'm pretty sure it was the night of the dance. Of the fire."

The shadow that was Bev stepped up beside her and placed a warm palm on her back. "You're alright, honey. You're back with us now. What did Alorah show you?"

Chrissy recounted what she had seen, hating how powerless she felt, both then and now. It had been frightening, made all the more so by the fact she hadn't been able to do a thing about it. In the moment, she knew it was a flash, a memory, and she had no way of influencing the outcome, and that made it even worse. The look of sheer terror on the girl's face would remain etched in her brain for as long as she lived.

She reached the end, and Bill spoke. "That's when I found her. Why didn't she leave then? Why would she stay?"

"That poor, poor girl," Sam's voice cracked with emotion.

"Alright." Bev stepped back to the center of the room. "I think it's time we begin. It's clear Alorah is already here and telling us her story, thanks in large part to Chrissy. Now it's time to speak with her. Rodney, it's time for you to ask your sister to come forward."

Rodney cleared his throat. "Uh, does it have to be me? She seems more interested in talking to Chrissy right now."

"She can only show Chrissy the past. It's you she needs to talk to. You're the one with the strongest connection to her. And, if my suspicions are correct, that connection is part of why she's still here."

"Okay, fine. Alorah? If you're here, can you come talk to us?"

The room fell into such a deep silence, Chrissy could hear the rhythmic whooshing of her blood pulsing through the tiny veins in her ears. Unrelenting and distracting, she held her breath, trying to slow her pulse and quiet the sound as she listened for any noise that might come out of the darkness. As time stretched on, nothing came but the scuff of shoes against tile as someone shifted their stance.

"Try again," Bev prompted.

"This is pointless."

"You need to try, Rodney," Chrissy said. "She's here, I know it."

"Okay, okay." He paused for a moment before trying once more, this time sounding far more genuine. "Alorah? Please. It's me, Roddy. It would mean a lot if you'd talk to us."

Again, the group grew still, waiting for something to happen.

"She's here." Bev said.

"What?" Alarm rose in Rodney's voice.

"She's here. With us."

Sam piped up from the other side of Chrissy; she could see his silhouette looking around. "She's in here? Where?"

"I've asked her not to show herself yet. She's still weak, and there's too much to discuss." Taking a couple of small steps forward, Bev reached out and took Rodney's hands in her own. "Speak to me as if I'm Alorah. I'll be channeling her. From here on out, everything I say will be her words. I understand this may seem strange or uncomfortable, and you're not inclined to believe it, but trust in your sister. Can you do that?"

"You're my sister," Rodney scoffed.

"Yes, I'm your sister, you dingus."

Chrissy's head jerked in Bev's direction. Her voice wasn't right. The familiar honeyed, calming tone was gone, replaced by a higher, almost youthful sound.

"This is bullshit." Rodney moved to pull his hands out of Bev's grasp, but the older woman tightened her grip.

"Knock it off, Roddy. You wanted to talk, so talk."

"You really think I'm going to believe this is real?" His voice went up with each word. "You're just screwing with me, and honestly, it's super messed up."

Bev brought herself closer to Rodney, her hands still clutching his. "I'm here, okay? You want proof? I know you snooped in my room and read my diary all the time. I kept it under my bed in a shoe box. I always knew you read it because you never put the lid back on the box, and you left sticky grape soda fingerprints on the pages more than once."

He stammered, unable to form any meaningful words.

"Exactly. Now, get over yourself and talk to me."

A bubble of laughter escaped Chrissy, which she tried to stifle with the back of her hand. Bev glanced over toward her, a small smile curling the corner of her lips.

"Hey, Chrissy. Would you please tell my dork ass brother to get with it?"

"Sure thing, Alorah," she said, breaking into a grin. "Uh, Rodney? I think your sister wants you to actually talk to her."

"I mean... What do I say to her?"

"I'm right here, dumbass."

"Right," he said. "Sorry. This is too weird."

Chrissy gave him a gentle nudge. "You need to talk to her. We don't have a lot of time."

He took a deep breath. "Yeah. Alright, fine. If you really are my sister-"

"I am," Bev said with a huff.

"If you *are* Alorah, then...well, it's cool to hear from you."

"Oh my *gawd,*" Bev groaned. In spite of the dark, Chrissy could picture how far her eyes must have rolled into her head. "You're speaking to someone who's been dead for twenty-two years, and all you have to say is it's cool to hear from me? You're such a dweeb."

"Well excuse me for not knowing what to say to my dead sister."

"I dunno, how about, 'Hey, sis. I sure have missed you. Sorry you're dead.'"

Chrissy bit back another laugh. "I knew I liked you."

"Of course I've missed you, Lor. You think I didn't? Growing up without you was hell. Mom and Dad fell apart after you...after the fire. They couldn't stand to live here with the constant reminder of what happened, packed everything into the wagon and left. Not that it helped. Dad bounced a year later, and Mom never recovered." A tremble crept into his voice. "You left us, Lor. You left, and everything fell apart."

Bev softened. "I'm sorry, Roddy. I didn't want to go."

"I know."

"But you're still mad at me."

"No." Rodney sniffed. "Maybe. It's stupid to be, but yeah."

"You need to stop being so angry."

"I'm not. I'm one of the most laid-back people out there."

Bev snorted. "Yeah right. On the outside, maybe, but I can feel it. You're pissed off. At me, at Roach, at Bill, at the world. At yourself." Rodney made a sound of protest, but she shook her head. "You know I'm right. But it's time to let it all go."

"Let it go? You want me to just let go of the fact that you were murdered? And that it was my fault?"

"Oh, what*ever*. Like you had anything to do with what happened that night."

"But I did." His voice strained with emotion. "I was so mad, I told Mom and Dad I would run away if you stayed home with me. I was such a pain in the ass, they decided it wasn't worth it. If I hadn't been so horrible, they wouldn't have let you go."

"You really were a huge turd, but that doesn't make it your fault."

"If I hadn't been so awful, you wouldn't have been there. It's all because I-"

"I was going to sneak out anyway."

"You what?"

"Yeah. I was going to go to the dance either way."

"You were going to leave me alone? Alorah, I was ten!"

"See? Can't blame yourself now, can you?"

Rodney sputtered.

"I'm serious, though. It wasn't your fault. It was never your fault. And it wasn't mine, either. You need to let go of all the anger inside you. You hide behind that laid back, surfer dude vibe — which, seriously, what is *that* all about? — but I can feel how angry you are. If you don't let it go, you're going to be miserable your entire life. And even if you are a total dingus, I don't want that for you. You're my baby brother. I want you to be happy."

Nobody spoke, but Chrissy could make out quiet sniffs coming from Rodney's direction, as well as where Sam stood to her left.

"'Kay, so now that that's over," Bev said, still sounding very much like a seventeen-year-old, "what's the plan? You didn't just come for a chat, did you?"

"Well, it was one of the reasons, but not the only one, no," Chrissy admitted. "We want to help you move on from this place."

Bev snorted. "I mean, that would be rad, but I can't. Not as long as *he's* still here. If I go, there won't be anything to keep him from going completely nutso. I can't let that happen to Merlin."

Exhaustion and sorrow colored her voice, making Chrissy's heart ache for the heavy burden she had endured for so long, a burden she never should have been forced to carry in the first place.

"We're going to make him move on too."

"How do you plan on doing that?"

"That's what we'd all like to know," Rodney muttered.

"Bill has a plan." Chrissy glanced over at the large figure that had remained silent the entire time. "Don't you, Bill?"

"Yes."

When he didn't reveal anything more, Bev spoke again. "And you think it'll work? Whatever it is?"

"Yes."

"Wow. Big talker." Sarcasm dripped from Bev's lips.

"Bev told me to think on it and come up with a plan. I did."

"And you honestly, really truly, think it will work?"

"It will," Bill said without hesitation.

Bev turned to the others. "What do the rest of you think?"

Nobody said anything for a beat.

"Well," Sam weighed his words carefully, "if Beverly believed Bill could come up with a plan, I suppose I do."

Chrissy nodded. "Same."

There was a sound of annoyance from where Rodney stood.

"Roddy?"

"I'm not sure."

"Roddy, I don't think I can move on unless I know you can get rid of Roach. If you don't believe they can do it, I won't leave."

"It's kind of hard to trust the guy who murdered my sister and dozens of other kids and who has lied to us about who he is from the very beginning, ya know?"

"I get it. I mean, I'm the one who's dead. But if *I* can get over it and trust that Bill has a plan to end things, why can't you?"

Rodney let out a long, drawn-out breath. "Fine. But I don't like it."

"You don't have to like it, you just have to do it." Bev once again turned her attention to the rest of the group. "So, what do we do? How am I supposed to go?"

Sam shuffled forward. "I believe I can help with that, young lady. Beverly gave me instructions. She said you must find a way to cut every tie binding you to the school."

"Didn't I just do that? I told Roddy it's not his fault I died."

"Indeed you did. But now each one of us has to cut our own ties to *you*."

Chrissy's brows shot up in surprise. "Each one of us?"

"Beverly said we have each built our own unique connection to Alorah. We all need to release her."

"How do we do it?" Bill asked.

"You can either speak the words 'I release you,' or conjure up an image of scissors cutting through a ribbon that is connecting you to her." Sam then raised his voice. "Alorah. I'm so sorry for what you went through, both before and after the fire. I appreciate all you have done to keep this school, and Merlin as a whole, safe from that evil boy, but you are not obligated to stay. I release you."

Silent tears flowed freely down Chrissy's cheeks. In her mind's eye, she visualized a vivid, bright pink ribbon, the ethereal strands connecting her to Alorah, an invisible bond that had formed between them. With a heavy heart, she pictured a sharp pair of scissors, slicing through the ribbon and severing the tie.

Across from her, she heard Bill muttering 'I release you' under his breath. From Rodney, a silence so full of unspoken thoughts and emotions too complex, too raw to put into words.

"Have we all done it?" Sam asked, answered in the affirmative by each member of the group. "Wonderful. Alorah, it is time for you to say your goodbyes. You have been released from your ties, and you are no longer responsible for keeping Derrick Roach in check. Find peace."

"What a relief." Bev stepped forward and threw her arms around Rodney. "Thanks for coming to help, Roddy."

"Any time, sis. I'm just sorry it took so long."

Next, she turned to Chrissy and wrapped her in a hug as well. "Thank you for seeing everything. That had to have been mega weird for you."

Chrissy laughed through her tears, giving a small sniffle. "I won't lie, it's been a bit of a shock. I'm still not sure what you were trying to tell me."

"I thought you should know everything that happened, what Roach is capable of. He's dangerous."

"I can see that." Chrissy stepped out of her embrace and held her gaze. "We're going to get rid of him, I promise."

"I wish I could have known you before I died. I feel like we would totally be BFFs." She grinned, and although she knew it was Bev before her, she saw a hint of the girl sparkling behind her eyes. "Thanks for everything. Take care of my idiot brother."

"I'll do my best."

Bev turned to face Sam. "Thank you for caring and for talking to me all these years, Mr. Cleeves. And thank you for bringing Roddy back here."

Sam pulled a tissue from the depths of one of his pockets and dabbed at his eyes. "You're most welcome."

Finally, Bev stepped across to face Bill. She held his gaze for a few moments before placing a soft hand on one of his shoulders. "Gary...I forgive you, and I'm sorry it ended up this way."

Covering his face with his hands, Bill let out a single choked sob.

"Well, I guess that's about it for me. Things might get a little gnarly when I leave, I'm guessing. Roach is definitely here. He's been sticking to the other side of the school — he does *not* like me — but once I head out, who knows what he'll do. Be careful. All of you."

"We will," Chrissy said. "Thank you, Alorah."

"Love you, Lor," Rodney said softly.

"Love you too, dweeb."

A soft breeze stirred inside the bathroom, and Bev closed her eyes. For a fraction of a moment, Chrissy felt a sense of calm wash over her. As soon as the humming stopped, the atmosphere shifted. An unsettling chill worked its way from her toes to the top of her head. It was electric and altogether unpleasant.

"He's coming."

THIRTY-THREE

Bev's voice settled back into its natural cadence. "She's at peace, but we are far from done here."

Chrissy wrapped her arms around herself, attempting to rub some warmth back into her body. "This isn't going to be fun."

"No, it's not." Bev turned towards Bill. "This next part is up to you, Bill. How would you like to proceed?"

Anticipation hung heavy as they all waited to finally hear what he had planned. Chrissy could imagine him shifting, uncomfortable under their gaze, even in the dark.

"Well," he started, the word cracking with nerves. He paused to clear his throat. "I don't know where to begin. I just know how it ends."

An annoyed groan escaped Rodney's lips, cut off by the bathroom door blasting inwards. It swung violently on hinges that shrieked from the sudden force. A scream clawed its way from Chrissy's chest, joining with the startled gasps and yells from Sam and the others.

"What the hell was that?" Rodney asked.

"He knows Alorah's gone," Bev said gravely. "We'd better get started before things become-"

The piercing cacophony of shattering glass prompted another scream from Chrissy. Instinctively, she raised an arm to shield herself from the onslaught, sharp stings of glass caressing the exposed skin of her arms and face. Chaos erupted in the cramped confines of the room.

"The mirrors!" Sam yelled.

"We need to leave," Bev said.

A warm, dry hand grabbed Chrissy by the wrist and pulled her toward the door. Panic seized her as she searched the darkness with her free hand, clamoring for purchase on anyone within reach to drag them to safety. When she connected with another body, she clutched the fabric of their shirt, yanking them forward as the bathroom door swung open.

They fell out into the hallway where the sunlight filtered in, a flood of light after the dark. Rodney still had Chrissy by the wrist, and she discovered she was holding a fistful of Bill's shirt in her other hand. Blood streamed down the arm connecting her to Bill, flowing from several shallow cuts that crisscrossed her arms from the hem of her sleeve all the way down to her knuckles. She let go of him with a gasp, noticing a small red stain blooming where she gripped the fabric.

"Oh crap. I ruined your shirt."

Bill glanced down, the blood not seeming to register.

"Is everyone okay?" Bev asked.

"Chrissy and Sam got the worst of it," Rodney said, clutching Chrissy with so much force, she thought the delicate bones in her wrist might snap. But she welcomed it, as his grip was the only thing keeping her upright.

"I-I think I'm alright," Sam said, voice trembling. "I've never seen anything like that."

Wincing, Bev plucked a bit of glass out of her forearm. "I'm afraid that was only the beginning. I think it would be best if you left now, Sam."

The older man stood tall, even as blood poured from a small cut above his brow. "I came to help, and help, I shall."

Bev reached out, cradling one of his gnarled hands in her own. "You've helped already. Things are about to get dangerous. We needed you to help Alorah, and you did a wonderful job, but now it's up to Bill to finish this."

Conflicting emotions flashed behind his eyes as he looked to each of them. "I don't want to let you down."

"You should go," Bill said.

The hairs on the back of Chrissy's neck stood up, and her skin broke out in goosebumps. Dread slithered into the hallway, bringing with it a palpable chill that seeped into every corner.

"You aren't letting anyone down," she said. "But you need to go now."

The air crackled, and the rest of the group shifted, uneasy, like a herd of deer scenting a predator lurking nearby. Sam appeared to sense it as well, and that seemed to make up his mind.

"Very well, but I won't be far. I'll wait in my car at the end of the block. If anything happens..." He trailed off as he shook his head and hurried towards the stairs.

His shuffling footsteps drifted up from the stairwell and faded. It was only when the echo of the front doors shutting reached them that Bev turned her attention to Chrissy, giving her a once-over. "Are you alright to continue?"

"I'm fine. What do we do now?"

At the far end of the hall, locker doors flew open and slammed shut with a bang that echoed like gunshots. All four of them jumped. A tumultuous clash of metal against metal reverberated through the hallways. They stood frozen in place as the force moved down the rows of lockers like a wave, closing the distance with every bang.

"Well, whatever we do, I don't think it should be here," Rodney said.

"You're absolutely right," Bev said. "Follow me."

They bolted for the stairs, and Chrissy skipped every other step as she flew down, with Rodney so close behind, he stepped on the back of her boot. Her arms shot out, finding the handrail as she nearly went tumbling down the last flight.

Reaching the bottom, Bev rushed to the front doors, throwing her body into them. When they refused to budge, her movements grew frantic. She pounded on the wood, hands slapping against the door in a useless attempt to force it open.

"It won't open." Her eyes darted from the door to the stairwell.

A cold knot of fear settled into Chrissy's stomach at the fear in Bev's normally calm voice. She shot forward, adding her own weight to the door. Her legs strained as she dug in, muscles quivering with exertion as she tried to force the stubborn thing open.

"But Sam just went out through here," Chrissy said, the pitch of her voice rising along with her panic. "Sam! Sam, can you hear us?"

"Calm down, Chrissy. We can go out through one of the windows," Rodney said. "They're all busted out anyway."

The way he said it, so unruffled and confident, eased some of the tension, and she allowed him to draw her away from the doors. The empty windows beckoned, but as she reached out towards the promise of freedom, a sudden force yanked her backwards. At the same time, Rodney took a huge, stumbling step back. Spinning around, they came face to face with Bill.

"What the hell, Bill?" Rodney shouted. "What do you think you're doing? We have to get out of here."

"You can't go out that way. It's not safe." Bill cast a glance over his shoulder. "He won't let you leave."

"What do you mean?" Bev asked, her voice inching towards terror. "Is he making you do this? Is he making you stop us from leaving?"

"He isn't making me do anything. I just know him and what he's capable of."

"No, we have to go. We can't stay here. We have to leave now."

"He won't let you."

Chrissy extended a trembling hand towards Bev, her fingers hovering tentatively as she tried to calm her, though her own nerves were frayed. The building was so cold now, she could see her breath. Fear drummed a relentless beat in her chest, and the urge to turn and jump out through the window was strong, but Bev seemed to be losing her grip entirely. Sweat glistened on her forehead, mixing with the blood from her cuts, running in red rivulets down her temples as her eyes rolled wildly in her head.

"Beverly." Struggling to keep the tremors from her voice, she tried to talk the woman down. "I think we should listen to Bill. He knows Roach better than the rest of us, and he has a plan, remember?"

The woman who had been the face of strength and resilience since Chrissy had met her was crumbling before her eyes. Her hands flew up, pressed tight against her ears, as tears streamed down her face. "He's in my head. I can hear them all screaming. All my friends... They're all dead, and we will be too!"

The words sent a cold dagger through Chrissy. "No, it's going to be alright."

"I can't stay here." Bev's dark eyes met Chrissy's, pleading.

“We need you to get rid of him,” Rodney reminded her. “You helped with my sister, and now, we need your help to finish this.”

“I can’t. I’m sorry.”

Bev jerked away and made a dash for the nearest window, arms stretched forward, desperate to escape whatever torment Roach was stirring up inside her head. She threw a leg over the window frame, a manic smile spreading across her face. As she pulled herself through the frame, her grin faltered. She froze. Shards of the long-ago broken window flew upwards from where they had lain for decades on the floor and danced through the air around Bev.

Chrissy watched in horror as bits of glass, some as large as her hand, coursed through the air. They slashed through Bev's flesh, leaving jagged trails of crimson on her legs, arms, and face. Smaller, dust-sized particles joined in, adding countless tiny lacerations to the larger gashes already seeping blood.

Over and over, Chrissy screamed Bev’s name, trying to free her from the grip of shock, but she wouldn’t move.

Pushing his way into the whirlwind of glass, Bill gripped Bev around the arm, yanking her out of the window and back inside. The shards came crashing back down to the floor, motionless, and Chrissy stared down at the heap that was Bev as red rivers traced their paths across every inch of her skin.

Bill fared slightly better, but the arm he used to pull her back into the building was sliced up, blood dripping from his fingertips onto the floor below him.

“I told you," he said after a moment, shattering the silence. "He won’t let you leave.”

THIRTY-FOUR

THE SOUND THAT CAME from Bev was almost inhuman as the initial shock wore off and pain set in. Everything inside Chrissy longed to reach out and comfort the woman, but there wasn't a single inch of her body not covered in lacerations. Any touch, soothing or not, would only result in more pain.

"We have to get her out of here," she said. "She's losing a lot of blood. I wouldn't even know where to begin trying to apply pressure."

"This needs to end." Rodney said. "Bill, whatever idea you came up with, you're going to have to do it now."

Bill blanched and looked down to where Bev lay writhing on the floor. "I don't know if I can."

Rodney advanced, closing the gap between them. "Well, looks like you're going to have to. Listen, dude, I'm pissed off. You're a real piece of shit. But Bev can't help us now, not like this, so it's all on you. You didn't step up and stop Roach before, but you can now. She's going to die if you don't."

Bill's eyes glazed over. He shook his head, and for a moment, Chrissy's heart sank. He wasn't going to do it. But before despair fully set in, his head snapped up, and he met Rodney's stare.

"Fine. But you need to get her ready to move," he said, tilting his head towards Bev. "Once it starts, you'll have to leave fast."

Rodney reached out and gripped Bill's upper arm with a short nod. He turned back to face Bev. Her wails had dwindled to mere whimpers and rasping breaths that rattled each time her body trembled.

Crouching down next to her, Rodney's tone softened as he explained the situation, that she needed to get to her feet and be ready to leave. Her pain was so great, he kept having to repeat himself, gently coaxing her to start moving.

Bill set off down the left-wing corridor. Apprehension surged through Chrissy as she watched him head towards the gymnasium, swallowed by the shadows. She took a step after him, then looked down to Rodney.

"Can you manage getting her out on your own?"

He looked up, surprised, until he noticed Bill's absence. "We'll be fine. But Chrissy, you don't know what's going to happen or what he's going to do."

Bending down, she brushed her lips over his before stepping back. His face clouded over with worry, but he jerked his head in the direction Bill had gone. "Hurry."

Rows of lockers flashed past as she jogged after Bill. Every pounding beat of her heart sent a flood of adrenaline through her, going into overdrive as the warped gymnasium doors came into view. A few feet ahead of her, a classroom door flew open, and she nearly lost her balance as she came skidding to a halt. Bill appeared in the door, eyes wild with fear.

"What are you doing?"

Chrissy opened her mouth to respond, and a noxious aroma filled her nostrils, the sudden overpowering scent making her cough. He took a step closer, the smell seeming to cling to him as it wafted out of the classroom behind him.

"You need to get out of here."

"What are *you* doing?" she threw his question back at him, coughing as the gasoline began to burn the back of her throat.

"I don't have time for this."

Pushing his way past her small frame, he moved down the hall. A bright flash of red drew her eyes down to what he held in one hand. Grabbing hold of his arm, she tried to pull him back, but the large man easily broke free of her grip. He rounded on her, and she recoiled at the crazed look behind his eyes.

"You wanted me to end this, so that's what I'm going to do."

Immediately, the knowledge this was somehow Roach's doing sprung to the front of her mind. It was the only explanation that made any sense. Keeping several feet behind, she trailed after Bill as he continued sloshing the gasoline around the halls and classroom doors, trying to reason with him.

"This isn't you, Bill. You need to stop this. We can find another way out."

He shook his head. "I know what I'm doing."

"What? What on Earth is this going to accomplish?"

"I have to finish what I started."

"What you started?"

Bill upended the gas cannister, shaking the last few drops out onto the hallway floor. That was it. He was out. Time to leave. He only had a few gallons, Chrissy realized. Even if he was able to ignite it, she doubted there was enough to do much damage to the already-destroyed wing. But as she allowed herself to believe she might be able to grab him and leave, he pulled open a locker, reached in, and produced another cannister full of gas to resume his dousing of the school.

"How..." Her eyes widened. "Is this what you were doing when you disappeared this morning?"

"I told you I had to get things ready for my plan," he said tightly.

"This is your plan? You're going to burn the school down? Again?"

He cringed at her words and raised a shoulder in a half shrug but continued splashing the noxious liquid over the walls and doorways. She wasn't sure how much gasoline he had hidden around the place, but he had gone missing for quite some time. If he was as intent on destroying the school as he appeared, she could only imagine that several more cannisters were stashed throughout the building.

"Bill," she tried again, stepping over a yellow-tinged puddle, "whatever Roach is telling you to do, you don't have to go through with it. We can leave right now. You just need to stop this and come with me. Please."

Bill turned, seeming to respond to the pleading in her voice, and Chrissy sagged with relief, sure she had gotten through to him, and not a minute too soon. The gas was making her eyes burn and run. But as she peered up into his face, all her hopes came crashing down. Shifting the gas can to one hand, he reached out and placed a hand on her shoulder, staring into her face with a mixture of tenderness and grief. His own eyes blazed red from the fumes, but when he spoke, his voice was choked with emotion, and she realized the tears streaming down his face weren't caused solely by the gasoline.

"This isn't because of Roach. I've missed out on too many things — messed up too many things — because I was scared. I have a chance to put things right here, and I'm not going to screw it up just because I'm still terrified."

"But-"

"There's no way this ends well for me, Chrissy. I'm going to jail after this is over. An arson charge isn't much compared to what I have ahead of me." He gave a short laugh, which dissolved into a fit of coughs. "You need to leave. Once this starts, you need to get Rod and Bev out. I think Roach will let you, or at least he'll be too distracted by what I'm doing to put much effort into trying to stop you."

Tears slid down Chrissy's cheeks as she realized there was nothing more she could do, nothing more she could say, to get Bill to come with her and find some other way to escape. With angry resignation, she swiped at her face. Bill's smile, bittersweet and full of sad determination, was the last thing she saw before he turned his back to her and returned to his task of saturating the school.

Chrissy started down the hall back to where she left Rodney and Bev. Stopping for a moment, she called back to him. "We'll see you outside after it's all done."

Keeping his back to her, he raised a hand in acknowledgment, and Chrissy made a run for it.

Audio Transcript

The following footage was pulled from a video camera recovered from the scene. Most of the footage was distorted or destroyed in the fire. Technicians were able to pull the following audio from the recording.

[00:00:05] BILL: Uh, alright. So, this is Bill, uh...Bill Weston. I'm recording now, the morning of August 28th, 2009. This is, I don't know, part confession, part [unintelligible]. Tonight, I'm going to do something that neither Chrissy Rodriguez nor Rodney Smith are aware of. They have nothing to do with this, and I want to make [unintelligible]. I'm willing to face the consequences, but it must be known that they had nothing to do with it. I've hurt too many people, and I won't [unintelligible] for anything I do.

[00:06:12] BILL: The other reason I'm creating this is for you, Chrissy. You want proof, and I'm going [unintelligible] some for you. I know it doesn't make up for all [unintelligible], but, uh, well, I suppose it's something. I hope you'll find it in your heart to forgive me, but, uh...

[00:08:41] BILL: Alright. I'm gonna end this now, I guess.

[01:12:23] BILL: ...know you didn't want any recordings of this, but I [unintelligible] you can find something to use anyway.

[01:13:10] [Sound of footsteps]

[01:13:56] BILL: ...just tried to stop me, but I convinced you to let me do what needed to be done. It's...4:27 p.m., and this is Bill...or, I guess, Gary Maslon. Might as well...

[01:33:02] BILL: Alright. Bev showed us how to release [unintelligible]. I'm going to try to do the same with Roach.

[01:37:04] BILL: I think it's time we had a chat, Derrick.

[01:37:38] BILL: What? Now you're too shy to come out and play? You can't even [unintelligible].

[01:40:11] [Audio becomes distorted with static for several minutes]

[01:49:16] BILL: ...more like it.

[01:49:50] UNKNOWN MALE: [Laughter]

[01:50:17] BILL: It's time to end this, Derrick. You need to leave. It's been [unintelligible].

[01:51:33] UNKNOWN MALE: [unintelligible] it here. With that skank gone, I can do whatever I want. I don't have to [unintelligible].

[01:52:49] BILL: Not gonna happen. You've caused enough grief and pain while you were alive. I'm not going to let you [unintelligible] now that you're dead. I release you. You have nothing [unintelligible] keeping you here. It's over.

[01:53:27] UNKNOWN MALE: [Laughter]

At this point, the footage and audio are destroyed beyond repair. The footage picks up again 30 minutes later.

[02:22:01] BILL: Shit.

[02:22:26] [Loud banging]

[02:24:09] BILL: Shit. Okay... [gasps] ...So, uh, for whoever is watching this...I'm currently in room...12A? I don't know. The art room. I didn't look at the number before I-

[02:24:51] [Loud banging resumes]

[02:24:00] BILL: I started the fire...started it down there, end of the hall. Left wing. Seemed appropriate to start there...

[02:24:33] [Coughing, followed by more loud banging]

[02:25:03] UNKNOWN MALE: [unintelligible] fitting that it goes down this way.

[02:25:19] BILL: At least I know... [coughing] ...you're going down too.

[02:25:24] UNKNOWN MALE: [unintelligible] encore performance [unintelligible] greatest achievement. [Laughter]

[02:25:51] BILL: Fuck you. [Coughing] I said, I release you. You can't stay here anymore.

[02:26:04] UNKNOWN MALE: If I have to go, might as well [unintelligible] you with me, Gary.

[02:27:12] [Banging resumes]

[02:29:59] BILL: Looks like I'm not going to [unintelligible]. He's got me trapped in here with him. I didn't want... [coughing]. I wasn't supposed to...

[02:32:27] BILL: I'm so sorry.

3 Years Later

THE LARGE BUILDING LOOMED ahead at the end of the street, dreadful and familiar in the fading light of the late summer sun. Chrissy suppressed a shudder as she stared up into the windows, now sporting stained glass panels all along the second story. A warm hand settled on her shoulder, giving a reassuring squeeze.

"It's all going to be okay. We'll go in, say our hellos, and leave as soon as you're ready."

Taking a deep breath, she steadied herself. "I just can't believe we're back here. I never thought..."

"I know." Rodney turned his own gaze to the old building at the end of the street. "It looks good, though."

Chrissy had to agree: the restoration of Merlin High was impressive. Everything she read about the project told her the city went to great lengths to keep the exterior of the school as it had been before the most recent fire. There was no saving the gymnasium after the fire of 1987 — the structure had been damaged beyond repair, and the subsequent years of neglect did nothing to help. The exterior survived the second fire, although it had been a complete loss inside. The city gutted the place and entirely renovated the interior.

Ready to face the old school, Chrissy stepped out from the small red sedan. Rodney joined her, and the two stood in front of the building, staring up into its face.

"Feels weird being here without the old Ghostmobile," Rodney said.

"Yeah. I miss the old girl, but you have to admit, the fact that the air conditioner actually works in Ghosty Two is kind of a big plus."

"It makes summer investigations a hell of a lot more enjoyable." He reached out and took her hand. "You ready?"

"As ready as I'll ever be."

With a reassuring squeeze, the pair made their way to the building's entrance. Chrissy noted the new fountain surrounded by pots overflowing with flowers of every color in front of the building. The old weed-choked parking lot had been turned into a sprawling emerald lawn, benches dotting the winding path circling the grounds.

Music and chatter poured through the open doors, welcoming the public into the newly renovated halls. As Chrissy crossed over the threshold, she half expected to feel the heaviness from before to wash over her, or to break out in goosebumps, but the building felt like any other.

"It looks so different," Rodney said, taking in the bright, airy hallways as they followed the signs to the ballroom.

"It's like an entirely different place."

The old, checkered linoleum floors had been replaced with marble slabs in dark green — a nod to the building's former life — and the classrooms had been ripped out to expand the space, making room for the rows of books now residing there.

The space bustled with activity, and it seemed as though the entire town had come to get a look at the new Merlin Public Library.

When Sam called two years back to tell her about the mayor's plan to convert the high school into the city's new public library, Chrissy had been thrilled. It would continue to be a place of knowledge, and the town's history would be preserved, sad as it may be. It just felt right, and already on the drive in, she noted signs of life returning to the surrounding neighborhood.

At the end of the left wing, the building opened into the new addition where the gymnasium had once stood. They stopped in front of the open doors, where a gold plaque bore the name of the room; the Alorah Smith Ballroom.

"Lovely, isn't it?" a voice spoke up behind them.

Rodney swiped at his eyes, and the couple turned, finding themselves face to face with Sam Cleeves.

"Sam," Chrissy offered the old man a warm smile. "It's so good to see you. The school looks amazing!"

Sam's eyes drifted across the hallway before he gave a small, satisfied shrug. "It does. I tell you, I wasn't sure about the whole thing at first, but the committee did a fine job breathing new life into it."

"They really did. When we got your email about what they had planned, it seemed like the perfect end for Merlin High."

Rodney cleared his throat and tilted his head towards the sign bearing his sister's name. "Was that your doing?"

"It was," Sam said with a touch of anxiety. "I hope I didn't overstep. I just thought... I suppose I should have consulted with you first."

"No way. She'd love it."

Sam beamed, and the three stood in silence for a moment, lost in their own memories.

Turning towards them with a glint in his eyes, Sam broke the silence. "Now tell me, what has been happening with the *Othersiders* team?"

Grinning, Rodney grabbed Chrissy's hand, raising it in the air to show off a small diamond. "Well, we're getting hitched."

"That's wonderful news!" He clapped his hands together. "How did that happen?"

"I was in the process of losing my house when we came out here," Chrissy said, linking her arm in Rodney's. "By the time the police finished their investigation and we were able to return home, I had officially been kicked out. Rodney offered to let me crash on his couch, and-"

"And I never let her leave."

"Pretty much," Chrissy laughed.

"Well, I'm just pleased as punch for the two of you."

"Thank you, Sam," Rodney said.

"And what are the two of you doing with your delightful show? I admit, I couldn't quite bring myself to watch the episode you released about Merlin," Sam said, his tone growing somber. "Still too fresh, you know?"

Chrissy cast a sidelong glance at Rodney before speaking. "Well, I had planned to scrap the entire thing. Too fresh, like you said. Too close. But after the footage Bill shot was recovered, I thought maybe we could come at the story from a different angle."

"Bill's involvement was going to come out at some point, about what he did both then and in the 80s," Rodney said. "She figured if we let some time pass, we could release what we knew about Roach and tell Bill's side. It was part paranormal investigation, part true crime style documentary. I struggled with it at first, but in the end, it seemed important we tell the truth about everything."

"The media got a lot of things wrong about Bill," Chrissy added. "When they reopened the investigation into the original fire and discovered how Roach's father covered up his son's involvement, Bill was just forgotten."

"Even though what he did was unforgivable, he was our friend," Rodney said. "And he did put a stop to Roach in the end. It didn't feel right letting the world think he was the evil psychopath the media portrayed him as. It took me a long time to get there myself."

Sam nodded. "No. He did some terrible things, but... Well, I'm afraid I have to go and make the rounds, and I don't want to keep you from the delightful spread inside any longer. It has been wonderful to see you two again, and congratulations on the pending nuptials."

The old caretaker shuffled off towards a small group that had come in, greeting each of them with a hearty handshake. Rodney gave Chrissy a bump with his elbow and guided her into the ballroom.

The former gymnasium had been transformed into a spacious room with cream-colored walls, every window and doorway framed in dark wood. Three ornate chandeliers hung from the ceiling, illuminating the dozens of tables and the buffet running the length of the wall at the far end of the room. Rodney broke away, making his way towards the food, as Chrissy continued to take in the room.

The delicate scent of lilacs caught her attention, and she turned around in search of its origin. Behind her, in a butter yellow dress, looking as stunning as ever, stood Bev.

"Bev!" Chrissy threw her arms around the woman. "I wasn't sure you'd be here."

"I wasn't sure I would be, either," her warm voice whispered against Chrissy's ear before she stepped back. "You look beautiful. Engagement suits you."

"Thank you. You look wonderful, yourself."

She waved a hand dismissively. "I make Frankenstein's monster look like a beauty queen."

"Don't say that."

"It's alright, honey. I'm not ashamed of the scars. They make me look tough, don't you think?" she asked with a wink.

"Toughest woman I know."

Rodney appeared, balancing a plate of canapes and two champagne flutes. His face broke into a wide grin when he noticed Bev standing beside Chrissy. "Hey! You made it! If I'd have seen you, I would have brought another drink. Hang on, I'll go grab you one."

"Don't be silly," she said with a laugh. "Not really a fan of champagne, anyway. I will take one of these, however." She plucked one of the small bites from his plate and popped it into her mouth.

The three exchanged pleasantries, discussing the explosion in popularity *Othersiders* had been experiencing thanks to Chrissy and the book Bev had begun to write about her experiences communicating with spirits. When there was a lull in the conversation, Rodney excused himself to refill his plate.

"I'm glad to see you so happy," Bev said, brushing the crumbs from her fingers.

Chrissy's eyes wandered to where Rodney stood at the buffet, surveying the new additions. "Life is good."

"How's Rodney dealing with your gift these days?"

"It was rough at first, even after everything that happened. He didn't like the idea of me using it for the show, but we've come to an agreement. We don't mention what I'm able to do, but we use the information I receive to help move more spirits on. So far, it has worked out alright."

"I'll say. I've seen how well *Othersiders* has been doing. Heard you're in talks with a cable network."

Chrissy's cheeks flushed. "Nothing's set in stone yet, but I have to admit, this new gift has opened up loads of opportunities."

She took a small sip of her drink, keeping her eyes on the crowd milling about, filling the room with excited chatter. "Do any of them know what really happened?"

"There have been rumors, but they're mostly laughed at and turned into urban legend, as is so often the case with these kinds of things."

"It's kind of sad. Nobody will ever know what Alorah did...what Bill did. What you did."

Bev gave a carefree shrug. "Does it matter? The souls who were here have finally been able to move on. That's the important thing."

"I guess."

"Well, I should get going. It was hard enough dragging myself back into this building. I think I've had my fill."

Chrissy enveloped her friend in another hug. "Of course. Please come and visit us sometime."

"I'll do that. And you better believe I'll be at the wedding."

Bev crossed the room, stopping Rodney to say her goodbyes as he made his way back. She watched the two, Rodney with his plate overloaded with food, Bev in her yellow dress, scarred arms and legs bared for the world, and let out a soft sigh. Maybe she was right. Bill's story had been told, and whether anyone chose to believe it or not didn't matter.

Soon, Rodney appeared at her side. As she took a small pastry off his plate, a strange sensation nudged at the base of her neck, almost like someone was staring at her. Turning, she scanned the room but didn't see anyone looking in her direction. With a shrug, she turned back to him.

"What's up, babe?" he asked around a mouth full off phyllo dough.

"Nothing." She reached up and brushed a bit of the flaky pastry from his lip then shivered. "Did it get super cold in here?"

"Maybe a little. Do you want my jacket?"

"No," she said slowly. The strange sensation on the back of her neck intensified and started to spread. She looked down at her arms to find every hair standing on end. Her body gave another involuntary shiver at the sight.

Rodney looked at her, and his forehead creased with worry. "Whoa. What's going on? You're all goosebumpy." He took off his jacket and wrapped it around her small frame.

"I'm not sure, but something feels off. Can we go, please?"

"Yeah, of course." He put his plate on the nearest table, taking Chrissy's champagne flute and setting it down before hurrying her out of the room.

Stepping out through the building's main entrance, the warm night air helped cut the chill, and she took a deep breath. As soon as she slipped into the passenger seat of the little sedan, her breathing returned to normal, and the goosebumps all but vanished. The strange sensation lessened, but a faint echo of it kept her eyes darting across the front of the school.

Rodney slid into the driver's seat and turned to her, his voice filled with concern. "What happened in there? Was it one of your flashbacks?"

Chrissy shook her head. "I don't think so. It was probably just a minor panic attack. I thought I was over what happened here, but...I guess not."

"Well, we don't ever have to come back."

She smiled and leaned across the armrest to plant a small kiss on his cheek. "Let's go home."

As Rodney put the car in drive, Chrissy found her eyes pulled back to the old school, now bathed in the stark brilliance of floodlights, standing bright against the deepening night sky. The car maneuvered in a tight three-point turn, and she watched as the building grew smaller and smaller in the side view mirror until they turned a corner, leaving it firmly in the past.

In the left-wing hallway of Merlin High, a towering shadow filled one of the window frames, watching as the car disappeared, the sound of its engine fading into the night.

Acknowledgements

Writing a book is hard work. It takes time and energy and so many coffees. But, it would be a million times harder without an incredible group of people who have helped along the way.

First, I want to thank my incredible partner, Anthony. The best sounding board and first reader anyone could ask for. Without you, I would still be trying to puzzle out this book.

To my mom, who has always bent over backwards to show her support. I know spooky isn't your thing, but you read all my drafts and told me to keep going when I wanted to give up.

Thank you to my amazing editor, Alexa, who helped polish this book up and make it much easier to read.

Thank you to Molly, the outstanding designer of the cover of this book, for taking the mess of ideas I gave her and creating the perfect cover.

To the people who have cheered me on through this messy journey: Alexis Spanevello, Nathan and Cristin Hessing, Olivia Day Wallace, Luke Southard, Therese Thompson, and everyone who has sent me encouraging messages. You're all incredible people.

Most of all, thank you, reader, for giving an unknown indie book a chance. Your decision to pick up this book means more to me than words can express. Thank you, thank you.

About the Author

V.S. Lawrence grew up in Utah being scared of everything. As an adult, she started putting her fears on paper and crafting spooky tales. When not writing, she can be found reading a good horror novel, wandering aimlessly, or cuddling her dog, Rigby. She is still scared of everything.

To stay up to date with future releases and news, you can sign up for her newsletter at https://vslawrence-author.com

www.ingramcontent.com/pod-product-compliance
Ingram Content Group UK Ltd.
Pitfield, Milton Keynes, MK11 3LW, UK
UKHW020659080725
6779UKWH00038B/613

9 798223 965145